STATE
OF
GRACE

STATE
OF
GRACE

Robert Tine

The Viking Press · New York

LIBRARY OF CONGRESS CATALOGING IN PUBLICATION DATA
Tine, Robert
State of grace.
I. Title.
PZ4.T5888ST   [PS3570.I48]   813'.54   80–14538
ISBN 0–670–66851–6

Printed in the United States of America
Set in Janson

Part One

FOR THREE DAYS Carlos had been on the pier. He had not slept, he was hoarse, and the smell of rotting fish and of sweat had worked itself into his skin and clothes. Maria sat next to him, patiently trying to make coffee on a spirit stove. It had been raining since the night before, warm unhealthy rain, and the wick was damp. He looked at her sadly; she looked so tired, her feet in their cheap sandals so filthy.

Spread out in front of them were perhaps a thousand people—silent, wet, fevered, hungry. Some stared at him. A hundred yards away, wedged between the demonstrators and the ship, the continental carrier *Bahia Blanca*, out of Boston of Panamanian registry, stood a line of police, self-conscious and uncomfortable in their bulky riot gear. They were tired too. Behind them rose the sheer cliff of the ship's side, an acre of peeling black paint. Lolling along the taff-rails were a few members of the crew. Carlos supposed they were Americans but couldn't be sure; they waited patiently, like theatergoers. There was violence in the air.

The correspondents for the major news services were calling the demonstration "the first serious challenge to Peru's military regime." Carlos they called "charismatic," the "radical reef that might sink the *Bahia Blanca* and puncture the government of Generalissimo José Sarmiento below the waterline." Seventy-two hours earlier they had filed stories that quoted Carlos saying the cargo of the *Bahia Blanca* would be unloaded only if the government was prepared to shed blood. The correspondents filled in the details: a consignment of arms had been ordered from Senatron Corp. of

Framingham, Massachusetts, the leading manufacturer of what the correspondents called "counterinsurgency hardware." The order was primarily lightweight automatic weapons and the cost was $4 million cash. This, they pointed out, was at a time when a third of the population was feeling the effects of a debilitating famine.

Carlos had led the crowd from the university in the center of Lima to Basin B at Calloa, the deep-water port a few miles from the city. They had sung and shouted and made speeches on the first night, some of the *Bahia*'s sailors clapping time to the songs. The police had done nothing. Was there a chance, the demonstrators asked themselves, that they could win?

By the second day they were hot and tired but firm. By the third, tense.

The chief of police loved his fatigues. In them he felt like a man of action. In America, in Texas, at the Counter Insurgency and Riot Control Training Institute, tall hard men in fatigues had taught him that the best time to clear a crowd was after they had been soaked—preferably by rain, but if not, then by hose. Water demoralized, they said. This crowd, he noted with satisfaction, had been soaked for eight hours. He glanced at his watch, a maze of dials. It was time to get started. Clipped to the console of his Jeep was a squalling walkie-talkie. He laid it lovingly against the side of his face and, tingling with excitement, gave orders.

The police began moving in on the crowd all at once, like a line of electronic toys that had been switched on. The first ragged line of demonstrators pushed back against them angrily. A confused animal roar rose from the crowd, so silent a few seconds before. Involuntarily Carlos added to it a harsh hoarse rasping from his throat. He saw clubs flying, and people began falling. As the first shots were fired, he

4

noted absently that he was saying a prayer—as though spoken by someone else.

He blundered wildly into the melee, wrenching free from a press of dirty green and brown. A hard, hot pain raced across his jaws—someone said, "Got him!" in a voice high and cracked with excitement—and it snatched at his cheeks and eyes. His mouth tasted the metallic sweetness of his own blood. As he fell, he thought he saw Maria lying on the ground.

1

POPE GREGORY DIED, as the newspapers would say later, much as he had reigned—quietly, with the minimum of drama, as serene in death as in life. There were no grand words from the deathbed, no death rattle, no final agonies; his breathing, which had become labored early that afternoon, ceased altogether early in the evening.

His Holiness's physician checked for a pulse and found none. He nodded absently to himself and glanced at his watch. The statement that would be issued to the world would, pro forma, include the detail of the time of the pope's death. The doctor stood back from the bed, as an artist steps back from painting, and looked at the elderly cardinal who hovered next to him. The cardinal's eyes searched the doctor's, as if it were up to him whether or not Gregory lived on.

"I'm sorry," the doctor said, and pointing to his chest added, "the heart . . "

The cardinal nodded sadly and leaned against the bed. He reached for Gregory's waxen hand and gripped it, as if to reassure him, and wept silently. They had been good friends.

It was a peculiarly calm scene. The doctor methodically filling out the death certificate, the cardinal bowed with silent grief, the nursing sisters rustling slightly in starched habits, self-conscious, in the background. All of them knew that Gregory's death was for the best. He had been ill a long time, and everyone knew that it would be only a matter of time before the end came. Some thought it a miracle that Gregory had held on for so long. Others, of a more practical bent, thought it was unfortunate that Gregory had been able to hang on as long as he had. His illness had left the Church rudderless.

And so the spectators who watched the last minutes of the reign of Gregory XVII, sad though they may have been at the passing of a good and quiet man, were calm, resigned. Only the fierce winter wind beating on the windows added a touch of drama.

As soon as her taxi pulled away from the airport, Rafaella felt a bubble of excitement rise within her. The driver eyed his beautiful passenger in the rear-view mirror, dutifully thanked a saint or two in gratitude for having delivered her to him, and tried to draw her into conversation.

"How long will you be in Rome? You want someone to show you around?"

Rafaella, like all Italian women, had the knack of cooling casual ardor.

"I live here," she said, "and my husband will show me anything I haven't seen already." The cabdriver smiled and sighed. There were a few things he wouldn't mind showing her.

"He's a lucky man, your husband," the driver said, taking in the long auburn hair curling around the woman's face and her soft blue eyes. A rare combination in Italy.

"I never let him forget it."

She had no husband and the driver knew it. She knew the driver knew. It was part of the game, a game Rafaella had learned in her teens and had been playing ever since. The driver, defeated, contented himself with keeping only one eye on the road, the other on the mirror, and driving fast, as if to get to Rome as quickly as possible and rid himself of the torment of Rafaella's slim and tempting form.

The road cut straight through the *campagna*, marked at intervals with industrial buildings. One, a scattered and haphazard collection of sheds and warehouses, gray in the

8

winter light, was dominated by a sign. Huge blue letters: BIANCHI.

That's all he has to say, thought Rafaella, just his name.

She was in her father's territory. Alessandro Bianchi's name was on hotels, ships, heavy machinery, appliances, shoes, shoe polish, and more; Bianchi was a household word. It meant money, and it meant power.

Rafaella stared out the window and told herself she was free of it. She loved her father but had grabbed for independence; and she held on, moving to New York and working her way up to contributing editor for *Renaissance Magazine*. She was good at her job, there was no doubt about that; she deserved her success, but the Bianchi name loomed.

A lot of people hated Alessandro Bianchi. His means of doing business were far from gentle, and he had a reputation for always wanting and always getting things his way. His toughness was legendary, and his trademarks were unmistakable—ruthless competitiveness and the ability to pull off showy but effective financial maneuvers such as takeovers and stock dumpings, all with their attendant double-crossings. Doing business with Bianchi was known in some circles as "snake-charming."

Although his methods were distasteful to many—the snake did not charm easily—no one could deny that they worked. He had been born in the south, in Sicily, and had risen from poverty to wealth in the decade following the war, when many fortunes had been made.

A light rain began to fall, and Rafaella only half heard the rhythmic slap of the windshield wipers. The driver yanked her back to the present.

"Of course," he said reflectively, "you're not really my type."

Rafaella looked blankly at his smiling eyes in the mirror. "What?"

"You're not really my type," he repeated.

She laughed. "Oh, no? What's your type?"

He launched into a lengthy description of a woman who, it seemed, combined the disparate qualities of Mary Magdalen, Mata Hari, and Sophia Loren. Most of what he said was lost in the growling of the Fiat engine and the rushing of the wind, but Rafaella didn't really want to hear and the driver didn't mind. He enjoyed replaying a treasured fantasy.

They approached the city. The dead winter scrubland gave way to a more or less continuous ribbon of houses, shops, restaurants—a little squalid but, Rafaella thought, reassuringly familiar.

Her assignment delighted her. *Renaissance Magazine*, an expensive, prestigious, and glossy quarterly, dealt with any interesting subject; nothing was considered outside its scope. One of the magazine's regular features was an in-depth report on a single country, a series of articles covering one nation's politics, arts, food, business, people. Rafaella's assignment was simple: Italy. The articles would take six months to write, maybe longer, and she couldn't wait to get started. She decided to write the hardest one first: the Church. It was impossible to cover Italy and not deal with the Vatican, a subject that didn't interest her much, and about which she knew very little. Her father had been consistently irreligious during her youth, although she had been sent to a convent school, as all rich little Roman girls were. She wanted to get the Church out of the way, and she had to cover it thoroughly. Gordon Soames, the publisher of *Renaissance*, knew everybody, even a cardinal, so at least she had a contact. He would be the first person Rafaella would see.

Rafaella had inherited little from her father—certainly not her looks—but she did have his iron will to work. Although she ached to see him, for she had planned her arrival as a surprise, she decided to check into a hotel in the center of the city rather than moving into the vast Bianchi estate on the outskirts of Rome. She knew that once they got together the Church article would be that much harder to write. She would wait a few days before calling him, until she was pulled into her subject and had achieved some momentum.

As she stared out the window of the taxi, now locked in traffic, she felt impatient, anxious to be there and get going. She had work to do.

"Peru," Martin was saying, "is a Catholic country. Yet we stand idly by while people are tortured, jailed, disappear. The Church there is as much a pillar of the regime as the army or the security police. Does the Holy See say a word? No, of course not. Not a whimper."

"It's not quite as simple as that, and you know it," said Anthony. He regarded the younger man with weary affection as they sat in the study of Anthony's rooms. In the early darkness the lamp on Anthony's desk isolated the two men in a small circle of light, giving Anthony no other focus for his gaze than the intense and scornful face of Father Martin Sykes; his secretary was beginning to try his patience.

Martin was leaning forward in his armchair. His strong jaw and powerful frame were outlined by the light. He looked exactly like what he was—a strong, young Irish-American who had never quite lost the rawboned look of a high school athlete. Anthony, by contrast, was tall and slender, and unlike many of his rather portly fellow cardinals, he wore his robes well, looking almost graceful in them. His face was deeply lined and his hair tinged with gray. He looked all of his fifty-eight years, although the laugh lines around his mouth served to offset his severe, straight North Italian features. His mother had been American, and he spoke English easily and without an accent.

"It is simple, Anthony. Nothing is easier to ignore. Look"— Martin tapped a pile of blue-bound reports on his lap—"here are the reports from the papal nuncio in Lima, Monsignor Sanz-Guerrero. All written within the last year. There's a great deal of information here. The number of Catholic schools, the number of marriages performed, numbers of every conceivable—and irrelevant—Catholic activity. Is there one word about the coup? No. The famine? No. There's not even a word about the regime's anti-clericism. This must be the first time the Church has supported a government that was anti-Church. If you look hard enough, you'll see that Monsignor Sanz-Guerrero notes with distaste that the outflow of monies from Catholic charities has increased by thirty percent. You know what that means?"

"What does it mean, Martin?" Anthony responded irritably. Martin had an annoying tendency to lecture.

"It means we're spending more money on food for the poor than ever before. Sanz-Guerrero doesn't like that. Not a bit."

"Then, you'll admit, the Church is doing something."

Martin leaned forward in his chair. "But we could do so much more."

"Martin, there's a limit—"

"No there isn't!" he interrupted. "There shouldn't be. Cardinal Van Doorn sits over there in the Prefecture for Economic Affairs, increasing the Vatican treasury by . . . who knows how much? And what do we do with it? Nothing. I don't know where it goes. You don't. No one does. Just Van Doorn, and he won't tell anyone."

"Martin, you know as well as I do that the Prefecture reports to the Holy Father directly."

"But the Holy Father has been in a coma for months. . . ."

Anthony shrugged his shoulders. "You're preaching to the converted, Martin. And before you get started on your favorite subject—"

"Cardinal Van Doorn is not, by any stretch of the imagination, my favorite subject. I just don't trust him. He's a cipher, and he has only his best interests at heart."

"Now how do you know that?"

"It's obvious," Martin said shortly.

"Martin," said Anthony, "don't make an enemy of Van Doorn. He's a powerful man. You are my personal secretary, he's head of one of the most powerful Vatican agencies; there's only so much I could do to protect you."

"I don't need protection," he replied hotly.

"Well, maybe you don't. But I do," replied Anthony quietly.

Martin knew Anthony was right. Despite the younger man's impatience, Anthony Cardinal D'Orlando, head of the Vatican Committee to Aid Victims of Injustice, had drawn a lot of fire from the other fellow curial cardinals. Anthony had traveled widely—to Africa, South America, the Far East—and he never failed to report on, or denounce, political or religious oppression. His outspokenness had made many Vatican bureaucrats uneasy. He walked a fine line between doing his duty and going too far. In certain quarters he was thought of as a dangerous man, considering the Vatican's low political profile.

Anthony sighed wearily. "The telephone is ringing. Why don't you answer it?"

"Yes, Your Eminence."

It was at times like these that Anthony D'Orlando wondered why he kept Martin on. He could be so tiresome—a doctrinaire radical. His sense of humor was often too scathing to be funny. And he certainly didn't do anything for Anthony's already delicate position with some of his fellow cardinals. From time to time one of them would suggest that perhaps the Vatican was not the right place for Father Sykes. Perhaps he needed a more rigorous post, some place where his zeal would be better appreciated. But Anthony defended him, reasoned with the cardinals, reproached Martin severely when he needed it, and smoothed things over. The young man was a time bomb, though—one day he would go too far.

But no one could deny that Martin was brilliant. His career at the seminary, and later at the Harvard School of Divinity, had been almost unparalleled. Indeed, in recent memory Martin's only serious intellectual rival had been Anthony himself. And no one could deny that Martin was passionately concerned about the Church, though many of Anthony's fellows would have deemed the young man's brand of Catholicism closer to communism or the black arts.

Martin returned, sat down. "Father Gioia wishes to speak with Your Eminence."

"Cut out the 'Your Eminence,' Martin. I believe we're on first-name terms."

"I'm sorry, Your Eminence. If I didn't call Your Eminence 'Your Eminence,' I would feel as if I were living a lie."

"Why me, God?" sighed Anthony. "Why me?"

When there was bad news to be heard in the Vatican, Father Gioia delivered it. It was not an official post, but the general feeling was that he enjoyed it. Father Gioia was known in some quarters as the "Ill Wind."

Wishing to receive whatever was to come in private, Anthony did not pick up the telephone on his desk but left Martin sitting in the study and went out to the secretary's desk in the antechamber. It was dark there; a chill hung in the air, soothing his tired eyes. Moonlight shone through a tracery of frost on the ancient window.

"Your Eminence, I am sorry to disturb you, but there is something you should know."

"Not at all, Father. What is it?"

"His Holiness," he said matter-of-factly. "He passed away a few minutes ago."

It had been anticipated for weeks, but Anthony could feel the shock of it running through his body. His legs weakened. He closed his eyes and sat on the edge of Martin's desk. "I'm sorry. I don't know what to say."

"There is nothing to say, Your Eminence. Good night."

Slowly, Anthony walked back to the study. Martin sprawled in his chair, reading.

"Gregory is dead."

Martin looked up sharply, put down his book.

"I'm sorry to hear that," he said. "He was a good man, if misguided."

"He made me a cardinal."

"He wasn't always misguided." Martin smiled slightly.

"I wonder what happens now?"

"We will mourn him, and then the way will be clear to make you pope."

Anthony felt a flash of anger. "His death means very little to you, does it?"

"It means a great deal. He will have my prayers. Those of you who were lucky enough to have him as a close friend will also have my prayers. But he has been ill—in a coma—for almost a year. His death, as sad as it is, had to come. The Church now has a chance to save itself. It means that in the closing years of the twentieth century, it can elect someone from the twentieth century to lead it. That person is you. I've surveyed the college, and the only person who can convince the half a dozen or so Catholics left in the world that there is life in the Leviathan is you. The Church will die, Anthony. It will if they dig up some conservative like Salvatore to sit on the throne."

"Martin, please," said Anthony wearily, "do you never stop? He isn't even buried, and already you're talking about the election."

Martin looked around the dark room, shaking off the sting of the rebuke. "I'm sorry, Anthony, but people have been talking of little else for six months. They are talking about it right now, if I know them. There are a lot of power-hungry men here, Anthony. Since Gregory fell ill and the college started ruling in his place, they have been quietly campaigning for the conservatives' cause. I cannot understand why you defend them. They are no friends of yours. The work you have done in the Commission to Aid Victims of Injustice has drawn nothing but fire from them. They say that what you are doing is not the province of the Church. Since when has the Church ignored suffering? The Church should have no part in saving lives, according to them."

"They are just doing what they think is right, Martin."

"That is the traditional defense of the reactionary. They are saying these things because they are terrified that your work will catapult the Church out of the nineteenth century. They can't stand to see the Church move and leave them behind. They're old men. Cornered. Scared and dangerous."

Anthony rose. He looked at Martin for a moment.

"I think you had better go and telephone that reporter. Tell her that I won't be able to see her tomorrow."

"Anthony, I'm sorry I shot off my mouth again. . . . I'll call that woman. What was her name?"

"Bianchi, Rafaella Bianchi."

"Is she any relation to *the* Bianchi?"

"His daughter, I believe."

"And how do you know her?"

"I don't. She works for a friend of mine, Gordon Soames."

"Well, I'll get in touch with her. Are you going to bed? You haven't eaten."

"I'm not hungry. Good night, Martin."

"Good night, Anthony. I'm sorry."

"Forget it."

Father Sykes watched Anthony leave. Picking up the telephone, he said quietly, "God help us."

Jet lag had destroyed Rafaella's desire to get to work immediately. She had managed to check into her hotel and make an appointment to see Anthony D'Orlando before falling asleep. Martin Sykes's phone call roused her, and she tried in vain to sound as if she had been wide awake.

"Ms. Bianchi? This is Martin Sykes. Cardinal D'Orlando asked me to call to ask that he be excused from his meeting with you tomorrow."

"Yes, of course, I'm sorry to hear that. Is there any particular reason?"

There was a brief pause on the end of the line.

"Well, I'm sure you have heard that His Holiness Pope Gregory died this afternoon, or rather this evening, and Cardinal D'Orlando thought that, under the circumstances . . ."

"I'm sorry, I hadn't heard. My flight got the better of me,

and I fell asleep shortly after I phoned. Can you tell me anything about it?"

"Pope Gregory died quietly in his sleep at five-fifteen this evening after eleven months in a diabetic coma. His confessor Salvatore Cardinal Di Nobili was present, as was His Holiness's personal physician, Doctor Viazzi. I'm afraid no one knows more than that. The secretariat of state will issue a statement tomorrow."

"Is it possible to reach Cardinal Di Nobili?"

"Cardinal Di Nobili is an extremely old man, and he was a close friend of His Holiness. I think it would be better if he weren't disturbed." Besides, thought Martin, he has probably never heard of the telephone.

"What are the reactions like at the Vatican? I would imagine that people are very upset."

"People are upset, one could hardly expect them to be otherwise."

"Pardon me for asking this—I'm sure I sound rather blunt—but wouldn't you say that people are rather relieved also?"

Martin thought for a moment. That was exactly the way he would have put it. Before he could answer, Rafaella spoke.

"I'm sorry. I shouldn't have said that."

"No, what you say makes a good deal of sense. People have been kept hanging by Gregory's illness. Yes. People are relieved. But there's a little more to it than that."

"What would that be?"

Martin hesitated. "Oh . . ." Anthony had warned him about saying too much. ". . . well, people are likely to be a little frightened."

"Frightened of what?"

"Of change, Ms. Bianchi," he said expansively. "The Church is old and made up of old men. Change is always likely to be a little unwelcome."

Rafaella thought of a number of questions that she would like to ask, but hesitancy was creeping into Martin's voice, a sense that he had gone too far.

"I don't suppose," Rafaella said, "that *you* would like to have dinner?"

"What?"

"Are you hungry? I would like to take you to dinner."

"Why would you want to do that?" Martin was a little puzzled. Dinner invitations were rare for him, particularly from heiresses.

"I'm not altogether sure how the Vatican works. I have done some preliminary research, but it's something of an impenetrable subject for an outsider. I would appreciate some help."

"Now?"

"Yes, if you can. Please don't, if it puts you in an awkward position." Rafaella was unused to not being pounced on by men; she wasn't sure the sensation was so disagreeable.

Martin thought for a moment.

"Yes, of course. I'd be delighted. Where are you staying?"

"I'm at the Hassler."

"That's on the Via . . ."

"Via Gregoriana."

"It will take me about forty-five minutes to get there."

"Perfect. I'll be in the lobby. How will I recognize you?"

"I will probably be the only one there wearing a Roman collar."

The Hotel Hassler-Médici stands at the top of the Spanish Steps, a discreet monument to old money. Martin had never actually been inside before, and he was curious. He was totally unprepared, though, for the opulence of the lobby, and was acutely aware of the frankly disapproving looks of the hotel staff. A young priest in a shabby black suit and a collar was a noticeable alien in the lavish room. The concierge half expected the priest to produce a tin and begin collecting money. Disapproval changed to astonishment when Rafaella approached Martin.

"Father Sykes? I'm Rafaella Bianchi."

Martin grasped her hand gratefully. Rafaella established his reason for being there.

"How do you do? Why don't we drop the 'Father'? My name is Martin."

"Please call me Rafaella. Shall we find a restaurant?"

They made for the door, Martin leading.

"Phew," said Martin, once outside. "Money frightens me to death." As soon as he spoke the words, he tried to get them back. "That is to say . . ."

"That is to say," said Rafaella, "that you feel as if you have made a dreadful faux pas. After all, the daughter of the richest man in Italy should love the stuff, right? Well, at the risk of sounding *really* spoiled, allow me to point out that I am a working girl. And besides, according to the Hassler view of things, the Bianchis are terribly *nouveau riche*. The trouble is, there isn't enough old money in Italy these days to keep the place filled. They'll take any *riche* they can get. Forget it, okay?"

Martin still felt awkward. He continued to mumble apologies.

Rafaella stopped that. "Where would you like to eat?"

"You tell me."

"We can go to Ranieri's. It's just down the street, and you'll be interested to know that it has been patronized by popes."

"It must cost a fortune."

"Not at all."

Martin suspected that Rafaella's view of inexpensive and his own were not quite the same. He was surprised, however, for Ranieri's, as it happened, was not too bad at all.

A dinner of veal, zucchini in garlic, *papardelle*, and plenty of crisp white wine served to melt, to a certain extent, the natural reserve that exists between strangers. Martin found himself admitting that Rafaella was a bit of a surprise. He had expected a rich girl, frivolous beyond words, whose position was due to wealth rather than brains. Yet she had succeeded in drawing information out of a reluctant subject

—he had told her more than he should have about Anthony, his fears for the coming election, and the conservatives.

She leaned forward and lit a very thin cigar in the candle flame. A plume of fragrant smoke unfurled across the table. Martin smiled. At least she had the taste to smoke a good cigar. But why did so many women feel that in order to be taken seriously they had to impersonate men? Still, it was not unappealing in one so doomed in the task of appearing masculine.

"It gets a lot of funny looks, even now, even in New York. I gave up cigarettes, but I have to have something. Would you like one?"

"Just a puff," he said, taking her cigar and drawing a pungent mouthful of smoke, noticing as he did that it had a floral undertaste. It detonated a charge of remembrance deep within his brain—how long had it been since he had tasted a woman's lipstick?

He passed the cigar back. "Is there anything else you want to know?"

"There's a lot more, but I don't want to rush it. For the time being, though, I could use some nuts-and-bolts information. The funeral of Gregory—when will it be and what actually takes place?"

"There is a period of mourning, of course. It begins officially tomorrow. Then in about ten days there will be a funeral. I'm afraid I don't know much about it—there hasn't been one since 1978, before my time. I could arrange to have you introduced to the man in charge of the arrangements, though. Cardinal Breakespeare-Beauchamp, the papal master of ceremonies. He's always looking for an audience for his vast store of arcane church history."

"He wouldn't mind?"

"I doubt it. But you've been warned. He can be quite long-winded."

"Good. Now tell me about you."

"Me?" said Martin, still smiling. "You know, the young priest, convinced that the Church isn't doing enough, impatient with my elders . . . the usual. Just before I was ordained, an old priest at my seminary told me: only fools think they have all the answers. I forget that now and again."

"So that's the usual? I find that hard to believe."

"There are hundreds like me. We pace a lot and never miss an opportunity to raise our voices to decry materialism and social injustice."

"Nothing wrong with that."

"No, probably not . . . but the bull-in-the-china-shop approach upsets a lot of people."

"What about Anthony? What's his approach?"

"Oh, Anthony is a different case altogether. He's quiet and reserved and very determined. But unlike priests of my type, he has moments of indecision. We, on the other hand, *know* we're right. That's why we never get anything done. And that's why Anthony never fails to get his point across, to *get* things done. Even his enemies respect him."

"Enemies? Do cardinals have enemies?"

"Of course. The days of Vatican intrigue and infighting didn't die with the Borgias. There's a wide range of troubles, running from petty squabbles about who has a better office or a bigger staff all the way to severe battles, ideological rifts. . . . This cardinal won't speak to that one . . . the pope—when we had a pope—makes it clear that His Eminence So-and-so has fallen from favor. You'd be surprised at what goes on behind that placid facade."

"How come no one ever hears about it?"

"Mainly because no one really cares. Until today, did you care if the Cardinal for Non-Christians was locked in battle with the Cardinal for the Eastern Church? Of course not. Besides, nothing happens quickly at the Vatican. A gentle rebuke in *L'Osservatore Romano*, the Vatican newspaper, might be answered a year and a half later in a speech by a cardinal to the Association of American Catholic Women's Clubs. You have to be awfully interested to follow things that closely—and you have to read between the lines to know who's mad at whom. It's like learning a new language."

21

"I have a feeling that this assignment is going to be a little harder than I expected."

"Well, it's not as straightforward as covering Capitol Hill, but I think you'll manage."

"As long as I have some help."

"I'll make sure you do."

They had a polite tussle over the check. Rafaella won, covering it with her expense account.

They strolled back through the cold streets, over which a solemn silence had already gathered.

"Tomorrow," Martin said, "Rome will be filled with the tolling of church bells. And mourning. Rome will be draped in black."

"Will they be mourning Gregory, or simply mourning a pope?"

"For both. More for the office, I think. Gregory was considered a cold man; someone once referred to him as *amleto*—Hamlet-like. He stands in danger of being overshadowed by his successor."

"Cardinal D'Orlando?"

"Anthony would outshine Gregory. But there are people at the Vatican who say he would just cast a shadow on the Church."

At the Hassler, he took his leave of her outside.

"Good night—Father. It has been very pleasant and very informative."

"I hope I have been of some help."

"How formal!" Rafaella laughed. "I intend to hold you to your promise of an introduction to Cardinal . . . what was his name?"

"Beauchamp. Alban Cardinal Beauchamp."

After the revolving doors had swept her inside, Martin turned and looked out over the cold city. He glanced at his watch. Ten-forty-five. He had fifteen minutes to get back to the Vatican before the gates closed. As he hurried through the streets, he realized that for the first time in a long while he felt relaxed, yet exhilarated. It had been a pleasant evening, and he knew he was looking forward to seeing Rafaella again.

A few minutes before midnight, Gerard Cardinal Van Doorn put down the latest copy of *The Economist*, took off his steel-frame glasses, ran his fingers through his short, brush-cut hair, and looked expectantly at the telephone. As if on cue it rang. The cardinal allowed it two shrill rings before he picked it up. He placed the receiver against his ear and settled back into his red leather wing desk chair.

The voice on the other end of the line, distorted slightly by distance, was a familiar one. Gerard did not know the young man's name, although he received a call from him five nights a week. Gerard had no curiosity about the man, because Gerard already knew all he needed to know about him —he was the trusted aide of Gerard's trusted New York stockbroker. Of course, the broker was not Gerard's personal financial man—Gerard had taken a vow of poverty—but rather he was the man who looked after the Vatican's substantial American investments.

Gerard had nicknamed the voice "Amex." Two hours after the closing of the New York Stock Exchange, the young man called a number in Rome and read off a list of stock prices to the voice at the other end. Finishing the litany of figures and company names—there were more than a hundred of them—with the closing figures of the Dow Jones and Amex indexes, the young man asked, as he always did—as he was instructed to do—if there were any questions. There never were.

The routine had changed little in the two years Amex had been placing the calls. Some of the names on the list had been dropped and new ones added in their place. Once in a while the young man had been instructed to call a number in Zurich or London. Once he had called Hong Kong, and twice Rio de Janeiro. But the same voice always answered, always two hours after the market closed, regardless of the time difference.

He did not know to whom he spoke, or what corporation or consortium that voice represented—if any at all. What he did know was this: a huge amount of money was involved, and a shrewd and steady hand guided the portfolio.

The calls always ended in the same way. The voice said, with a slight trace of an accent—probably German—"Thank you. Good evening." Amex in New York also said the same thing every night—"Thank *you*, sir," though he was never quite sure why.

Gerard Cardinal Van Doorn was the director of the Vatican organization once called the Institute for Works of Religion, and still referred to by many as simply "the Institute." The new name was more straightforward: the Prefecture for Economic Affairs—the Vatican bank. No matter what the Curia chose to call it, the people of Rome had their own name for it—"the pope's shop"—and Gerard was the pope's shopkeeper.

Money was in Gerard's blood. His family had been involved in banking in their native Holland for two centuries. A steady succession of Van Doorns had run the LeidenStaats Bank with a profitable, if sober, touch for as long as anyone could remember. Gerard's decision to enter the Church had come as something of a blow to his family, because Gerard had shown great promise as a banker even in his youth. Luckily the Church was a shrewd judge of talent, and Gerard had been placed at the Institute early in his career, and remained there.

There was a time when young non-Italian priests had found little comfort at the Vatican. It was an Italian club, and Italians were the ones earmarked for promotion, often at the expense of their foreign brothers. Gerard was aware of this immediately and, intensely ambitious, had resolved to do something about it. He waited until he saw his chance, and when it came he seized it.

The Vatican has a prison, and its last occupant, a youthful prelate named Giorgio Dammato, had been put there by the young Gerard Van Doorn. Dammato had been Gerard's supervisor at the Institute and was well thought of by his superiors. He was something of an extrovert and enjoyed moving in high society, both within the Church and outside it. Gerard noticed that Dammato had many more blue-chip business contacts outside the Vatican than his relatively low position merited. Overstepping the bounds of his authority, but far too clever to be caught doing so, Gerard began to watch Dammato closely. Well after work had ended for the day, Gerard spent long hours checking Dammato's work, looking for a single flaw—something out of order, a clue. It was not long before Gerard found himself following, with the single-mindedness of a bloodhound, a trail of money that began outside the Vatican, passed through Dammato, and vanished again outside of Italy. Gerard knew immediately what was going on, but he lacked proof.

Currency regulations in Italy were then—as they are now—very strict. Italian businessmen, anxious to get money out of the country for investment purposes in more lucrative markets, found that the government, so lax in most areas, continually upset their plans. The Vatican, a separate state, didn't have this problem—its money was free to come and go. Dammato, using the Church as a blind, was exporting cash for Italian businessmen, and probably raking off a fair amount in commissions for himself. If this fact were revealed, and if Gerard were the one to reveal it, Dammato would be removed, and the way would be clear for Gerard to move up. After all, he would have done everybody a favor. But he needed the proof.

Alone, one night, Gerard found what he needed. Dammato had transferred $140,000 to none other than the Leiden-Staats Bank in Holland. Gerard had no trouble getting the necessary evidence from his uncle, the director of the bank, to show that the money Dammato had transferred belonged not to the Church, or even to Dammato himself, but to an electronics firm in Turin. Dammato's fall had been as swift as Gerard's subsequent rise. He gained a reputation for being a smart young man, a financial force to be reckoned with.

The Dammato incident had brought the young Dutch cleric to the attention of Bernardino Nogara, a shadowy figure, a layman who had ruled the Vatican treasury for thirty years. Gerard became Nogara's protégé, and it was from this quiet, elusive millionaire that Gerard had learned the secret of Nogara's and, later, Gerard's own success: never restrict one's investments because of religious or moral considerations. It was a good rule, and a profitable one.

Gerard was a man given to secrecy, and the Vatican's manner of doing business suited him. The Vatican publishes no balance sheets, issues no list of its holdings. The Church fears that investors would think the pope infallible in matters of finance as well as in faith. From Van Doorn's point of view, the pope had nothing to do with it. All of the Vatican's money passed through the Prefecture, whose reasons for discretion were even simpler than the Church's: it was nobody's business but his—and, technically, the pope's.

In the later years of his reign Gregory had never bothered much about finances. He had been content, as the years passed, to be assured by Gerard that the Church, whatever its ills spiritually, was in sound shape financially. Only Gerard knew how sound. Of course, he did not run the Prefecture by himself—he had dozens of directors, subdirectors, executors, and assistants—but only Gerard knew the key pieces of information necessary to fit all the pieces of the puzzle together.

Shortly before Gerard's appointment as director the Church had suffered huge losses; most of the large corporations of the United States and Europe would have been bankrupted had they sustained similar disasters. Only the almost limitless resources of the Church and Gerard's canny resourcefulness had restored the Church once again to the position of strength it had enjoyed. It had been a scare, and it was a cataclysm that Gerard was determined to avoid in the future. He had a simple plan to combat such an eventuality: he must be allowed to arrange the papal purse as he saw fit—without intervention from anyone. The Church, he decided, must eschew profligate spending completely, and it must continue to follow Nogara's Rule.

It is not surprising that in the seven years that Gerard had been head of the Prefecture for Economic Affairs he had come to regard the agency as his own private domain. Where other Vatican bureaucrats were deeply offended if His Holiness did not show an overwhelming interest in the affairs of their departments, Gerard was delighted.

As he hung up the phone, Gerard's only concern was making sure that someone with Gregory's lack of interest in fiscal matters be elected to replace the pope who had died that day. There were disturbing rumors that Anthony D'Orlando would almost certainly be named. Gerard knew that that could not be allowed to happen. He knew those liberals: D'Orlando would be giving out money to anyone who came to the back door, cap in hand. Besides, D'Orlando would be unlikely to keep a conservative like Gerard on in so delicate a position. Chances were that immediately after the election the Prefecture would be ruined by some new, liberal director, and Gerard's work would have been in vain. D'Orlando was not acceptable—worse, he was dangerous.

Gerard stared out the window. The new pope would have to be a conservative, an old-fashioned one. Someone who thought the Church existed on grace and manna. Someone, he thought, like the old war-horse Salvatore Di Nobili.

2

VATICAN PROTOCOL ALLOWS nine days in which to mourn a pope. A million or more people attend the lying-in state, filing by the lifeless figure somewhat lost, it seems, in the heavy folds of the papal regalia. The crowds come throughout the day and night, the bells of St. Peter's providing an endless mournful accompaniment. Each mourner stands in line for five or six hours to spend only a few seconds—perhaps long enough to mumble a prayer—in front of the scarlet-draped bier watched over by four Swiss Guards. Those who would like to linger are forced on and out by the crush of mourners behind.

Anthony D'Orlando attended the private leave-taking that was arranged for the curial cardinals the day after Gregory's death. He also participated in the solemn procession that bore Gregory's body from the Apostolic Palace to St. Peter's. But that did not prevent him from standing now, under a slate-gray sky, exposed with the crowd to the November cold, to pay his respects once more. He had joined the crowd on impulse and did not notice the movement, the cold, or the passage of time. He needed time to think.

He had had a visitor that morning, an old friend, Alain Cardinal LeBrewster. He was an affable, portly man who had a reputation for being the hard cutting edge of the liberal element in the college of cardinals. He held immense power. He had come to offer Anthony the papacy.

LeBrewster used joviality and irreverence to hide the fact, as best he could, that he was a consummate, wholehearted politician. Manipulation and intrigue came as easily to him as

the drawing of breath, and his friends and enemies alike—
and he had hordes of each—remarked that there were striking
similarities between LeBrewster and another French cardinal, one of a bygone age—Richelieu. But unlike Richelieu,
LeBrewster's word, when he gave it, was binding; his intentions were honorable. The more conservative were wary
of him, but held him in immense, if guarded, respect.

The secular world held no horror for him, and it was
thought in some quarters that he was far too comfortable in
the company of the rich and powerful for a man of God. He
knew of this rumor, as he knew of every other, and dismissed
it. "The saintly, such as myself," he would say smiling
broadly, "must have at least a working knowledge of sin."

His power within the Church and outside it was a fact that
could not be ignored. Two factors made his influence absolute: it was all-encompassing, stretching from the heights of
the college of cardinals to the grass roots, the parishes, di-
oceses, and seminaries, the Church's own rank and file. Le-
Brewster paid attention to details and he reaped a bountiful
harvest in friendship, information, and, ultimately, influence.
But far more important was the ultimate source of his authority—the papacy itself. Alain LeBrewster had been close
to Gregory in a way few men had. It had been his task,
whenever possible—and it had never been easy—to pull Gregory from the clouds, to temper the pope's idealism with cold
reasoning and cruel fact. He had not always been successful,
yet he had achieved his goal often enough to show the in-
siders, if not the world, that to a great extent the course that
the Church was sailing was due as much to Alain LeBrewster
as to Pope Gregory XI.

But LeBrewster had realized that his hard-won victories
would mean nothing if the election following Gregory's
death were not carefully orchestrated. He had felt the pulse
of the college carefully; he had sought opinions, confirming
a suspicion here and there, making a note of the biases, playing a hunch in the guise of seeking guidance. From his re-
searches he had forged a coalition—a delicate one, he knew,

but still the single largest bloc of votes in the college: the Pan-Europeans, a group of cardinals, liberals for the most part, representing all of Western Europe, North and South America, the Far East, and Oceania. He emerged from his wanderings as a pope-maker, a man to whom the majority of the college would look to for guidance, as the conservatives relied on Salvatore Di Nobili. LeBrewster's supporters hoped, and his detractors feared, that he would be able to deliver votes in conclave like an old ward boss. The time had come to put his power to the test.

LeBrewster lit the first of many cigarettes he would smoke that afternoon.

"Anthony, you know why I am here."

Anthony nodded. "I can guess," he said.

LeBrewster straightened himself in his chair, exhaled heavily, and looked squarely at Anthony.

"Much as you hate to admit it, the time has come. What you decide to do after hearing me out is crucial. Crucial not only in terms of you and our aspirations, but crucial for the Church. Crucial to the Catholics—and the non-Catholics—all over the world." He gestured toward the crowd outside the window. "They are waiting to see what we will do. To see whom we shall choose. This time they cannot be ignored, as they have been in the past. They are looking for two things in the next pope, and we must provide them: a man of action and a man of strength. We believe that you have those attributes—and we are not alone. Already the Romans are saying that you are *papabile*."

"My secretary tells me of it continually."

"And I am willing to wager that you do not allow yourself to hear him."

"It is a difficult thing to listen to, you must realize that."

"Don't think of the Crown, Anthony. Think of your chance to do good. I have not come here to glorify you, but to place in your hands the power to help, to save."

"I would like to know," Anthony said, "why you are not

using your considerable power to support your own candidacy."

LeBrewster laughed and stubbed out the cigarette. "You know, if I thought I had the slightest chance of winning I wouldn't be here now. But people think I have too much power as it is. They are quite prepared to take my advice—"

"That's a pleasant way of putting it," said Anthony.

"—but no one, certainly not you, Anthony, would be happy about taking orders from me. Besides, the ultraconservatives would never support a man they suspect of owning a dinner jacket." He laughed at his own joke and continued. "Anthony," he said with conviction, "I could not be elected, but you can."

Anthony said nothing and looked down.

"How modest the good father is," said LeBrewster, a touch of acid in his voice.

"Please do not think that I am not honored. I am. But I assure you that it is not false humility that makes me say that I feel unsure."

"Of course you are unsure," said LeBrewster. "I would think you the most extraordinary fool, or the most unbearable of egotists, if you assumed that you were immediately equal to the office. But listen." He leaned forward, lighting another cigarette. "For months now I have been traveling—Africa, South America, the United States, Europe, everywhere—and what have I seen? In South Africa we have civil wars, white against black. In central Africa, drought and famine. There are dictatorships in nearly every country, from the Tropic of Capricorn to the Sahara. A rice crop fails in the Far East—more famine, more death, more unrest—a powder keg. South America is no better. There is one country, *one*, on the whole continent that is not ruled by a military government. In Peru there is a dictatorship only a few months old, and already it is more brutal and more repressive than anything we have seen since the war. And all this on a continent generally considered to be *Catholic*.

"But there is more. I am told that the problems of Europe and America are different—a little more subtle. Where is the subtlety in terrorist bombings? In kidnappings? Society is coming apart at the seams. And where are the Catholics in the midst of all this disorder? They are not in church. We all know that. And why not? Because they cannot believe. *Cannot*, Anthony. They cannot believe because they see that their church is doing nothing at all to help. We do nothing for the Italians, nothing for Europeans, and nothing for the man languishing in a detention cell in Zaire, Argentina, or Peru. But there is one country that prospers. Ours. The Vatican. One hundred acres of peace, tranquillity, full bellies, full churches, full employment, no crime . . . we don't even have a parking problem. And why are things so rosy here?" LeBrewster shrugged his shoulders and answered his own question. "My friend, that's an easy one. We, alone, have the grace of God beaming down on us in an uninterrupted stream. He is looking out for us, taking care of us, making sure that we don't get our lovely vestments dirty. True? No, it is not true at all. We are rolling along without a care in the world because we have been looking out for ourselves. Because we have kept out of the troubles that we should be deeply involved in.

"It's time to get our hands dirty, Anthony, to get mired in the troubles and anguish of the ordinary human being—white, black, Catholic, Muslim, and Jew. It's time to forget that there are some who are Catholic and there are some who are not. We should see only people, whether they believe or not. And for that mission we need a strong man, a good one, and yes, a young one. A leader. You, Anthony. *You.*" He sat back in his chair and pulled on his cigarette with the air of a man who has spoken his piece.

"I presume you have canvassed the college on your views?"

LeBrewster nodded.

"And what was the reaction?"

"I cannot claim that I met with complete agreement," said

LeBrewster, "but certainly more than enough to insure your election.

"You must realize, Anthony," he continued, "that we cannot afford a long, divisive election. We cannot afford to wrangle for days in the conclave. It is time for quick, decisive action."

"What makes you so sure you can hand the office over?"

"It is a simple question of arithmetic," said LeBrewster. "There are one hundred and thirty-four cardinals. Because no one over the age of eighty can vote in an election, we can reduce that number by four right at the beginning. Provezano, Belotti, Solferino, Marcobi—all conservatives. Four votes we don't have to worry about. We need two-thirds of the college plus one to elect a pope. I know of sixty-seven votes committed already."

Anthony looked doubtful. Sixty-seven was a huge number to be voting as a unit before the conclave began.

"Believe me, Anthony, I know this for a fact. Of course, they won't come on the first ballot. Some have courtesy obligations and have had them for years. But by the third or fourth ballot, they will be voting for you. Added to these are the fourteen African votes from Mokate, making a total of eighty-one. And I don't think the other seven votes will be hard to get."

"Forgive my naïveté, Alain, but I always had the impression that the Holy Spirit had something to do with it."

"And so it does. Do you think we came up with this idea merely because we wanted to prove to the conservatives that we are more powerful than they are? Do you think we want you to become pope merely to give old Salvatore Di Nobili heart failure?"

Anthony smiled. "Poor Salvatore. Does he hate me that much?"

"He doesn't hate you, Anthony. He's just afraid of you. He doesn't understand your methods or your goals."

The tolling of the bells outside was the only sound to be

heard. The afternoon was making an abrupt change to evening. LeBrewster sighed heavily.

"Anthony," he said quietly, "don't let your modesty stand in the way of this. I'm afraid it's a luxury the Church couldn't afford to let you have. The Church is weak. It is time for new blood, for vigorous leadership. These last few months have been terrible for the Church. While Gregory lay dying the strength was sapped from us. You have a duty to accept, a duty to restore the strength. Of course," he shrugged, "if you genuinely feel that you cannot do it, that you would be doing us a disservice in accepting, you must refuse. But all I ask of you now is to think about it. Be sure of yourself. Examine your motives. We can talk again; there's no need to answer now. Now, I think I should be going. . . ."

Anthony and LeBrewster shook hands gravely. "Think," said LeBrewster. "Think hard."

Anthony smiled. "Alain, have you heard the Roman proverb . . . ?"

"Which one?" said LeBrewster, laughing. "There are so many."

"He who enters the conclave a pope, comes out a cardinal."

LeBrewster grinned. "Let that be the least of your worries."

The crowd had moved, carrying Anthony with it. He was inside St. Peter's now, and it was poorly lit and cold. The size and decoration of the building, so awesome when one entered from the warm summer sunlight of the square, seemed tawdry now in winter, bleak and comfortless. The vast space caught the coughs and shufflings of the crowd, quiet with grief though it was, making for a muffled cacophony of coughs and whispers. At the far end Anthony could see the white and red bier that held the embalmed corpse of the man who had, years before, spoken the words to Anthony which came rushing back to him now: "God will decide how we are to serve him in this world. . . ." Abruptly Anthony left the line and made for the door, his indecision dissolving.

3

SALVATORE CARDINAL DI NOBILI would have been astonished to find that he had a nickname; moreover, a ludicrous but fitting one. Having been considered a serious contender for the papacy on four occasions—without success —Vatican wags called him *la damigèlla*, the bridesmaid.

Gerard couldn't help thinking of the nickname as he dined with Salvatore. It had been a plain meal, as all meals in Salvatore's quarters were likely to be. Neither of the men had taken much notice of what they had eaten, usually consuming anything put in front of them. They were not, however, without their own culinary weaknesses. Salvatore was something of a snob about wine—though he took great pains to conceal it—and, despite the spartan mediocrity of the food he served, a good bottle of wine was assured. Gerard had an incurable sweet tooth, and he chafed now, after dinner, when he realized that a single, not very sweet pear was all he was going to get for dessert.

They sat in the cold vaulted sitting rooms of Salvatore's apartments, surrounded by pieces of heavy brown mahogany furniture. Gerard thought of the four long, steep flights of stairs he had climbed to get there and wondered how Salvatore had managed to find people willing to carry the furniture up for him.

The cardinal's manservant placed a tray of coffee on a low table between them and lighted the fire before he withdrew. It gave off little warmth but a great deal of smoke. Gerard sat erect in his armchair, drinking his coffee, his elbows tucked in at his sides. He took frequent sips from the cup and wondered just how to bring up the subject he had come to discuss. He had no great love for Salvatore; he found the old man, for the most part, quite tedious—a cardinal of the nineteenth century, his eyes closed to the world around him, seeing only the Church and, a short distance above that, God. However, Gerard knew that Salvatore found Gerard's duties at the Prefecture for Economic Affairs incomprehensible and had never made any attempt to understand them or to meddle, which suited Gerard admirably.

The two sat in silence for a moment.

"I am tired, Father," Salvatore said finally, sighing heavily.

"I'll leave you," said Gerard.

Salvatore motioned for him to stay. "No, that's not what I meant. . . . I am old, too tired of life to see much more. Gregory's death made me realize that. You know, I've seen four popes reign. . . ." He drank his coffee in a series of great gulps, forcing the tiny cup over his nose, all the while staring straight ahead, forgetting his guest.

Gerard shuffled his feet and cleared his throat. There was no sugar in his coffee, and there was no bowl on the tray. "Then, of course," he said, "there is the matter of the election."

"Yes," said Salvatore, looking neither right nor left, "the election."

It had once been said that Salvatore Cardinal Di Nobili was the only piece of genuine gothic amid the baroque splendor of the Vatican. There was some accuracy to the remark, for Salvatore did seem to suggest the gray grandeur of a gothic cathedral. His voice, as the students he lectured long and arduously at the Pontifical Gregorian University knew only too well, seemed to rise straight from the depths of a dark granite vault.

"The election," said Salvatore, "will take care of itself. It always does."

That, thought Gerard, is the statement of an old fool.

"I'm afraid, Father," said Gerard, "that I have had some news of a rather disturbing kind. It seems that some of the more liberal of our colleagues are trying to influence the election almost before it begins."

"There are always rumors of that sort before a conclave," said Salvatore. "They never mean anything."

"I think it would be wise to pay attention to these, Father."

Salvatore looked at Gerard. "What would you tell me, Father?"

"It seems that there has been a coalition made. A group of our colleagues are already pledging their support to a single candidate." Salvatore merely grunted and looked into the fire once more.

Who? Ask me, who? thought Gerard. That will give you a shock. They sat in silence for a few minutes. The question was not forthcoming.

"It seems," said Gerard, trying again, "that they are trying to put forward Anthony Cardinal D'Orlando."

Salvatore showed signs of life. "D'Orlando? He's barely sixty."

"Not even, Father. He's fifty-eight."

Salvatore seemed to sink again. "A very young man for the throne. But his candidacy is to be expected. He's been very . . . very visible recently."

"I think he is a shameless campaigner. He knows what he wants, and he shows himself a little too eager to get it," said Gerard vehemently.

Windblown rain brushed against the window, accenting the chill in the room. Salvatore was a long time replying.

"Perhaps. Perhaps. There was a time, Father, when certain elements thought that I was, as you put it, a shameless campaigner. Perhaps I was—I was very anxious to become pope. Not, as so many suspected, out of vanity, but because I thought I could do what was right and good. I have no doubt that Cardinal D'Orlando feels as I did." He paused. "But I admit that I share your concern. Cardinal D'Orlando may think he's doing good, yet I cannot but fear that in his 'doing good' he might seriously damage the Church."

"Exactly, exactly," said Gerard, a little too eagerly. "I

don't think we would be at fault if we thought Cardinal D'Orlando a dangerous man."

"A little uncharitable, Father." Six months earlier Salvatore would have agreed wholeheartedly, but now this kind of talk only tired him. He felt old and weak for the first time. "But I don't think we shall have to worry. The college will not elect D'Orlando."

"I wish I could share your confidence, Father."

Silence hung between them again. Salvatore was completely unaware that his complacency had infuriated his guest; Gerard did his best to control his temper.

"I do know something which I have only recently begun to realize, Father," said Salvatore, sighing. "Our day has passed. The tenor of the papacy, indeed of the whole Church, has changed. You say they are going to elect D'Orlando. I say that is a little farfetched." He smiled slightly, to soften his blunt words.

"But whomever they elect, the spirit, if not the outcome, of this conclave was decided years ago, decided in favor of what is called 'liberal.' Liberal . . ." He pondered the word for a moment. "Perhaps we would say 'wayward.' But whatever one's terms, conservatism is passing. Now, to hold fast to the older order of things is, for many of our colleagues, something of a sin. They shall hold the reins of power. But we shall have a role. You and I and a few others must act as a brake, a net below the tightrope, to insure against wholesale abandonment of the values for which we have stood for so long. We must make sure that the man elected will be the man who will do the least harm while doing the greatest good. And this time, like our time, shall pass. The Church will survive, as it always has, and emerge strong and shining, a beacon of hope."

"Your complacency is a little frightening, Father," said Gerard sharply. "I disagree. We cannot sit back and wait for the liberal ravages to do their damage. We must put up our own candidate to oppose them. Show them we are strong."

"But we aren't."

Gerard paid no attention. "We need someone who will lead us down the path we have followed for centuries, not to ruin us today or tomorrow as they would. Father, I can only hope that you will become the candidate for the true Church."

"Me? I cannot think that there would be enough support. You flatter me, Father, but I could never agree."

"There *is* support," Gerard insisted. "There is discontent in the college. It can be tapped, harnessed, and turned in our favor."

"I would not like to think of myself as the candidate of discontent," Salvatore said quietly.

"You are content, then, with the state of things as they are? You are content with the path we are taking? There's no telling what D'Orlando could embroil us in. He has been dangerously political already. Urging confrontation with the Communists, poking his nose into affairs in other countries—Africa, Latin America. Where will he stop? There's no telling what could happen."

Salvatore smiled. "No, Father, I am not content with the way things are, and I have no doubt that, if Cardinal D'Orlando were elected, and if he were to follow the path he has already set for himself, I would be even more unhappy. But remember, I do not believe that Cardinal D'Orlando will be elected. Remember too that the throne often has a sobering effect on a man. I have faith, Father, and I urge you to have it also."

"Faith and complacency can often be mistaken for one another."

"How true, and believe me, I have looked carefully at my own feelings, and there is no mistake." He leaned over and placed his bony hand on Gerard's forearm. It was a curiously paternal gesture from one man so close in age to another. "My friend, you have shown me great respect, and you have made me very proud to know that you think that I am fit for the throne of St. Peter. But please, let us not talk of this now. We must pray the Holy Spirit will enable us to do our duty. Remember, we are the brake, not the throttle."

Gerard stood up. "There is nothing that can be said to change your mind?"

"No, Father. Five years ago, maybe. But not now."

"But we shall act together in conclave?"

"You have my word."

"Then I feel all is not lost," said Gerard.

"Father, you know that all is never lost in the Church. Come, I'll see you out."

Once on the street, Gerard could not help feeling that he had been defeated. Without Salvatore to block Anthony D'Orlando, Gerard was uneasy about his own position. It was probably only a matter of time now before he would be forced to say good-bye to the Prefecture for Economic Affairs, the arm of the Vatican that he had built, that he had made strong. He shook off the chill that enveloped him. He had forty-five minutes before his call from New York and the reassuring familiarity of the portfolio.

4

ALBAN CARDINAL BREAKESPEARE-BEAUCHAMP, an English-man by birth and a Roman by virtue of having lived in that city for almost fifty years, knew more about the details of the papacy than any pope, than any man living. He easily outdistanced his closest rival, a dourly Lutheran professor of church history at the University of Mainz, with whom Alban enjoyed a long and learned correspondence.

Alban habitually wore—except in the height of the suffocating Roman summer—an ancient black overcoat and a scarf of his college colors, left over from his student days. Two bright blue eyes peered out from beneath bushy eyebrows which had long since ceased to be individual growths and had grown together to form a single unruly line of hair, like a misplaced, ill-kempt moustache.

Hardly a scrap of church-related information escaped the donnish old man. Apart from the actual history of the papacy, Alban could also wend his way with great confidence through the labyrinth of papal nobility, knowing without even having to think the exact order of precedence, the extent of the privileges and honors each member could claim. He knew every ceremony, every rite, every order, every honor, and every censure the Vicar of Christ held within his power to perform, confer, or declare. He was a mine of information on the regalia, the music, the pomp, and the majesty that made up the papal court. Such scholarship—and it had taken years to master it all—had made Alban a cardinal and Master of Papal Ceremonies. His duties were to oversee the smooth execution of every ceremony the pope wished or the liturgical calendar dictated. It was to Alban that the responsibility for staging Gregory's funeral fell.

He stood in the great nave of St. Peter's, a stooped old man in a wrinkled black soutane, watching with bright eyes the preparations going on all around him. He had not forgotten that the occasion that gave rise to the industry before him was a sad and solemn one; he carried his grief deep within him. Yet he could never quite suppress the ecstasy that enveloped him when he stood in St. Peter's, surrounded by the soaring grandeur of it all, the day before one of his beloved ceremonies. Workmen were erecting barriers and platforms for the television cameras (an innovation Alban didn't much like) and setting up rows of utilitarian black plastic chairs for guests.

As jockeys and racing drivers walk the course they are to travel the day before the event, so Alban never failed to pace the length and breadth of St. Peter's the day before a major ceremony. He was always worried that something would go wrong; a single mistake, a papal marquis out of order, would have been an error over which Alban would die a thousand deaths—a mistake which would undoubtedly be obvious to the world and shame him to the grave. He was quite lost in the details, forgetting for the moment that he had promised to show a journalist around the cathedral and give some background on the papal funeral.

Martin approached him diffidently. "Excuse me, Your Eminence."

Alban gave a little start. "Oh, Father Sykes. Hello."

"Your Eminence, I have the honor to present Rafaella Bianchi. I believe that Cardinal D'Orlando spoke to you about explaining tomorrow's events to her."

"Oh, yes, of course." Alban was always a little flustered in the presence of women. "How do you do, Miss Bianchi. I find your interest most gratifying. I hope I'll be able to enlighten you somewhat."

"I am assured, Your Eminence, that no one knows more about the Church than you."

"Well, I am not quite sure that's true. There's Professor Knauer at Mainz, he's always catching me on points. Small points, actually. Just last week I had a letter from him in which he mentions that I said that Pope Pelagius denied the title 'Oecumenical Patriarch' to St. John the Faster on two occasions. The title was denied twice, as I said, but the second time it was denied by Gregory the First. St. John took the title anyway. But Professor Knauer was right, I had completely forgotten about Gregory. Very silly of me."

Martin had melted away during this confession, and Rafaella was not quite sure what to say. "But," said Alban, "it's rather an academic argument, and I suppose it's not very interesting to most people. Well, I was just having my little walk through, and you are more than welcome to join me, Miss Bianchi."

"If I am not imposing, Your Eminence."

"Not at all, not at all." Alban rarely had a captive audience for his favorite subject. "I expect Father Sykes filled you in on most of what will happen tomorrow."

"Hardly at all. He said he wasn't quite sure what would happen."

"Splendid," said Alban. "The catafalque is placed here." He pointed to a spot in front of the central altar dwarfed by Bernini's swirling canopy. "In front of what is mistakenly called the papal altar. Its true title is the confessorial altar, the place where we are to come to make the confession, not of our sins, but of our faith. It's quite extraordinary the number of people who refer to this altar, the largest one in St. Peter's, as the papal altar. I suppose it's a forgivable mistake, though. . . . The body is vested in scarlet with the pallium—that's a circular band of white wool made from the wool of lambs blessed on St. Agnes's Day—and the fanon, a vestment worn on only the most solemn of occasions, about the shoulders. On His Holiness's head is the golden miter of the Bishop of Rome. On this side aisle we will find the members of the papal nobility—the pontifical family, as they are called. There is a strict order of precedence which I won't bother to go into. It would only bore you . . . or would it?"

"No, not at all, I assure you."

"Well, if you're quite sure," he said quickly, delighted. "Heading the procession is the papal cupbearer. His duty at one time was raising the cup of wine, at mealtimes, to the lips of the pope. Of course, his function has long since been dispensed with, but not the office, I am pleased to say. Behind him comes the master of the sacred hospice, another title that carries no duties but dates from the thirteenth century. His responsibility was to oversee the proper eating and sleeping arrangements for the pope and cardinals should they be away from the Apostolic Palace. Now the master of the hospice has but one function. Should a queen come to visit the Holy Father, the master of the hospice will take her to him on his arm. I'm afraid that it is not a function he is called on to perform very often. Behind him comes the prince assistant, in black velvet knee breeches. He stands, very prominently, on the right-hand side of the papal throne. Or rather, he did when we still had papal thrones. Pope Paul did away with them."

"Surely the chair on which the pope is carried is a throne?"

"Not exactly. It's a lavish, ornate chair, of course, but its function is purely practical. People cannot see His Holiness when he arrives at a mass or an audience, so the portable chair, or *sedia gestatoria*, solves that. It is not an implied badge of rank as the throne would be."

"And the papal nobility, are these men cardinals?"

"Dear me, no, they aren't priests or clerics of any kind. These posts are held by members of families who come from what one would call the Roman aristocracy. They are the very old families of Rome: the Colonnas, the Della Roveres, the Chigis, the Orsinis—these families are almost as old as the papacy itself. In fact, all of them have, at one time or another, contributed a pope to the church. There were two Orsini popes. These families don't hold these positions in perpetuity, though. There are changes every so often. A few years ago the prince assistant was ejected, and his post was given to another family."

"Really? Why was that?"

"I don't know the exact details . . . a scandal of some sort . . . something about an actress," Alban muttered, embarrassed. "Where was I? Oh yes. Behind the prince assistant come the heads of the various orders of papal knights. The leading knight is the grand master of the Knights of the Order of the Hospital of St. John of Jerusalem. This is a very ancient order of knights, and the grand master is accorded, in certain Catholic countries, the rank of royalty. The present master doesn't travel much now though. He lives here in Rome, on the Via Condotti, and his house is a separate state. He can issue his own passports, make his own laws, even issue his own license plates. I must say, the Italians are very kind about giving away bits of their country."

"What does the grand master do—within the Church, I mean?"

"Oh," said Alban a little bewildered, "nothing. . . . Now behind him comes the grand ducal knight of the knights templar or, to give them their full name, the Poor Knights of Christ and of the Temple of Solomon. . . ." They continued to walk, and Alban never stopped talking. Finally they found themselves back in front of the main altar.

"The dean of the sacred college will read an account of His Holiness's life, mentioning, of course, his major achievements while pontiff. The account is rolled up and put in a metal container and placed within the coffin. But other things are put inside the coffin as well. Examples of all the medals struck during the reign will be placed in there. Then all the cardinals will come forward and each will sprinkle holy water on the remains. Then the coffin is sealed. Actually, I should say coffins. There are three of them."

"Why three?"

"Well, the innermost is made of cypress, which is a fine and rich wood. But it's not very durable, so a coffin made of lead is built around it to contain it. The outermost coffin is made of elm, which is very strong; a lovely wood, very pretty. After all the coffins have been sealed, they are carried to the crypt by eight Swiss Guards. At one time the coffin was carried by the pontifical honor guard, but they were disbanded in 1970. And they had been in service for so long, too. That was a great pity." He was silent for a moment.

"People laugh at me, but I do wish they wouldn't change these things." There was genuine distress in his voice, and he looked at Rafaella as if she were his oldest friend. "I don't wish to criticize the Holy Father, of course, not at all. I just think I am a little too old for change." He smiled weakly.

Rafaella was somewhat disconcerted by so heartfelt a confession. He sensed her unease and resumed his commentary.

"Sometimes, when the pontiff has been a bit, well, portly, the weight of the body plus the weight of the coffins is too great to be carried. Then the remains are lowered into the crypt on pulleys. We don't anticipate that problem this time. And that is the end of the funeral. Barring, of course, the unforeseen."

"I'm sure everything will work out well. I'm sure there's never been a mistake."

"I wish that were true. The funeral of Pope Pius the Twelfth was very unfortunate. I don't even wish to think about it."

Rafaella wanted to ask what happened, but she could see that the memory upset the old man. "I'm sure you needn't worry."

"Actually, it was very interesting, and Cardinal Breakespeare-Beauchamp is terribly nice," said Rafaella, as she faced Martin across the table in a busy café in the Via Conciliazione. "Tell me, what happened at the funeral of Pius the Twelfth? His Eminence mentioned it as if something terrible happened, but he wouldn't go into it."

"The funeral was pretty bad, according to people who

were there. A Swiss Guard fainted."

"That's not so terrible."

"He fainted because attempts to embalm Pius had failed. Apparently the smell . . ."

"Oh, no!"

"Here, have some coffee."

She sipped. "He also said something about there being seven arms of Saint Barbara. That can't be true."

"There are seven convents claiming to own one of Saint Barbara's arms. There are two heads of Saint Lawrence—in fact there's one in the Vatican library; he was the patron of librarians. There are about sixty churches claiming to have one of Saint John the Baptist's fingers. And we have enough wood from the True Cross to build a log cabin. The people of Lareto in the north of Italy claim to possess the Virgin Mary's house—a group of angels flew from Nazareth to Lareto carrying it and placed it there."

"Now, you can't honestly believe that any of these things are genuine."

"Well, personally, I don't. And in all but a few cases, the Church doesn't believe them either. That's why there is a whole department at the Vatican that does nothing but look into these relics. For Alban, it's a hobby. His other interest is tracing the lineage of the papal nobility."

"That's not a subject I'm very well versed in. I grew up with a father who hates the shreds of nobility that Italy has left. He snubs them; they snub him."

"I would imagine that Alessandro Bianchi doesn't have to worry too much about papal nobles. Their titles are honorary; even less than that, they're hollow. The Bianchi power on the other hand is concrete and well-known."

Rafaella nodded. "True, but that's not enough. Maybe you don't see it as much because you're a foreigner, but there is as strong a class system in Italy as there is in England. My father may be richer and more powerful, more influential than the prince of this and the duke of that, but a noble heritage still counts for a lot here. It means being accepted, part of the power structure. Alessandro Bianchi will always be the rich, uncouth brigand from Sicily, and he knows it; and believe me, he feels it."

"But how could it possibly bother him?"

Rafaella sounded a little angry. "Of course it bothers him—how could it not? He tried to get on their good side once. Have you ever heard of the Jockey Club?"

Martin nodded. The Jockey Club was Rome's most exclusive club, a quiet mahogany-and-marble playpen for what remained of Italy's wealthy aristocracy.

"After the war," Rafaella continued, "when my father was coming on strong in the business world, he tried to join the club. He was turned down. Now they beg him to join."

"That's understandable. He's somebody now."

"He was somebody then," said Rafaella hotly. "To them he's still the same Alessandro Bianchi, only now he owns all the buildings adjacent to the club. The club members are terrified he'll tear them down and surround the staid old Jockey Club with parking lots, gas stations, and, I don't know, strip joints . . . but he's not doing anything. He's just sitting on the holdings, making them sweat."

Martin caught a note of pride in Rafaella's voice. "Every rejection hurts him, and he never forgets one." She looked Martin squarely in the eyes. "Don't make the mistake everyone else has. Alessandro Bianchi is a human being, and since my mother died and he left Sicily, he has been a lonely man—except for me. And then I left him. For almost twenty years it was just me and him. . . . Okay, I know what they say about him, but believe me he's paid for what he has."

"Why did he want it so badly?"

"How do you know he did?"

"I just know what I hear."

"And what have you heard?"

Martin shifted uneasily in his seat. "I think it would be better if we didn't get into this."

"No, come on," Rafaella challenged. "Tell me."

Martin leaned back in his chair and drained his coffee cup

before answering. "There was a small company in the north, in Turin, I think. This company made building materials—door frames, window frames—the things that you never think about that go into a building. Apparently your father owns a construction company, I don't know what it's called . . ."

"Costruzione Bianchi," said Rafaella.

". . . Costruzione Bianchi, thank you. Well, for some reason it was decided that if Industria Bianchi acquired this small company, it would be to Costruzione Bianchi's advantage. There was a problem though. The little company was family-owned, and the family didn't want to sell. Your father was anxious that they sell, and he didn't care how he got them to do it. . . . They sold in the end."

"How?"

"He besieged the company with orders. It was such a small company that it couldn't keep up with them. Because the firm was swamped with work, the old customers—not great customers, just the steady orders—weren't getting their goods when they needed them, so they took their business elsewhere. As soon as they did that, your father had Costruzione Bianchi withdraw a lot of their orders, and the little construction company went into a tailspin. They ended up selling to Industria Bianchi very cheaply."

Rafaella looked away for a moment. The pained expression on her face made Martin sorry he had spoken so bluntly. "You sound more like a prosecuting attorney than a priest," she said.

Martin shook his head. "Still a priest," he said, "all of me."

"I'm sorry," she said, smiling slightly. "It's hard for me to remember. Apart from Father Sparveri at the convent school and the parish priest at Sette Bagni—that's where my father and mother were from, in Sicily—you're the only priest I've spoken to for any length of time. And you couldn't be more different from Father Sparveri. He used to frighten me to death. I must have been eleven or twelve years old, a virtuous, wealthy little Roman maiden, and he told me I had committed a mortal sin. I nearly died. . . ."

"What had you done?"

Rafaella looked sheepish. "Maybe I shouldn't tell you. Maybe it was a mortal sin." She laughed, remembering her old terror.

"Come on, let me put your soul at rest."

"Well—I can't believe that these old remembered fears don't die. Thinking back, I'm frightened all over again. Okay." She braced herself. "I tasted some holy water. What are you laughing at? I just wanted to see if it tasted different from real water. . . ."

Martin laughed. He buried his face in his hands and laughed till his shoulders shook. He groaned weakly, wiping his eyes. "*That* is certainly grounds for eternal damnation."

"Well," said Rafaella indignantly, "I was scared. I told my father and he was furious. He wanted to beat up Father Sparveri."

"That's not a very Christian attitude," said Martin, still smiling. "But I daresay the good Father Sparveri deserved it."

"My father doesn't pretend to be a Christian."

"Unlike a lot of people . . . I suppose I shouldn't really bother you about him. After all, you are upholding the commandment 'Honor Thy Father and Thy Mother.'"

"Look," said Rafaella suddenly, "come and meet my father. I'll arrange a dinner."

"Come on . . ."

"No. I'm serious. What do you say? Come and judge the richest and the most ruthless man in Italy for yourself."

Martin thought for a moment. "Okay. But it will have to wait until the conclave begins."

"You won't back out?"

"No, of course not. I look forward to it."

"Saint George and the dragon. I can't wait."

"Which is which?"

Rafaella just laughed.

5

Rome is not a city well suited to mourning. Suppressing the natural volubility of the place is not an easy task, and following Gregory's faultlessly orchestrated funeral, there was a citywide sigh of relief as the weeds were stripped away and the populace looked forward to the opening of the conclave.

Martin and Anthony stood in the courtyard of San Domaso, an open space deep in the center of the Apostolic Palace. The courtyard is a small one, and the bastion walls of the palace loomed above them; lights were burning in the windows that peered out over the yard. They could hear the choir singing *"Veni Creator Spiritus"* from within the Sistine Chapel. Anthony should have joined the assembled cardinals, but he lingered with Martin, as if to breathe his last free air. The beginning of the conclave, now only minutes away, hung over them, making both of them nervous.

"I suppose," said Martin, "that it is too late for me to enter the conclave with you." He had not really expected Anthony to authorize his entry into the conclave. Every cardinal was allowed to bring in a single assistant, but Anthony, characteristically, had decided that he needed no one.

"I'm afraid so. . . . If I were you, Martin, I would just spend the next few days doing as little as possible. There is going to be quite a bit of work to do when this is over."

A smile spread slowly over Martin's face. "So you've accepted the inevitable?"

Anthony hesitated a moment. "If the college has accepted it."

"We know they have. We knew that this morning."

At the Pontifical Votive Mass in St. Peter's that morning, LeBrewster had given the oration *"De Eligendo Pontifice,"* a speech in which a distinguished member of the college outlines the type of man the cardinals should seek to elect. He had called for "a man of God and a man of the times . . ." The speech is invariably taken to represent the wishes of the majority of the cardinals. There could be no doubt to whom LeBrewster was referring.

A bell began to ring in the tower above them. It was the signal that the area was to be cleared of all those not entering the conclave. Anthony and Martin shook hands, as if one of them was going on a journey.

"I shall pray for you," said Martin.

"Pray for us all," said Anthony.

Six years of living in Italy had taught Martin the finer points of Italian driving. With no traffic against him, it didn't take long for him to get out of Rome and into the rolling countryside. He pulled his tiny Fiat up in front of the huge gates that marked the entrance to the Bianchi estate.

Security was stringent. His car was searched by four men at the gate. He was asked for identification, and his invitation was confirmed by telephone with the house, which Martin still couldn't see. One of the guards drove Martin up the long twisting drive, the manicured lawns stretching away on both sides. At points throughout the garden stood tall pylons surmounted by spotlights. Martin wondered how many armed men hid in the shadows.

The house was extravagant. It was a voluptuously beautiful Palladian villa, perfectly proportioned, built of the brown-pink travertine stone that becomes even more beautiful as it grows older. Martin was surprised at the delicacy of the house. He had expected a cold, brash modern home, the architecture of the self-made man.

In the midst of the warm splendor of the house, Rafaella

looked even more radiant than usual. She had dressed simply, almost without care; a silk blouse hung loosely from her shoulders, and flowing trousers were gathered tightly at her slim waist. Her coppery hair was tied behind her head. She appeared at once businesslike and warmly feminine, and Martin, once again, felt shabby beside her.

"You're very punctual," said Rafaella.

"It's something you should expect from a seminarian,' said Martin with a smile.

"I'll remember that in future," she replied, laughing. "Come and meet Papa."

Instead of going further inside the house, Rafaella led Martin across a lawn that dropped away from the house. They followed a path that led them to a large garden shed set in a dark thicket of trees. Lights glowed through the windows. "Papa's retreat," she said, opening the door.

The shed was dominated by a huge wine press, a barrel-like contraption with spaces between the slats. What looked like the shaft of an enormous screw protruded from the top of the press; at right angles to the screw was a beam which forced the weight of the press down onto the grapes. Bianchi was bent over the lever like a rower, forcing it back and forth; the action made a heavy rasping sound. A thin brown liquid dribbled from the bottom of the barrel into a pan on the floor. The air was heavy with a sweet, sharp alcohol smell that caught in Martin's throat and made his head spin slightly. He realized he hadn't eaten since early that morning.

"Papa," said Rafaella, laying her hand lightly on her father's shoulder. "This is Martin Sykes."

Bianchi straightened and whipped a stained handkerchief from his back pocket to wipe his sticky hands. He was dressed in worn old corduroy trousers and a bleached-out shirt that might once have been blue, ragged at the elbows.

He was an unremarkable-looking man, short, stocky, and coarse-boned. His crinkly black hair was thin on top and gray around the edges, and he had the bulbous nose of a

Sicilian. Martin searched for some resemblance between father and daughter but found none. Apart from his nose, Bianchi's face seemed to be almost without features, yet he had the air of a man used to having others do exactly what he told them to do.

If he disliked Martin he did not show it. Martin, mindful of Bianchi's reputation, half expected to be greeted with the gesture that Italian males reserve for priests: one hand cupping the testicles, the other hand held above the head, with index and little finger raised to ward off the evil eye. He shook hands affably enough, but Martin could feel the man's eyes sizing him up.

"How do you do, Father Sykes," he said in surprisingly clear English. "I'm sorry I am such a mess."

"It's an honor to meet you," Martin replied, secretly glad that Bianchi looked disheveled. It made him feel a little more comfortable.

"Do you live in Rome, Father?"

"Please call me Martin . . . yes I do."

"Papa," Rafaella chided, "I *told* you he did."

"I'm sorry, I forgot. If you live in Rome I'll send you some wine when it's done, but if you lived farther away I couldn't. My wine doesn't travel well. If you carry certain wines too far they spoil. Don't ask me why . . . sometimes fifty miles is too far."

"Papa enjoys talking about wine more than he enjoys drinking it," said Rafaella with a grin.

"Ho! Don't believe that."

"Surely," said Martin, "it's too late in the year to be making wine."

"Rafaella, you've brought an expert with you!" said Bianchi, smiling broadly. "You're absolutely right. I am not making wine here." He gestured toward the press. "This is *grappa*. After you've made the wine, you take the mash that's left over and press it again; then you ferment the liquid that you get. People call *grappa* peasant brandy, but I like it."

"It looks like hard work," said Martin.

"Hard work is good," said Bianchi simply. "I watched my father make *grappa* every year when I was a child. Then one day I was old enough to help him. I hated it at first. I was impatient with the process. Now I like it." He raised his hands, palms open. "We change . . ."

"Do you do it all yourself?"

"Everything. If I didn't, it wouldn't be my wine. I even go to the market and select the grapes myself. Funny thing about grapes," said Bianchi, scratching his head. "When I was a boy, I used to go to the market with my father to buy grapes, but he'd never get the ones I wanted, the nice big, juicy fat ones. He would always get the ones that were a little on the brown side, two steps away from rotten. I couldn't understand that, but now I know why. The brown ones are fermenting already; they are good wine grapes but terrible eating grapes. Now I look for the same thing."

"I didn't know that," said Martin.

"Don't encourage him," said Rafaella. "He'll stand here all night and talk about wine. Papa, go and get cleaned up. . . ."

"You see how she treats me," Bianchi said to Martin, slipping a strong arm affectionately around his daughter's waist.

"Papa!" Rafaella shrieked, breaking away from him. "You'll get that sticky grape juice all over my clothes!"

Martin was amused at how easily Rafaella managed her father. He wished that captains of industry the world over could see the terrible Alessandro Bianchi pushed around by his daughter. It was touching, in a way.

The three of them returned to the house. Bianchi disappeared upstairs to wash and dress, and Martin and Rafaella settled in a small paneled drawing room that was warm and surprisingly intimate, considering the size of the house. A drinks tray stood on a table, and Martin accepted a Campari from Rafaella, as she poured herself a Lillet.

"You see," she said, curling up in an armchair, "my father has no horns, no pointed tail, doesn't carry a gun, and doesn't talk like a gangster."

"He was charming," said Martin, thinking that any guns Bianchi might need were carried for him by the men at the gates.

"But you're not convinced," Rafaella added.

"What difference does it make?" Martin replied.

Sicilians can be charmingly voluble or ominously silent. Bianchi was talkative throughout dinner, cracking jokes and telling anecdotes. Martin found himself straining to catch every word the man said. The meal, the lavishness of the dining room, the heady wine—one of Bianchi's own—acted on Martin's brain like a narcotic. He found himself liking Alessandro Bianchi.

Gradually conversation turned to the Church, and Martin noticed that Bianchi said less and less. His reticence put a barely perceptible strain on the meal; Rafaella seemed unaware of it.

"I attended the Pontifical Votive Mass this morning," she said. "I looked for you, but the Basilica was too crowded."

"You've certainly been spending a lot of time in church," Martin said to her, glancing at Bianchi.

"Well, I'm trying to get as much background as I can. The other subjects I'll be covering while I'm here are a little easier to grasp than the Church. In fact, I'm afraid you'll have to rescue me again. During the Mass this morning, someone made a long speech in Latin. What was he talking about?"

"That was Cardinal LeBrewster. The speech, 'De Eligendo Pontifice,' is an outline of the type of man the cardinals should be looking for. He called for 'a man of God and a man of the times.' There's no doubt he meant Anthony Cardinal D'Orlando."

"I would have thought that such a description fit Cardinal Van Doorn best," said Bianchi quietly.

Martin was surprised that Bianchi could name a cardinal. "Do you know Cardinal Van Doorn?"

"Father Sykes, few important businessmen in Italy—probably in the world—don't know Gerard Van Doorn. Being on good terms with him is considered a very sound investment."

Martin had the feeling that this was the Bianchi demeanor the world knew. His smiling, jocular manner was gone. There was a slight, almost intangible tone of menace in his voice.

"Cardinal Van Doorn? Have you told me about him?" Rafaella looked quizzically at Martin. She was surprised to hear her father speak so highly of a churchman.

"Cardinal Van Doorn controls the papal purse."

"He does a lot more than that," said Bianchi. "He could, if he wished, control the Italian economy—the profitable part of it, at least—but Gerard prefers to invest his money elsewhere."

"Surely," said Rafaella, "the Church's money is wrapped up in things that are extremely valuable but could not be sold. You couldn't sell the *Pietà* or the ceiling of the Sistine Chapel."

"That is what so many people think, but in actual fact, when the Church catalogues its wealth, it doesn't even include its treasures," Bianchi replied.

"There's no doubt that the Church is wealthy," said Martin, "but surely you overrate the power and size of their holdings."

Bianchi shrugged off the contradiction. He had no real interest in arguing about the extent of Vatican power. Bianchi knew where it began and had a fair idea of where it ended; clearly the young priest did not.

"Of course," he said, "you priests would like to think that your power comes exclusively from God. That is not quite true—not in the real world, anyway. Before Van Doorn took over the Prefecture for Economic Affairs, the Church's pocketbook had taken a savage beating. It is a testament to the men who labored making it strong before the disastrous early seventies that it withstood it at all. Between 1972 and 1974, the Vatican lost enormous amounts of money through dangerous and foolhardy maneuverings. Van Doorn was handed a Vatican financial machine that hardly worked at all and was told to fix it, to get it back on track. Believe me, he has mended it well. Now the Prefecture and its investments run like a sewing machine. Van Doorn moved mountains—mountains of money. That, Father Sykes, is power. More powerful than a sip of wine, a slice of bread, and a Hail Mary."

An older priest might have been nettled by this irreverence. Martin ignored it. He wanted to hear more—getting solid information about the Vatican treasury was a difficult task.

Bianchi obliged him. He settled back in his chair and looked at the young man. He looked like a man about to tell a fairy tale to a group of children. "Tell me, Father, have you ever heard of Michele Sindona?"

"I'm sorry. I haven't."

"It's a remarkable thing for me to realize that people know so little about the organization they work for. If you ask one of the workers in my factories 'Who do you work for?' he will tell you 'Bianchi.' "

"And if you were to ask me the same question," said Martin, "I would say 'the pope.' "

"And you would be only half right, Father. . . . Tell me, are you paid?"

"Yes. Five hundred thousand lira a month. Six hundred dollars."

"That's hardly princely."

"It's not a job you take for the money."

"True, of course. But on six hundred dollars a month you pay no taxes, so you aren't doing so badly."

"And you, Papa? Do you pay taxes?" asked Rafaella, smiling. Among the rich and poor alike, tax evasion was almost a national sport in Italy.

Bianchi ignored her. "You have never wondered where that money comes from?" he asked Martin.

"I haven't wondered," he replied, "because I know. The Church is given money, is bequeathed money, and, true, it has certain investments. But the Church is not a corporation. We don't pay our stockholders dividends."

"At least not here on earth," said Rafaella.

Martin and Bianchi smiled. "We hope their dividends come in the hereafter," Martin said.

"Let me ask you another question," said Bianchi. "Before Van Doorn, who ran the Prefecture for Economic Affairs?"

"Cardinal . . . let me see, Cardinal Vagnozzi."

"That is what the Vatican Who's Who, *Pontificio Annuario*, would have us believe. The person who was actually in charge of the money was Pope Gregory himself. Gregory was a Sozio. The Sozio family have been important bankers in Lombardy for generations. He had always been interested in the financial side of the Church, so when he became pope he took on the heaviest responsibility of the job. He developed a master plan. He wanted to move the Vatican wealth out of Italy, into the safer, less volatile markets of Western Europe and America. But he needed help. He turned to a man outside the Church, a friend of his, a man known for his charitable works as well as his ability to turn a profit. Michele Sindona." Bianchi paused to light a cigar.

A white-coated servant entered silently, bearing a tray with a silver coffee pot and demitasse cups; he placed the tray in front of Rafaella, who poured the coffee. Bianchi looked up from the flame that he held to the end of his cigar.

"Pietro," he said to the servant, "*grappa* for Father Sykes and for me. Rafaella?" Rafaella shook her head. The servant nodded and withdrew.

"When Gregory the Eleventh was still Monsignore Tarquinio Sozio, Sindona helped him raise the cash for one of his pet charities. I don't remember what it was—a hospital, an orphanage, a home for some ancient nuns—it doesn't matter. Sindona worked very hard and did very well for the monsignore. So Gregory trusted him, and when the time came, he asked Sindona to help him. The Church has a history of asking laymen to advise them on their money. Perhaps that is a comment on the honesty of priests—I don't

60

know. There was another layman, Bernardino Nogara, who ruled the Vatican treasury for decades. He trained Gerard Van Doorn. Nogara was conservative and brilliant, which is a rare combination of virtues in an Italian. Usually Italian conservatives are as brilliant as a heap of *baccalà* drying in the sun. Nogara was dead by the time Gregory went hunting for a new brain. When Sindona came along, all the followers of Nogara were pushed aside. Sindona wanted a free hand, and I don't blame him, considering what he wanted to do. Many of the Nogara men resigned, but not Gerard. He knew that Sindona would make mistakes, and Gerard has always been good at capitalizing on the mistakes of others. He knew that Sindona was not clever enough to handle the type of money that Pope Gregory gave him to control."

"How much money are we talking about?" said Martin, reaching for the tiny glass of pale brown liquid that had been placed silently at his elbow. The *grappa* burned his tongue at first; then he felt the warmth of the liquor spreading through him.

"I don't imagine that anyone will ever know for certain. The initial investment was probably in the region of five hundred million."

"Good God!" said Rafaella.

"God had very little to do with it; if He had, perhaps this story would have a happier ending. Sindona worked quickly. He got busy transferring money here and there, making some very fine investments in the process. The Vatican built and owns the Pan Am Building on the Champs-Elysées in Paris, the Stock Exchange in Montreal, even the fabled Watergate complex in Washington."

"Come on . . ." said Martin.

"Absolutely true, I assure you. But Sindona made a lot of mistakes, terrible investments, and he broke a lot of rules. He got the United States Securities and Exchange Commission after him. The hallowed Bank of Italy began investigating him—though they are hardly a terrifying organization. But Sindona made a fatal mistake: he upset the Swiss. It's always foolhardy to get the Swiss upset about banks. Sindona got scared. He offered a million dollars to that Nixon committee that there was such a fuss over . . . the reelection committee. He wanted the S.E.C. off his back, but that man —what was his name?—Stans, Maurice Stans, refused the donation. One by one the Sindona banks began to fold. Maybe you've heard of the Franklin National Bank in New York? It was run by Sindona—run right into the ground."

"I remember that," said Rafaella. "It was in the New York papers for days, but no one ever mentioned the Vatican."

"Of course not," said Bianchi, smiling as he swirled the *grappa* in his glass. "The Vatican knows better than anyone how to keep its name out of the papers. Anyway, the Bank of Italy stepped up its investigation; they were even talking about a prison term for Sindona, who by this time had bought himself a million-dollar co-op apartment in New York. The Swiss closed a Sindona bank in Geneva. By the time the watchdogs had finished, Sindona was out of business and the Vatican was in the hole by—who knows how much?"

"Would you care to guess?"

"It would be impossible to say. Some say that losses were as low as—a relative term, in this case—one hundred million dollars. Some say it was as high as ten percent of the Vatican's total value."

"Ten percent," said Martin. "That must be an enormous figure."

"I would say," said Bianchi, relighting his cigar with studied nonchalance, "that that would be in the region of one billion dollars."

"That means," said Rafaella, "that the Vatican is worth about ten billion dollars. Good God."

"No one knows exactly how much the Church is worth— except Gerard of course. But that is not the end of the story. Sindona had fled to New York, and the Church was left with mounting losses and a very worried, very old, very ill pope. Gregory had hoped that he could defend the Church against any troubles that might arise if Communists gain full power in this country. Gregory looked at history and saw that when the Church had fallen from favor it was its purse that suffered most."

"That's true," said Martin. "When Henry the Eighth declared himself head of the Church of England, he seized the wealth of the monasteries first, and decided that seizing people's souls could wait for a while."

"Exactly," said Bianchi. "And believe me, if the government took over the Vatican holdings in Italy the economy would get its greatest boost in years. But because of the Sindona affair Gregory was sure he had left the Church defenseless. He was tired of money; it had brought him nothing but trouble, and he had been let down rather hard by a man he trusted. He wanted a discreet man of the cloth to take the troubled finances out of his hands. He turned to Gerard Van Doorn . . . he should have years ago. Gregory never knew what Van Doorn did for the Church. After turning the finances over to him, Gregory would hear very little about it. That was the way he wanted it."

Martin stared at Bianchi intently. "What did Van Doorn do?"

Bianchi let Martin hang a moment before answering him. "I don't know. Van Doorn would have made an excellent spy. He is security-conscious and very meticulous. He is not infallible—that quality is reserved for one high-ranking churchman at a time—but he is careful. So careful that he has built an almost impenetrable wall of secrecy and silence around his doings."

"I'd like to know more about them," said Rafaella, thinking of her article.

Bianchi smiled knowingly. "You will never get a thing. The Vatican doesn't talk to the press about money."

"But one must be able to find out something," said Martin. "Why do *you* care?"

Martin was taken aback by the question; he had never meant to show that Gerard's doings were of interest to him.

Bianchi smiled affably. "You do not have to apologize,

Father. Even for those of you who have taken a vow of poverty, money remains the most interesting thing in the world. We are all fascinated by it; we want to know where it comes from and where it goes. It is nothing to be ashamed of. To answer your question: there are thousands of ways of investing money and a million or more ways of hiding those investments. Gerard is operating on many levels, through clever and discreet middlemen. To recoup his losses he must play tough—he might even break some rules—but he will never be caught the way Sindona was. Let me tell you something. You Vatican priests should watch Cardinal Van Doorn."

Martin had always watched Gerard. "Really? Why?"

"Because if Gerard were to fall under the wheels of a busload of pilgrims on the Via Conciliazione, the Vatican would never be able to recover the information in Gerard's head. It would be very bad for business." Bianchi laughed quietly.

"I hadn't thought of that."

"You had not thought of it because you did not know it. You see, Van Doorn is certainly a man of the times. We have had the Stone Age, the Bronze Age, the Iron Age. We are living now in the Money Age, and no one knows that better than Gerard Van Doorn."

"He might make an excellent chairman of the board," said Martin, "but the Vatican has more important business than business."

"Of course, forgive me, I forget. There are the souls of millions to consider. All the profits are an accident. The Vatican built the Rome Hilton and the Rome International Airport as monuments to the great glory of God. Correct?"

"Now, Papa, you must be exaggerating," said Rafaella. "How do you know they built them?"

"The omniscient press," said Bianchi sarcastically, gesturing toward his daughter. "You should pay more attention to rumors, my love, the more scandalous the better. You can never tell when it might pay you handsomely."

"Trite though it may sound," said Martin, "we are more interested in people than profits."

"Of course you are." Bianchi smiled patronizingly. "But you must understand how it looks to a poor peasant from Calabria or Abruzze, or a rich peasant like myself from Sicily. The way the priests live and the riches of the Church lead us devout peasants"—he crossed himself ostentatiously—"to think that money may have a soul after all. But I can see your problem. If the Church pleads poverty, the people will lose all respect for you. When you wheel and deal, they hate you. Believe me, Father Sykes, I sympathize, I sympathize. It's a problem all the rich have to face. . . . Now if you'll excuse me . . . it's been interesting talking with you, Father Sykes. You must come again. Rafaella rarely brings home men of the cloth."

After Bianchi left them, Rafaella and Martin had a last cup of coffee in the drawing room.

"If we were arguing," said Martin, "I think he won."

"He wasn't arguing, he was just putting you through the paces. He doesn't respect men who just agree with everything he says."

"He certainly had a number of interesting things to say." Martin was trying to remember everything Bianchi had said about Gerard. It suddenly dawned on him that in less than twenty-four hours Anthony would be pope. "I must go. . . ."

They stood at the top of the steps in the cold fresh air.

"Thank you," said Martin. "It's certainly been memorable."

Rafaella smiled at him, as if enjoying a private joke. "Tactful, discreet, idealistic," she said, "a dangerous combination." She leaned forward and kissed him lightly on the cheek. "Good night." She turned and entered the house quickly.

On the drive back to Rome, Martin could feel the place where her lips had touched, like a burn.

6

GERARD VAN DOORN looked over the two ranks of his fellow cardinals as they sat on their thrones, a tiny canopy over each holy head, and realized that they reminded him of nothing if not a herd of goats. He couldn't drive the uncharitable thought from his head, so he surrendered himself to it. LeBrewster was the sleek and cunning goat, a satyr. He led the rest, the mangy, bleating animals of the herd, their hooves planted firmly in the milking pail, the sullen gleam of stupidity lurking behind each eye. He knew that before long these mindless old men would be taking away from him everything that mattered. Each cardinal held a ballot, and with that scrap of paper they were eagerly waiting to buy a bill of goods—shoddy merchandise—that had been sold to them as neatly as a television advertisement sells soap.

Next to Gerard sat Cardinal Pidgeon, the genial cardinal from Boston. Angling his head, Gerard could make out a portion of the name—D'Orla—written on Pidgeon's ballot. From across the room Gerard could feel the eyes of LeBrewster upon him. Gerard looked away from Pidgeon's ballot, his eyes traveling up to the ceiling and down to the floor, trying to appear as if he weren't looking anywhere, or at anything in particular. He felt like a schoolboy caught peeking at his neighbor's answers.

The result of the first ballot was as expected. Anthony fared well, receiving forty-four votes. The votes for Salvatore—twenty-seven—showed that there were still some sparks of life in the conservative cause. The question now was, would they die out or burst into flame? The other votes, made out of courtesy more than anything else, were scattered among another fifty cardinals. Alban had received three, and although he knew that he had no chance to win and, indeed, had no desire to, he felt greatly honored. He beamed.

Salvatore looked glum; he listened halfheartedly to an American cardinal who whispered agitatedly in his ear.

Gerard sat rigid, his worst fears confirmed. He hadn't expected the vote to go any other way, but like a condemned man he had hoped . . .

Anthony felt uneasy, as if every eye in the room were fixed on him. He half-heard LeBrewster whisper to him: "Now they know which way the wind blows."

Several hours later, a large crowd had already gathered in St. Peter's Square. They had arrived in time to see the black smoke of the burning of the second set of ballots. The smoke hung over St. Peter's long enough for several thousand people to photograph it.

The second ballot had been telling but not decisive. Anthony's votes had increased to sixty-eight. Salvatore's total had dropped drastically, to nine. Alban had lost all of his votes.

Sic transit gloria mundi, he thought.

Following the second ballot, the cardinals adjourned for lunch. Salvatore decided not to eat and went directly to his room. He was not very surprised to find Alban Beauchamp waiting for him.

"Forgive me for disturbing you, Salvatore, but I wonder if I could speak with you for a moment?"

"Of course, Alban, what can I do for you?" He attempted a smile to reassure his old friend, but the gesture hung hollow on his tired face.

"I am sorely in need of guidance."

"I suspect that we all are, Alban."

"I have looked to you for guidance for so long, Salvatore. For so many years . . ."

"I have been honored, Father."

"I am worried. What are we to do? It seems that we cannot make our voice heard. Please, Salvatore, tell me what to do."

"Forgive me, Alban, but I would not presume to tell you or anyone else how to vote. I cannot make up your mind for you." Salvatore felt so tired. He was sure that the conclave would last an eternity.

Disappointment cut deep across Alban's mottled face. "No, of course not, Father. Excuse me . . ." Alban wandered back to his room to await the bell that would call him back to the chapel and the third ballot. He felt that he was without bearings now. Salvatore had always had an answer in the past, and Alban had come to rely on him. A cloud had passed over his polestar.

The ballot that LeBrewster had said would be the last had begun. Each cardinal had filled out, perhaps for the last time in his lifetime, a form upon which were printed two lines of Latin:

Eligo in summum Pontificem
Rev. D. Meum D. Card _____

"I elect as Supreme Pontiff the Most Reverend Lord, My Lord Cardinal _____." One hundred and seventeen cardinals had written Anthony's name in the blank space.

One by one, in order of seniority, led by Giacomo Pompomnazzi, the dean of the sacred college, the cardinals had come forward with their ballots, declaring: "I call to witness Christ Our Lord, Who will be my judge, that I am electing the one who, before God, I think should be elected." The ballots were placed on a patten; the patten was tilted, and the ballots fell into a chalice below. When the voting was completed, three scrutineers examined the ballots, and the name on each was announced only after each scrutineer had seen it. It was a time-consuming process. Alain LeBrewster kept a tally in his head. When the number of votes for Anthony passed eighty-seven, he slumped back in his throne, relieved. The coalition had held. Anthony was Pope.

Giacomo Pompomnazzi had been a cardinal longer than anyone else, and his seniority qualified him for the position of dean of the sacred college. Arthritis in his right hip made walking difficult, but he walked proudly, if slowly, to where Anthony sat.

"My Lord Cardinal D'Orlando, do you accept your election which has been performed canonically, as sovereign pontiff? If so, so signify with the word '*accepto*,' and from that moment forth assume the powers of the throne of St. Peter."

Across the room Anthony could see Salvatore. He thought he could see tears in his eyes. "*Accepto*."

"And by what name does Your Holiness"—the title he had said and heard said so often shocked Anthony—"wish to be known?"

Anthony took a deep breath. "I take as my regnal name the name I now hold, Anthony, for Saint Anthony of Padua."

There was a gasp of surprise around the room. It was not unheard of for a pope not to change his name, but it hadn't happened in six hundred years.

"Anthony, servant of the servants of God," said Pompomnazzi. At that moment, the canopies that surmounted all of the thrones in the room were lowered, Anthony's alone staying aloft. The reign of Anthony I, Pontifex Maximus, had begun.

7

BECAUSE NO ONE KNEW who would emerge from the conclave as pope, and because cardinals come in various sizes, the Vatican had provided three white silk soutanes—large, medium, and small—as temporary dress for the newly elected pontiff.

Anthony was hurried from the chapel into a nearby antechamber. He could hear the roaring of the crowd quite clearly now. They had not stopped cheering since the first wisp of white smoke had appeared.

The medium fit best in the shoulders, but it was too short; the large was the right length, but it practically enveloped him.

"The medium," said LeBrewster. "No one expects a pope to be well dressed."

As Anthony put on the embroidered red velvet slippers, the scarlet cape, and the white skullcap, he realized that only a few days earlier he had seen identical garments on Gregory's shrunken corpse. He would live in these clothes, he thought, lie in state in them, be buried in them. But that was many years off. After all, longevity was one of his qualifications.

Alban approached. "Your Holiness, you must return now to the chapel to accept the homage of the cardinals."

The cardinals came forward, in order of seniority, to kiss Anthony's hand; most of them were smiling. Some smiled broadly, some merely politely. Salvatore did not look happy, yet the fervor with which he grasped Anthony's hand served to convey that whatever differences he may have had with

Anthony D'Orlando, he was the pope's loyal servant.

Pompomnazzi appeared with the Fisherman's Ring and reverently placed it on Anthony's finger. As he did, the strains of the *"Te Deum"* arose, the cardinals singing with tired and cracked voices, falling far short of filling the room. Anthony thought they sounded very old.

As the last notes died away, the name of the new pope was announced to the crowd. The cheering split the air; it was a popular choice.

Anthony was rushed into the Basilica. The heavy miter of the Bishop of Rome was placed on his head, and the crozier, the bishop's staff, was thrust into his hands.

Alban had forgotten his earlier bewilderment in the excitement of the moment. He capered about excitedly. "No, no, Your Holiness, the crozier must be held in your left hand, leaving the right free for the benediction. That's right, that's right. Giacomo Pompomnazzi, you must stand on His Holiness's right. Governatore Spagnola on the left. That's right. Good. Now . . ." He breathed deeply and called to one of the papal attendants, "Giorgio, the curtain. Open the curtain." The tall white curtain was swept aside, and with the motion, the roaring of the crowd increased.

"If it please Your Holiness . . ." said Alban, gesturing toward the window like a headwaiter.

Anthony stepped onto the balcony and was immediately buffeted by the sounds of hundreds of thousands of voices. People packed the square, and there were thousands more filling the wide Via Conciliazione. People hung from every window, every balcony; they crowded every rooftop in sight. Anthony was struck with stage fright. He grinned widely and nervously and stood frozen.

"If Your Holiness would wave," Alban discreetly stage-whispered.

Anthony waved and the crowd roared back. Somewhere below him he could hear a brass band, distinct from the noise of the crowd. Flags appeared among the crowd, vibrant flashes of color standing out from the mass. He held up his hands for silence, as a microphone was placed before him, the sound of feedback shimmering briefly through the air. Gradually, the sound of the crowd began to subside; only a low roar rose off the multitude.

Anthony raised his hand to confer the papal blessing.

"*Urbi* . . ." He did not recognize the sound of his own voice booming out over St. Peter's Square ". . . *et Orbi.*"

Unlike many of their fellows, Gerard and Salvatore did not follow Anthony to the balcony. Gerard walked briskly from the chapel. He had many things to attend to, and he had been without financial news for several days. He was hungry for it. He had no doubt that Anthony I would be sending for him soon and asking for his resignation. Perhaps the new pope would submit Gerard to an even more insidious Vatican indignity. He was afraid that Anthony would name an assistant to Gerard without consulting him. It was a traditional vote of no-confidence, and protocol demanded that it be met with resignation.

Salvatore stood waiting for Gerard in the gallery of tapestries. He stood almost against the wall, as if he didn't want to be seen, in front of the tapestry depicting Boniface ransoming the city of Rome; Salvatore seemed almost to be part of the scene. Gerard would have swept by him if Salvatore hadn't spoken up.

"Gerard, I am sorry. I should have listened to you."

"I'm afraid it's a little late for that, Father." He wanted to continue, to say that he had no further use for the old man, but Salvatore looked so pitiful that he stopped himself.

"We still have a role to play."

"Oh yes," said Gerard archly, "and what might that be? Court jesters? Or something more dignified that adds up to the same thing? The loyal opposition. Am I correct?"

"I told you, I told you the night you came to see me, we must act as a brake, a—"

"Oh yes, a brake, a net below the tightrope. . . Too late, Father, too late."

"It's not too late. We have a duty."

"We had a duty, and we failed. Now if you'll excuse me, I must leave you . . ."

"May I come to see you, when the furor has settled down? Please?" Salvatore was grasping Gerard's forearm tightly.

"You may come and see me, Father. I shall have plenty of free time. But I warn you, the furor won't settle down. It is only just beginning." He left Salvatore alone, staring after him.

8

UNEXPECTEDLY, the cold gray sky had broken to allow some pale sunlight through to take the chill off the winter air. It was the first pleasant day in weeks, and the Romans took advantage of it, filling the squares and parks. A single topic of conversation went round and round like a carousel: the new pope, quickly nicknamed *Il Papa Americano*—conveniently forgetting Anthony's Italian birth, since a foreign pope was a pleasant diversion in an otherwise bleak winter.

The pontificate of Anthony I was only a day old and already he was being credited with the change in the weather, a slight rise in the stock market, and Italy's early successes in the European Soccer Cup. The intractably anti-clerical were laying squarely on Anthony the blame for the new tax on cigarettes.

Those who had a specialized interest in the new pope had no time to mull over Anthony's vices or virtues. Souvenir-makers were working around the clock to produce ashtrays, postcards, scarves, pens, and pennants with Anthony's face on them. Old Pope Gregory stock could be bought at rock bottom prices.

A newspaper interviewed a burly *sediario*, one of the men whose job it is to carry the Pope in the *sedia gestatoria*. "Don't tell me how much of a saint he is," the *sediario* had said. "Just tell me how much he weighs."

The change that had been Gregory's last months was over. Italy once again had her national good luck charm, one that would live for years—intelligent, saintly, *simpatico*. It was a good choice the cardinals had made this time.

Gerard sat in the huge anteroom of the papal apartments, plainly unhappy but calm. He had typed his letter of resignation himself last night after receiving his final call from New York. If Gerard had been an emotional man, or even a sentimental one, he would have spoken a little with Amex, asking him if he was married or if he had children or some other pious, humdrum question to show that Gerard regarded the voice as more than just a human stock ticker. But Gerard did not care. He assumed that his successor would instruct the broker in New York about any new arrangements, and maybe Amex would be able to catch an earlier train home. Gerard did not know. Starting today, it was really none of his affair.

Father Gioia had drifted up to Gerard in the corridor and mentioned, politely, that Gerard was the first person Anthony had asked to see. Anthony was not wasting any time in clearing him out. Gerard, waiting impassively to be shown into Anthony's office, scarcely noticed the arrival of Martin Sykes.

"Good morning, Your Eminence."

Gerard turned his steely gaze on the young man. "Good morning, Father Sykes," he said without enthusiasm. To Gerard, Martin and men of his stamp were poison. Better no young priests than this foolishly radical type.

"I met a friend of yours, Your Eminence."

"Really," said Gerard. "Who might that have been?"

"Alessandro Bianchi."

The muscles in Gerard's face tightened slightly. "You're moving in very august circles, Father Sykes. And despite what you may have heard, Signor Bianchi could hardly be called a friend of mine."

"He spoke very highly of you."

"Did he? That is good to know."

Further conversation was interrupted by the arrival of Marco Garetti, Anthony's valet. He was a tiny man, scarcely more than five feet tall, and only in bad humor when his soccer team, Lazio di Roma, was doing poorly; then he was unbearable. He doted on Anthony, referring to him as "Signor Santo," Mr. Saint. He was acting as usher until the papal household could arrange itself to Anthony's orders.

Assuming what he called his cardinal's face, an air of exaggerated sobriety, Marco turned to Van Doorn: "The Holy Father will see you now, Your Eminence. If you would follow me please . . ." He winked at Martin and ushered Gerard through the double doors.

Gregory had redecorated the airy pontifical offices, banishing the ponderous marble busts, and repainting the voluptuously red walls a neutral beige. Anthony was content to leave things the way they were: the more inoffensive the decoration, the better. The only addition he had made was a soft and gray portrait of the Virgin by Domenico Puligo. Perhaps the finest work of a second-rate artist, it was all that remained of the D'Orlando collection; the rest of it—some pictures were of the highest quality—Anthony had long since donated to the Pinacoteca, the Vatican picture gallery. The Puligo had been the last painting his father had bought, a gift for Anthony's mother when she had been received into the Church. It had hung in her dressing room, a personal picture.

Anthony arose from behind a large, rather ornate desk when Gerard entered.

"Cardinal Van Doorn," he said, extending his hand. "Good morning, come, sit down."

Gerard dipped in something between a bow and a curtsy and kissed Anthony's hand.

"All this respect is going to be the hardest part of this task."

"It is a common problem, Holy Father. Gregory had much trouble with it. It will become natural in time."

They sat facing each other, Gerard in an armchair, Anthony on a couch. Anthony studied Gerard's face for a mo-

76

ment; his features revealed nothing.

"The rumor here," Anthony said, "is that you and I are arch-enemies. It is a rumor so strong, so prevalent, that I half expected to find your letter of resignation waiting for me this morning."

"Yes. I apologize," said Gerard, busying himself with the snaps of his leather portfolio. "I would have gotten it to you sooner, but I thought it best to give it to you in person." He extracted the letter and held it out.

Anthony got up and walked to the window. Gerard put the letter on the table in front of him.

Anthony looked through the window, studying the square below him. The two fountains threw unruly sprays of water into the air. Between the two arms of the colonnade he could see the hawkers of slides and postcards tormenting tourists unmercifully—pilgrims, priests, and nuns alike.

"I was once asked," he said, "if these windows were bullet-proof." He tapped one. "They're not."

Anthony stood directly behind Gerard, who turned his head to watch him from the corner of his eye.

"Tell me, Your Eminence, have you given any thought to your successor, who he might be?"

"Of course, Holy Father."

"And who will it be, do you think?"

"If the truth be known, I could not guess."

"There will be no successor," Anthony said firmly. "I would appreciate it if you would withdraw your resignation and stay on in your post."

Gerard was immensely surprised. He took off his wire-frame glasses and polished them furiously. Relief flooded through him, leaving in its wake a fresh set of fears to gnaw at him.

"This is totally unexpected, Holy Father. I'm not sure what to say."

"There is not much to say, Father. Will you stay?"

"I must have certain assurances . . ."

Anthony looked at Gerard quizzically. "Assurances?"

"Am I to be kept on until someone is found to take my place?"

"You will stay at the Prefecture for Economic Affairs until you can no longer do your job, or until you reach the mandatory retirement age of eighty."

Gerard smiled. "Then I accept with thanks, Holy Father."

"I confess that I find the ins and outs of finance a little mystifying," said Anthony with a smile. "I feel secure knowing you'll continue the work you have been doing for the past few years."

Gerard found himself disarmed by Anthony's praise and honesty. "My efforts are merely a continuation of works that were begun well before my time, Holy Father," he said.

"Tell me about the Prefecture. How does it work?"

The question chilled Gerard. Was this simple curiosity on Anthony's part, or was he trying to trap him? Gerard had no idea.

"You must understand, Holy Father, that a great deal of nonsense is talked about the overseeing of . . . of the Church's temporalities," he said hesitantly.

"Of course."

Anthony waited for Gerard to continue.

"Because we have no . . . no stockholders," Gerard said slowly, "or a board of directors, we are not constrained by problems that affect other financial institutions. We can afford to ignore a trend; we are not bound by a time period for a return on investment. Money can be invested, securely invested, of course, fifty, a hundred years into the future."

"And you find no shortage of sound investments?"

"No."

"Or a shortage of money to invest?"

"No." Gerard felt that Anthony was driving at something. Trying to catch him out, giving him enough rope to hang himself.

"There is, then, a steady supply of money coming in and going out?"

"Yes." Gerard shifted uncomfortably.

"Where is the money invested?"

"In gold mostly," said Gerard blandly, "and in land." It was not, he felt, quite the time to bring up anything more complicated than that.

"And what happens to the money that isn't reinvested?"

"It pays the bills, Holy Father." Anthony laughed and Gerard smiled. He began to feel relieved. Anthony's questions were refreshingly naïve.

"How much is paid out in aid?"

Gerard shut his eyes for a second. The relief he had felt a moment before vanished. This was the question he always dreaded: How much can we give away? "It's impossible to tell. Different agencies receive different budgets."

"But you must have some idea of the percentage of the whole, surely?"

"Really, Holy Father, it is so hard to say . . ."

"Twenty percent? Fifty?" Anthony persisted.

Gerard breathed deeply. "At a guess, I would say some ten percent of our budget goes for aid. An extremely rough figure, of course." Gerard knew the figure was lower, perhaps seven percent.

"Of course," Anthony echoed. He stared at Gerard for a moment, his brow creased. "It's not much, is it?"

"It's a large sum of money, Holy Father."

"But it could be higher."

"A little, perhaps."

"We shall see," said Anthony, rising and extending his hand. "Your Eminence," he said lightly, "I cannot thank you enough for coming."

"I am honored, Holy Father."

Anthony escorted Gerard to the door. "One more thing, Father. I would like to see a complete list of the Church's holdings. Also, I believe you submit quarterly statements to me, is that true?"

Gerard's heart sank. "Yes, Holy Father."

"One is due soon, I believe."

"In about two months."

"Perhaps you could submit it to me a little sooner than that. And the list of holdings as soon as possible. Thank you, Father." Anthony smiled.

Gerard smiled back, a little weakly.

He left the papal apartments in the same frame of mind that he had arrived. He felt grim. The interview, polite though it had been, had unnerved him. His control of the Prefecture was threatened—quietly, subtly, but threatened nonetheless. Without action it would slip from his own capable hands into those of amateurs, and amateurs could be dangerous.

9

SALVATORE DI NOBILI found comfort not in the gaudy majesty of Rome's great churches but in the plain, primitive solitude of the Basilica of St. Clement, deep in old Rome, a place of worship since the time of St. Peter. Salvatore felt himself to be only a whisper away from the simple faith of those early Christians. He could feel those far-off souls, whose bones lay in sacred anonymity in the catacombs, huddled in St. Clement's crypt listening to the Mass with one ear and for the footsteps of soldiers with the other.

Salvatore reflected that to so many the challenge of dying for one's faith seemed terrifying, yet he would gladly have changed places with any of the thousands who died in those long-ago persecutions. It was not that Salvatore thought himself a particularly brave man, it was just that things were so much simpler then.

He had spent the morning in St. Clement's, thinking and praying, and upon leaving had summoned his two friends Gerard and Alban to meet with him in his rooms at the Vatican. They sat before him now, around a plain square wooden table in Salvatore's cold and poorly lit study. Along one wall ran a bookcase filled with devotional works and volumes of church history. On the wall facing it was a rather bad painting of the martyrdom of St. Stephen. Over the severe metal desk was a print of the sacred heart. Gerard looked faintly disapproving, as he always did; Alban looked patient.

Salvatore picked up a heavy book in front of him.

"My friends," he said, flipping the pages back and forth to find a place he had marked, "no doubt you are familiar with

Giovanni de Mussi's *Chronicles of Piacenza.* . . ." Only Alban nodded, but Salvatore did not notice and continued, "Please let me read you a portion, a few lines only." He cleared his throat and read in a strong voice. " 'It were in truth better before the eyes of God and the world that the pope should entirely denounce the *dominium temporale,* for since Pope Sylvester's time the consequences of the Church's temporal power have been innumerable wars and the overthrow of cities. How is it that there has never been any good pope to remedy such evils; truly we cannot stand with one foot in heaven and the other on earth!' "

Dust rose from the book when Salvatore closed it. He was silent a moment to allow time for the words he had read to sink in. He looked very grave.

"That little passage," he said, "was written in the thirteenth century."

"Fourteenth," said Alban quietly.

"Excuse me, Father, it was written in the fourteenth century, yet we can see around us the evils of which Father de Mussi wrote so many years ago.

"*Dominium temporale* . . . earthly power," he continued. "Over the years we have attempted to gain earthly power and it has come, I believe, at the expense of our spiritual well-being. It is my belief that Our Lord Anthony would have us neglect our spiritual duties in favor of our physical ones. He, Cardinal LeBrewster, and some of the other more prominent church officials have always indulged their political interests too much for my taste. We have a duty to the faithful to minister the faith. Not to dabble in the world of politics."

"I'm not altogether certain," said Alban, "that I see the danger . . ."

Salvatore, as a professor at the Pontifical Gregorian University, was used to learned dispute.

"The Church," he said professorially, "exists in many countries strictly on the sufferance of the governments of those nations. It would be foolish of us to think that in certain parts of the world we are welcomed with open arms. Now that Anthony is pope his political dabblings could endanger the lives and the work of many of the priests and sisters in countries that might take exception to his actions. He has, in the past, been quite . . . quite vocal about certain things."

Alban nodded grimly. Gerard was unmoved.

"I am by nature," continued Salvatore, "a man of deep loyalties. When Anthony was elected, above my dislike for his philosophies, I was content with the choice because I felt that my fellow cardinals had spoken and that their choice had been sanctioned by the Holy Spirit. I was content to trust the judgment of my fellows, despite the disquiet I felt. I prayed that the office of the Vicar of Christ would exert a sobering influence on our Lord and Brother Anthony. . . . But I am not so sure. Anthony might be anxious to put the Church on an equal footing with the great temporal powers of the world. This would be madness. What need have we of *dominium temporale?* Do we not represent a greater kingdom than any of earth?" Salvatore's voice rose. Gerard suddenly noticed that he had never, in all the years he had known him, heard Salvatore shout.

Salvatore continued. "I think that our Lord Anthony will do little to salve wounds of this kind inflicted on our Mother Church.

"I have thought constantly of what could be done to offset the cataclysms that may befall us. Ahead of us is a hard path, a road strewn with obstacles." Salvatore looked as if he were overcome with his own words. His small audience shifted uncomfortably.

Salvatore steadied himself. "I have asked you here because I believe that we three represent a bulwark of the true faith. I suggest that we bind ourselves together, we three, in a brotherhood, a sodality dedicated to preserving the beauty of our faith and to offsetting the damage that may be done to the Church. We should take, I believe, as our patron, St. Clement, the third pope after St. Peter, who did so much in his short reign to halt the forces *within* our church that sought to destroy it. We must meet in secret, of course. Together we must decide what we can do to fight the poison that might infect the Church. We face a grave problem, and I admit that we have no authority to form ourselves into a brotherhood. But we have a duty to perform, a duty greater than any rule or fashion. The sodality must be a foundation from which the true church can rise if the ravages we fear have run their course." He sat down. The room was very still.

"Fittingly," said Alban timidly, "the symbol of St. Clement is an anchor."

"I presume," said Gerard, "that you are suggesting that we act as what the Americans would call lobbyists. We will meet to discuss our plans, and when we have decided on a single course of action, one of us will approach the Holy Father, or a prominent and, perhaps, sympathetic member of the college, and make our views known. Am I correct?"

Salvatore nodded. "And we would forge our own plans to suggest in place of ones that may be promulgated by others. We are not without power of our own. By making our views known in concert, rather than individually, we will be adding weight to our words. We will be safeguarding against having our voices shouted down by the multitude."

"It seems rather . . . irregular," said Alban.

"Anthony's will be an irregular papacy," said Gerard icily.

"More than that, it is important that we keep the spirit of what we believe alive," said Salvatore. "In times of unrest, in the times of the persecutions, a band of Christians would quietly keep the flame of the Church burning. When the danger had passed, as it always passes, the lamp would be brought forth and the world would be lit again with the light of the world, Jesus Christ, Our Lord. In the parable of the ten wise and ten foolish virgins, we are told that we must keep a little of the spirit of God in readiness for times of darkness. This is our function as a brotherhood and this is our duty.

"So, will we join together in our crusade?" asked Salvatore, through the haze of cigar smoke that wafted toward him.

Gerard had his hands full at the moment and he didn't really want to get involved in what promised to be a long-winded project, a project that would, ultimately, achieve very little. Yet something told him that the sodality might be of some use one day. "You can count on my support," he said.

"And, for what it is worth, mine," said Alban.

Salvatore smiled a trifle wanly. "Let us pray. . . ."

10

LISA BLAKE plucked her eyebrows every morning. It was more than just a beauty exercise; it was a moment to be enjoyed, and she loved doing it. She held the tiny blue-rimmed hand mirror close to her forehead and peered into it, intently watching the tips of the tweezers search out the minute, almost invisible hairs. When she removed one she carefully laid it on the back of the thumb of the hand that held the mirror, as fighter pilots are said to keep track of their kills on the sides of their planes. When she finished, she examined the nude gap between her eyebrows closely and then brushed off her thumb.

Lisa looked good. She had to—her livelihood depended on it. She was small and blond, with a fresh-scrubbed look that many men found attractive. Her eyes were bright and blue, her breasts small and firm, her legs strong and well formed. She could not honestly think what Bianchi saw in her, though. She thought his tastes would run to something more exotic. Perhaps it was that she didn't look like a whore. In makeup and high heels she gave off a delicious sense of childhood defiled. That must be what Bianchi liked. That quality was her fortune.

She had come easily to her profession. In the summer following her graduation from college, she had worked as a receptionist at one of Manhattan's smart hotels on Central Park South. She spoke French fluently and sometimes made extra money as a secretary for foreign guests at the hotel. One of them, an Iranian businessman, had invited her for a weekend in the Bahamas.

Up to that time her life had been normal enough. She had been graduated from college with honors and intended to start graduate school in the fall. She wanted a master's in psychology. She shared an apartment with her boyfriend, and although she didn't love him, she needed him and was happy to have him around. She had plenty of friends—too many, in fact, because she was a popular girl—and she made a point of saving enough money each year so she could ski for two weeks in Vermont.

She thought about all this, and then accepted the invitation from Farid, the Iranian. That winter she had enough money to enjoy her winter's skiing in Gstaad.

Bianchi had no time for corporate jets. On a trip from Rome to Milan they were good enough, perhaps, but on transatlantic flights he preferred commercial aircraft—with a difference. When he could, Bianchi booked every seat in first class—there were only sixteen of them—to assure his privacy.

Lisa was naturally frugal, so despite her newfound wealth, she had decided to travel economy to Switzerland. Bianchi was traveling first class on the same flight. She caught his eye while they were embarking. To anyone else, Lisa looked like a well-heeled college girl going to Switzerland to ski, but Bianchi's eye for a whore was as fine as a trainer's for a Derby winner. He had a stewardess invite her to come forward, and they had dinner together. As the short transatlantic night enveloped them, the cabin crew discreetly left Bianchi and Lisa alone, and by the time the plane landed in Geneva the next morning, Lisa was on the Bianchi payroll.

They spent a week together in Gstaad while officers of Bianchi's company pleaded with him to return to business. He ignored them. In that week his lust for Lisa only increased, and she was never at a loss to accommodate it. He was obsessed with her. He could not get enough of her; he toyed briefly with the idea of asking her to marry him. He rejected that and bought her instead.

She was to remain in New York; he preferred to keep the

deal private, for he had a certain celebrity status in Italy. She received the title deed for a co-op apartment in the Olympic Tower on Fifth Avenue, a blank check to cover the cost of furniture, a BMW, and a "salary" of seventy-five thousand dollars. For Lisa, the distance from the apartment on 114th Street to Fifth Avenue was covered in record time. She told her mother that she produced television commercials.

Sometimes she would lie in bed and cry and worry about the future, but mostly she just went out and had a good time. Lisa had lost none of her knack for making friends.

Bianchi always gave her a day's notice before he arrived in town. He knew she slept with other men and didn't care; he just didn't want to bump into them. He liked to think that she used them the way he used her. He wondered if they paid.

As Lisa reread the telegram, she fingered the fine chain around her neck on which was strung a solitary diamond—a present from Bianchi—and glanced at her watch, also a present from Bianchi. He would arrive soon.

She walked aimlessly into the living room and lay down on the sofa. It was a well-furnished room, the colors carefully chosen and not in the least overbearing. The furniture was modern but not flashy; Lisa had natural good taste. She stared at the building across Fifth Avenue and hoped that for dinner they would go to that French place on Fifty-sixth Street she liked so much.

She got up and made herself a drink. Not a strong one, for she rarely drank much. She crunched the ice firmly and let her thoughts drift idly to Bianchi. Despite their intimacy she hardly knew him. He was kind and attentive, not particularly talkative, and strangely silent when they made love. But she liked him. He had a way of touching her that made her feel . . . less, well, cheap, and she appreciated him for that. He was good in bed and had a tendency to sweat—she didn't appreciate that very much, but she couldn't do anything about it. The thing she liked best was the next morning, for as she dozed, he would get up and shower and shave and dress and then come back into the bedroom to say good-bye. He rarely stayed two nights in a row. As she lay there, he would gather her up in his strong arms—all of her—and kiss her. It was paternal. She liked the smell of his shaving cream. It was their tenderest moment.

She was surprised to read in *Time* magazine that an "unnamed source in the Italian government" had called Bianchi "the cossack of Italian business, ruthless and demanding . . ."

She had once met Bianchi's daughter at a party. That had been weird. . . .

The doorbell rang, and as she opened the door she could tell by his face that he was not happy. There'd be no French place tonight.

"Sandro," she said, and threw her arms over his shoulders and nuzzled him. He held her for a moment and then let her go. She took his hand and led him into the living room.

"I've missed you . . ." she said. It was a lie, Bianchi knew, but she handled it well.

"I'm glad," he said. He threw down his briefcase, slipped off his overcoat, and dropped onto the couch. He threw his arm over his eyes.

"I'm exhausted," he said, speaking to the ceiling.

"Can I get you a drink?" She did her best to sound sympathetic.

"Scotch," he said, his eyes still covered.

As she mixed the drink, standing with her back toward him, she asked brightly: "What did you do today?"

"Business."

"That's what you always say, 'business.' What sort of business?"

"Nothing very interesting . . ."

It had been, in fact, very interesting. Bianchi had spent the afternoon with Steven Roth, president of Roth Liebmann, Inc., 36 Wall Street.

"What?"

"For Christ's sake . . ." Bianchi was too tired to inject

much passion into the outburst. He just croaked the words. Lisa gazed up at the ceiling and assumed a hurt expression.

Roth, Liebmann, Inc. were known on Wall Street as the best "witch doctors" money could buy. Their power was almost mystical, but their business was simple: they would examine a company from top to bottom and then tell you if you were going bankrupt, why, when, and, if possible, how to avoid it. Some clients were given a clean bill of health, but most of Roth, Liebmann's business dealt with failure. Powerful men dreaded a visit to the stylish, airtight Roth, Liebmann offices. In the business world the bulky, thorough Roth, Liebmann reports were known as "doomsday books." That afternoon Bianchi had seen the Roth, Liebmann report on Industria Bianchi.

His eyes still covered, Bianchi felt Lisa sit on the edge of the couch. She leaned across his body; he could feel the shallow warmth between her breasts. Her hand rested lightly on his thigh. He stifled a desire to push her away.

Industria Bianchi was one of Roth, Liebmann's top ten accounts, so Steven Roth, the youngish, rather serious president, met with Bianchi personally.

Roth had the look of a man who made a lot of money consistently and quietly and thought long and hard before he spent it. He was carefully clean-shaven, his black hair cut well and modishly so, but in such a way as to attract no attention. He was dressed in Brooks Brothers chic: a somber, well-cut gray suit and an expensive oxford-cloth blue shirt. He wore a tie of some Ivy League university.

"Sandro," said Lisa, grazing his lips with hers, "please talk to me. . . ." She spoke with mock petulance.

Slowly Bianchi removed his arm from over his eyes and looked at her. He liked Lisa, but theirs was a professional relationship. Right then he didn't want her.

"Don't be a pain in the ass," he said evenly. Lisa looked hurt, genuinely so this time, and got up and walked out of the living room.

Bianchi continued with his replay of the afternoon. Roth

had called him a legend. "It isn't often one gets a chance to meet a legend. . . ." Remembering Roth's words, Bianchi thought of the pictures that were the public milestones of his life. His face smiling up from the cover of *Business Week*, his "captain of industry" portrait on the cover of *Fortune*. The article marked "Miracle Worker" that had been his profile in *The Economist*. Right then he could use a miracle.

Roth had been anxious to get down to work. Bianchi took a seat in front of the stark modern desk. It was a perspective he didn't much like, one to which he was unaccustomed. It made him slightly uncomfortable, as if he were driving late at night the wrong way on a one-way street.

"Mr. Roth, forgive me for asking this, but I would like your assurance that anything said in this room will be kept in the strictest confidence."

Roth had looked put out. "Mr. Bianchi, if Roth, Liebmann were in the habit of broadcasting its business, Roth, Liebmann would have very few clients." He spoke like a kindergarten teacher.

"I don't want word to get out that we're in trouble. I don't want a run on my stock."

"A run on my stock," he said aloud, measuring the words. Bianchi could hear Lisa moving around in the kitchen. The noises were meant to be heard. She had turned on the radio and was singing along with it in a high girlish voice. Bianchi hoped she had some money saved, because the way things were going . . .

He continued to turn the conversation with Roth over in his mind.

"Your position is not good, Mr. Bianchi, not good at all."

"How bad?"

"Over the last three years, Bianchi Industries losses have been extremely high. But with loans and government subsidies, you have managed to stay afloat pretty successfully."

Bianchi knew that already.

"Your productivity has been severely damaged by strikes, sabotage, inflation, and the general gloom that afflicts the

Italian economy. This, of course, has had the effect of putting a severe strain on the potentially very profitable foreign sectors of Bianchi Industries. Your holdings in the United States and Europe have been put in the unpleasant position of exporting capital to the Italian mother company which, in turn, must return capital to foreign Bianchi companies. A nasty situation . . ." Roth smiled. "A sort of money-go-round."

Bianchi knew that already too. He had fumbled for a cigarette, and before lighting it, he had thought to ask Roth if he minded; he dismissed his own good intention and tossed the match onto the desk in front of him. There was no ashtray.

Roth had glanced apprehensively at the place where the match had fallen, worried about the finish on the desk. It was a small victory for Bianchi, and he wasn't so much of a legend that he didn't enjoy it.

"These problems," Roth continued, "are not really different from troubles presently facing other European and American businesses. Worrisome, perhaps, but inevitable. You, for example, are producing heavy machinery—among other things—at prices that cannot compete, and you have no market to expand into. Your goods are subject to enormous tariffs from other industrial nations, and there is an ever-declining market for them in Italy. Every time one of your giant generators is manufactured it costs you money—money you'll never see again. Taken as a whole, things look rather bleak for Bianchi Industries." Roth sounded like a doctor who had just pronounced the growth malignant. Bianchi squirmed. The room was a few degrees too warm to be comfortable. Bianchi had noticed that America was overcooled in the summer and overheated in the winter. . . .

Lisa had come back into the room. She slumped into an armchair and stared at Bianchi, resentful, like a child trapped indoors on a wet afternoon. He looked at her for a moment and then the scene with Roth returned with painful clarity

"Given the broad base of Bianchi ventures—manufacturing, hotels, shipping, though nobody is making any money in shipping these days, except, of course, the Japanese"—if he had intended to sound reassuring he failed—"with a certain amount of borrowing, and, I'm sorry to say, divestment, Bianchi Industries might have weathered the storm."

"Might have?" Bianchi tapped his ash on the floor.

"Yes, there is another very disturbing factor to take into account," said Roth, now concerned about the carpet. "Something which throws the very delicate balance of your financing right out of kilter . . ." Roth thumbed through the folder that Bianchi had come to collect. "According to the information we've gathered, Bianchi Industries is on the verge of launching a new venture. Computers." Roth said the last word as if Bianchi had decided to invest in zeppelins. "And to this end you have expended two hundred and twenty-five million dollars. This has put an enormous strain on your company."

"But the money will be earned back."

Roth rubbed his eyes. "I think not, Mr. Bianchi. Our analysts expect that this venture, to put it bluntly, will have the same success that Ford had with the Edsel." There was a note of reproach in his voice. Bianchi sat rigid.

"The premier market for your wares is already served, in cutthroat competition, by IBM, Honeywell, Sperry-Univac, and one or two others. The profit potential for a newcomer in the field is almost nil. To tell you the truth, Mr. Bianchi, I am amazed that you allowed your company to go ahead with this. . . . Even in the unlikely event that you could market your line successfully, it would be ten years or longer before you could expect to see a penny in profit, and well before that Bianchi Industries could be facing a cash flow problem of disastrous proportions, running all the way from stockholder dividends to payroll." Roth smiled apologetically. He could tell by the look on Bianchi's face that he was lucky it was no longer common practice to kill the bearer of bad tidings.

He continued: "We feel that the flow of capital out of

your company can be stopped in two ways—both equally unpleasant. You could borrow extensively on the open money market at exorbitant interest rates—assuming you could find a lender. This would lower the value of your stock and put you deeper in the hole. Or you could retrench. Liquidate some of your holdings, which would cause you to run the very real risk of dragging some of your other holdings down, like a house of cards. Either way, you're sure to shake up investor confidence."

"A new stock issue?" Bianchi asked quietly.

"A stock issue large enough to cover the deficit would have to be huge—so large as to render your existing stock worthless."

"Bonds?" said Bianchi, knowing it was hopeless.

"I'm afraid you wouldn't get a very good rating from the brokers, and I'd say you're going to have trouble covering the notes you have out already. They're due in"—Roth glanced at his report—"March. Not too much time. Two months."

Bianchi was angry. Angry at Roth, angry at himself, angry at his board of directors and their damn computers. "You mean to tell me that in a company the size of mine there is nothing I can do to avoid even partial collapse?"

"Not unless you can come up with some very large sums of money, at extremely low interest, without anyone knowing about it. That seems rather unlikely . . ."

Bianchi stared at the blank white ceiling of Lisa's apartment and admitted to himself that it was indeed unlikely—impossible, probably—to get hold of that kind of money and retain control of his company. Abruptly he got up.

Lisa, crouched in an armchair, her chin resting on her drawn-up knees, gazed idly off into space. Bianchi rediscovered every so often just how beautiful she was. She looked young and frail, younger than Rafaella, even. He went to her and ran his hand softly along the fine line of her jaw.

"Let's go to bed."

Her eyes widened. "Sandro, it's only eight o'clock." She laughed. She liked, more than anything, to be desired.

"So what?" He pulled her up from the chair. She rubbed against him.

"So what about dinner?"

He guided her to the bedroom. Bianchi was in no mood to be playful or subtle. When Lisa had tongued his penis with short, dry, catlike licks, he filled his hands with her blond hair and forced her mouth over him. Lisa, like a dancer following her partner's lead, understood immediately and sucked him deep into her mouth. He came quickly and hard, thrusting forcefully against her mouth. She was afraid she would gag.

She kept him in her mouth until he grew soft and then slid up along his body and kissed him. Her mouth was soft and wet, like the muzzle of an animal. She nestled against him for a moment. Then he took her hand and caressed her with it, his hand over hers like a glove, gently weighing her breasts, then moving their hands across the soft sheen of her stomach till they came to rest between her thighs. He moved her fingers, giving her the motion to follow. Gradually, her fingers began to move of their own accord, touching the sensitive places she knew best. It was a long sensuous climb, but after a moment or two, Bianchi could feel her straining against their hands, her legs lifting slightly off the bed, her eyes half closed. Her hips rocked gently. Bianchi removed his hand and watched her closely. She continued her tiny movements, increasing the pressure on herself, oblivious to him, on the edge. Small sharp sounds came from her throat.

"Roll over," he said.

Her eyes flickered to his face. "What?"

"Roll over." There was a harsh passion in his voice.

Her fingers worked quickly as she heaved over, just her breasts and shoulders touching the bed. He knelt behind her and pulled her thighs apart. She moved her hands to allow him to enter.

"Keep them there. I'm going to fuck you the other way."
He was breathing hard through his mouth. He spat on his
hand and worked the saliva around his penis and then roughly
plunged himself into her. She moaned loudly. She knew he
liked her to be noisy, and she was an accomplished per-
former.

He awoke abruptly. The lights were still on, and Lisa was
asleep, worked up into a ball, her back to him. He swung out
of bed and picked up the phone. Lisa stirred, rolled over
slightly, bending only her top half; she opened her eyes and
looked at him, unseeing for a moment. She shut them again
and was asleep.

"I'd like to place a call to Rome," he said to the operator,
and gave her the number. He glanced at the clock on the
bedside table. It was eighty-twenty in the morning, Rome
time. As he listened to the ringing at the other end and the
static in between, he smiled to himself. It was ironic, calling
a cardinal from a whore's bed.

Part Two

CARLOS WAS BACK in his confessional, at his first church in Calle Maipu, but it was not right somehow. The walls were cold and wet, and it was dark and stuffy. He remembered that there had been a little light inside. He shifted on the hard bench seat, and as he did so he caught his own smell —vomit, urine, blood. He slid the screen back, and kneeling in front of the confessional was Maria.

He was happy to see her. "I love you," he said.

Her face was twisted grotesquely, and she spat at him, blood and saliva mixed.

He opened his eyes. He was still in the cell. His face hurt, as did his arms and shins. He realized, absently, that they were broken. Back there, in time somewhere, men had been beating him under bright lights, shouting at him.

A man stood over him.

"Ferreyra, get up."

He saw, but did not feel, the man kick him. Carlos rocked slightly from the strength of the blow. He heard the man— he wore a uniform with big sweat stains under the arms— shout to someone: "He can't get up."

There was silence for some time. Maybe a minute. Maybe an hour.

A man in a cassock stood over him.

"Father Ferreyra, can you hear me?"

Carlos moved his head. Yes.

"I am Monsignor Sanz-Guerrero, papal nuncio to the Republic of Peru. We met some months ago when you applied to be released from your vows."

99

Carlos remembered.

"I have come to tell you that the Church will not be responsible for your actions, and I have prepared a letter to the secretariat of state explaining what I have done. Do you understand? You applied to be released from your vows. I have decided to approve tentatively your application to spare your fellow priests and other religious in the country the danger of being associated with you. Your behavior has been reprehensible. You lived openly with a woman. . . ."

Somewhere, Carlos found a voice.

"Maria?" He did not sound like himself.

A voice behind Sanz-Guerrero said: "Dead."

And Carlos didn't hear any more.

11

Every Wednesday fifteen thousand people pack the vast, modern audience hall to the left of St. Peter's to attend a general audience with the pope. Anthony enjoyed these noisy, informal meetings, and he used the occasions to speak simply and straightforwardly to the pilgrims and tourists he referred to as his parishioners. At one such audience, he spoke of human rights, of the basic dignities to which every man was entitled. It was a strong statement but well reasoned, all but the closing line of which was pro forma. The pope ended by saying: "There have always been tyrants, but there have always been men who opposed tyranny. These men, the ones who fight tyrants, have Our prayers."

The world noted and then forgot Anthony's words, but certain elements in the Vatican reeled, Salvatore among them.

"I could not believe my ears. The pope telling the oppressed to rise up in armed struggle. How could he have said such a thing?"

"Salvatore," said Alban hesitantly, "I'm not altogether sure that's what the Holy Father meant to—"

"Of course he did!" thundered Salvatore. "And to make a major policy statement without consulting, without *informing* the curia! It's unforgivable." Salvatore hated being angry. It made him feel helpless, impotent; he wished he were the sort of man who threw things.

"Fathers," said Gerard, at once both bored and impatient. "I think it is time we all realized that this pontificate will be as close to us as it is to the ordinary parish priest. We will hear what the pope has decided to do from the pages of *L'Osservatore Romano*."

"Easy words for you to say, Father," said Salvatore. "You have your post, your position, your influence. We have nothing." He snorted angrily.

Alban was bewildered. His position was pleasant enough. He had no desire to wield much influence.

"Forgive me, Father, but I had no idea that you were so anxious for power," said Gerard unpleasantly.

"No, not for power," said Salvatore. "But"—and he pounded the table with his fist to accent each word—"*I will be heard.*"

"And do you think he would bother to listen?"

"He has to!"

"Does he? Remember, Salvatore, this is not some petty curial squabble. Anthony is pope. He can do anything he pleases."

"Then what can we do?" wailed Salvatore, his voice laced with anguish.

"Nothing," said Gerard, and they knew it to be true.

Salvatore motioned to Gerard to stay behind when Alban had gone. Gerard was tired and anxious to be off. He remained, but with ill-concealed bad grace.

"Would you like something to drink—coffee, perhaps?"

"Thank you, no."

Salvatore settled himself in a chair facing Gerard. He sighed heavily.

"Father," he said, "I am going to tell you something that I did not think I would ever tell a soul."

"Yes, Father?"

"I do not like that man." That man was Anthony.

"There is no reason why you should," said Gerard, removing his glasses. There were mussel-shell-shaped welts on either side of his nose where his glasses had rested. He rubbed his eyes vigorously, as if he hoped tnat when he opened them again Salvatore would be gone.

"No, no, Father, there is every reason why I should," Salvatore said quickly. "We have dedicated our lives to the service of God through the service of the Church. Anthony leads the Church . . . his election has been sanctioned by the Holy Spirit. By denying him, I, to a certain extent, deny the Paraclete."

"That's rather an extreme view," said Gerard. He didn't see much point in arguing it.

"When I became a priest . . ." Salvatore said slowly.

Oh no, thought Gerard.

". . . I wanted nothing so much as to *serve*. Completely and wholeheartedly. To follow without question the orders of my superiors, God, the Church. As I grew older and my knowledge and experience grew, I realized that I wanted to serve, yes, but also to *lead*, and in so doing, serve all the more."

Gerard was enough of a diplomat to realize that the situation called for a platitude. "You have led many by your example, Salvatore." He stifled a yawn.

Salvatore nodded sagely. "Yes, perhaps . . . but one can lead by example only to a certain degree. Without authority one acts in a vacuum."

"You are not without authority."

Salvatore waved his position and power away, as if he were trying to clear the air of smoke. "That is not at all what I mean. . . ."

You mean, Gerard thought, that you want to be pope. Too late for that.

"I mean to attain a position and use it to serve God and man directly, rather than being what I am . . . an obscure Vatican bureaucrat."

Gerard could tell that the truth of Salvatore's own words had cut him. He was surprised that the old man would describe himself so candidly. "Come, Father, I think you are being rather hard on yourself. . . ."

"No, no, I am being honest. . . . I came close to election in 1958. I almost received the secretariat of state in 1963. But I failed, somehow. Now I am ignored. . . . I am getting old, Gerard. I will die and be buried without trace, I will leave no mark." He paused for a moment. "In the Capuchin church, Santa Maria della Concezione—do you know it?" Gerard nodded. "There is the tombstone of Cardinal Antonio Barberini and on it is the epitaph *hic jacet pulvis cinis et nihil*—'here lies dust, ashes, nothing.' It will be a fitting inscription on my tombstone. Unless . . . unless I speak now. I will be heard. I must be . . ." Instead of pounding the table this time, the words were said quietly, without emphasis, almost chanted. He stared at a point on the threadbare carpet in front of him, looking sad. Gerard shifted uncomfortably; the leather armchair squeaked. Despite the chill in the room, the hide stuck to his back.

"When you came to me before the election," Salvatore continued, "I should have accepted. I should have declared myself for the papacy. Instead, I imagined myself to be . . . dead, I suppose, unable to go on. Now I realize that I had been summoned and I turned the summons aside." He shook his leonine head slowly. "Failure . . . it has haunted me. Your request was my last chance and I failed again."

Gerard's only concern was leaving. He could only leave on an encouraging note—it was good form, if nothing else. But what could he say? Salvatore, for once, had described the situation exactly as it stood. Time had run out. There would be no more chances.

"Please don't think me ungracious," Salvatore said, looking neither left nor right, "but I would rather like to be alone. . . ."

Gerard fled, much relieved but unsettled.

12

A LESSANDRO BIANCHI's black Mercedes 600 nosed its way
through traffic on its way into Rome from the airport.
The huge car, surrounded by tiny round-shouldered Fiats,
resembled an ocean liner being nudged out to sea by attendant tugs. Bianchi sat deep in the crushed velvet of the back
seat, the fatigue of the all-night transatlantic flight cutting
into him. His shoulders felt heavy and ached slightly. He
would have a shower in the bathroom adjoining his office before receiving Van Doorn.

He had thought about the cardinal all the way across the
Atlantic. Although each had known of the other for years,
they had only met a year or two earlier. It had been at a Fina-
bank reception in Zurich held to honor the head of a newly
independent African state, an inexperienced politician who
had come to Europe in search of foreign investments for his
poverty-ridden country. Van Doorn had stood slightly aloof
from the crowd; the crowd had stood slightly aloof from
Bianchi. Alessandro had introduced himself to the cardinal,
who was coldly polite. They chatted for a few minutes, and
Bianchi mentioned that investment in the guest of honor's
country seemed attractive. He was considering, he said,
financing the construction of a deep-water port there.

"That," Van Doorn had said, "would be most unwise."

Bianchi knew inside information when he heard it. Within
six months the African leader was dead and his country overrun with Cuban and Marxist guerrillas. Bianchi realized he
owed Gerard a favor. He paid his debt handsomely.

At the time, Bianchi U.S.A. had been on the verge of taking over a small American chemical company, the shares of which were quoted at a listless $12.00 on the New York Stock Exchange. The takeover offer would be $45.00 per share. Bianchi made sure that Van Doorn knew of the takeover well in advance and noted with satisfaction the purchase of a block of stock by a dummy corporation in Panama—a Van Doorn blind, as he had expected. The stock, of course, skyrocketed, Bianchi had helped Van Doorn turn a tidy profit—all, Bianchi noted, for the greater glory of God. The leak was illegal; Bianchi knew that, Gerard knew that. More than that, though, Bianchi's favor was not without strings attached. Van Doorn was just about to find out what those strings were.

Periodically his eyes flicked into a second rear-view mirror attached to the partition that separated the driver from the passenger. In it he watched a white Volvo following him at a discreet distance. He could make out the thick-necked, bulky forms of his four German bodyguards, men Bianchi referred to as his "Dobermans." Private bodyguards are illegal in Italy. Citizens needing protection from the left wing, the right wing, or both, are provided with police escorts. Bianchi wanted nothing to do with the police. They had proven themselves to be inept too many times; too many politicians and millionaires had been kidnapped or murdered when guarded by state employees. Also, there was the very real danger of traitors on the police force, men who might turn their guns on those they are sworn to protect. Bianchi preferred his Dobermans; he paid them well; they were professionals. If the government didn't like it, the government could go to hell. Bianchi had every reason to be pleased with his Germans. The four attempts at kidnapping him had been costly, bloody failures for the other side. Professionals though they were, Bianchi liked to keep an eye on them, hence the mirror. If the Volvo came within fifty meters of the Mercedes, Bianchi fined the four men a week's pay. Bianchi knew, and the Dobermans knew, and the terrorists knew that the most successful kidnappings had been the result of the guards and the guarded coming within the sweep of a single machine gun. Bianchi had never caught his men too close. He hoped he never would.

The Rome offices of Industria Bianchi were housed in a villa on the Via Sardegna, off the Via Veneto. In contrast to the company headquarters in Milan, a complex covering a dozen acres and overlooking three separate Bianchi plants, the Rome office was an anonymous affair, blending in well with the embassies and townhouses that surrounded it. Bianchi preferred to work out of Rome rather than from the chrome-and-glass bastion to the north; it was not good business, he knew. The chief should be at the helm, visible, in the place where most of the work gets done. But Bianchi had the southerner's aversion to the north. Of course, he spent a great deal of time in Milan, he had to, but he never felt comfortable north of Rome.

The Mercedes passed the pink splendor of the American Embassy and the ice-cream-cake frivolity of the Excelsior Hotel and slowed down for the right turn into the Via Sardegna. Bianchi ran an idle eye over the crowds on the Via Veneto. He remembered now, when he had first come to Rome after the war, a smart kid with some money in his pocket and all the right connections with the occupying American forces, he had almost blown everything on a good-looking but haughty whore he had gaped at on the very corner he was passing. He had romanced her like a lovesick teenager, but before he had spent all his money and missed some chances with the government contracts that were being handed out, he came to his senses, kicked her out, sobered up, and got down to the business of making money. She had cost him plenty, but it had been worth it. He smiled, remembering. What was her name? Leila? Sophie? Silvie? Something French, anyway. . . .

Before the car made the final turn into the courtyard of the Industria Bianchi offices, Bianchi glanced once more in the mirror. Kidnapping attempts often take place at the point least expected, on your front doorstep, and Bianchi often thought that the sharp blind turn into the courtyard would be the perfect spot. But nothing happened; the Volvo was there, making the turn fifty meters back. Another safe trip.

An hour later, Bianchi, his fatigue relieved by a shower and a cup of coffee, faced Gerard in his spacious, subdued office. Gerard, as usual, had the look of a mandarin.

"It was good of you to come on such short notice."

"Your call from New York had a note of urgency."

"I am afraid this matter is more than urgent."

"And what is 'this matter'?" He said the words as if they smelled.

"I need a loan," said Bianchi quickly.

"I cannot give you one," said Gerard even faster.

"Why not?"

"Because you are a bad risk."

Bianchi clenched his fists tightly. He flushed deep red.

"A bad risk? Me? There is no better risk in Italy." He spoke through clenched teeth. He looked angry but was really deathly afraid that the priest had found out about Industria Bianchi's problems.

"Calm yourself. You don't have to defend your credit rating to me. I know, better than most, what Industria Bianchi entails. A giant combine, standing next to ITT, Fiat, the cream of the world's multinationals, blue chip and all that."

"So?"

"So, why don't you go to a bank?" Gerard spoke coolly.

"I want the loan from you. First you say that I am a bad risk, and then you tell me that I can get credit wherever I want. What kind of game are you playing?" Bianchi almost, but not quite, shouted at his guest.

"Perhaps you could explain—"

"Risk! Huh, how am I a risk?" It was plain to Bianchi that his financial problems had not gone beyond the Roth, Liebmann offices. But Gerard had unnerved him. For one ghastly moment Bianchi was afraid word was out.

"You are a bad *moral* risk," said Gerard icily.

"A moral risk!" This time Bianchi shouted. "Since when

did that concern you? What about Nogara's famous rule? It's not the secret you think it is. Religious considerations should not influence investments."

"It is a rule I have followed unswervingly. If that means that Protestant England is a better risk than Catholic Spain, so be it. My conscience is at rest."

"It has gone beyond that."

"If there have been excesses, they have been unintentional." Gerard sniffed primly. All at once his demeanor changed. "Alessandro, how much money do you actually need?"

"One hundred, maybe one hundred and fifty million dollars," Bianchi said lamely, suddenly aware of the magnitude of the figure.

Gerard shook his head. "I'm sorry, it's impossible. . . ."

"Why?" Bianchi saw defeat looming.

"Try to understand, we have a new pope. A watchdog. Before, in the days of Gregory, I might have been able to help you. Now it would be extremely dangerous for me to move that kind of money without arousing a good deal of suspicion from Anthony. He watches everything I do. I suspect he has even set his meddlesome secretary to snooping about my affairs. I walk a tightrope. And, as I've told you . . ." he realized his words would be harsh ". . . you have rather a poor reputation. Anthony would not stand for an alliance between the Church and Bianchi."

"Gerard, if you do not give me the money Industria Bianchi will be bankrupted. Completely. Think what that—"

"What are you talking about?"

Bianchi told him everything. The decreased production, the money-go-round, the misguided attempt to break into computers. He told all that was in the Roth, Liebmann report.

Gerard was silent for a moment after Bianchi had finished.

"I have substantial investments in Bianchi Industries," he said quietly.

"And what does your pope say to that?"

"He doesn't know."

Bianchi saw the thought flash through Gerard's mind. Gerard would leave with one thing on his mind: to divest himself of Bianchi stock quickly.

"Gerard, I must have that money."

"And I cannot give it to you. . . ."

Bianchi leaned forward on his desk. He touched a button on the intercom.

"Maria, is the projector set up?"

"Yes, Mr. Bianchi. Mr. Penna is in the boardroom."

Bianchi snapped the intercom off. "I want to show you something," he said, getting up and going to the door of his office.

Gerard, faintly uneasy, followed.

A young man waited for the two men in the boardroom. A screen had been rolled down on one wall. To the left was a podium; facing it and the screen were two chairs. Bianchi did not introduce the young man behind the podium; he just nodded to him. Gerard and Bianchi sat down.

"Do you remember, Gerard, that you—the Church—owns voting rights in one of my companies, the one called Senatron?"

Gerard nodded. Senatron's vital statistics flashed through his mind like a stock ticker. An American subsidiary of Bianchi Chemicals. Based in Framingham, Massachusetts, or was it Farmingham? A small company that drew heavily on M.I.T. and Harvard talent, paid well. It had closed out the previous day's trading on the New York Stock Exchange— Amex's voice from the night before came back to him—at $54\frac{1}{2}$, up an eighth . . . so what?

"And you recall that I hold your voting proxy?"

Gerard nodded again.

"Good. I wanted to make sure that you remembered that. Mr. Penna here," he gestured toward the young man, "works as a liaison between Chimico Bianchi and our American holdings. He knows a great deal about Senatron. He'll tell you some interesting things."

"The films you are about to see range in time from the early seventies . . ." said Penna, quickly enough to reveal his nervousness.

"About the time of your initial investment," Bianchi reminded Gerard.

". . . to the present day. They were shot in various parts of the world. I think they represent a good idea of the range of Senatron products and the direction in which we are expanding."

Gerard felt more uneasy, as if he were already inside a trap and now just waiting for it to snap shut.

The lights were switched off, and the projector purred behind them.

Fuzz and visual static flashed across the screen, sorted itself out, and presented the words:

SENATRON, INC.,
A DIVISION OF INDUSTRIA BIANCHI CHEMICALS
MILAN, ITALY.

That gave way to the title:

SENATRON, INC. TEST FILM
DEFOLIANT/INCENDIARY #14 (Petroleum Based)
Quang Tri Province, 1971.

It was aerial footage, silent, showing the lush green vegetation of Vietnam, so well known, at one time, in living rooms of the Western world. Small diamond-shaped canisters were spiraling out of the plane, into the slipstream, across the view of the camera. They grew gradually smaller and disappeared. As they vanished, orange sheets of flame flashed across the jungle, one on top of another. There were eight flashes. They lit up the room, glinting off Gerard's glasses.

The plane banked to allow the camera a good view. Flames leaped hundreds of feet into the air, across an area half a mile square. Type appeared across the bottom of the footage:

INCENDIARY/DEFOLIANT EFFICIENCY RATING:
97 percent.

The camera hovered lovingly on the inferno.

"Mr. Penna," said Bianchi, "could anyone live through that?"

Penna shook his head. "As the United States Air Force said, there was a life support quotient of zero point two percent."

A new title appeared:

SENATRON, INC.
DEFOLIANT/INCENDIARY #17 (Acid Based)
Quang Tri, 1971.

The camera was on the ground this time. It focused on a sign that read:

Welcome to Cavalry Airstrike Battalion Division #2
KILLING IS OUR BUSINESS,
AND BUSINESS IS GOOD.

Gerard blanched.

American men in fatigues and sunglasses were crouched under the glass fly-heads of a set of helicopters. They were busy affixing some kind of canister to a brace on the undercarriage. In the background some more green-clad men clowned for the camera.

The scene shifted abruptly to the air. The camera followed the movements of four helicopters as they jerked their way over a malt-brown village that stood out from the dark green of the jungle.

"No," said Gerard softly.

Simultaneously, the canisters leaped off their holdings and

fell gracefully, end over end, into the village. Another sheet of flame. Blank screen. A title: *Time elapsed, 22 minutes.* When the image returned, the village no longer existed. A smoldering ruin, flames burning in pockets, stood in its place.

The camera came in low and tight; it seemed almost to gloat. A few figures wandered on the ground, burned.

INCENDIARY EFFICIENCY RATING:
100 percent.

These scenes had lasted only a few minutes, but to Gerard they seemed an eternity.

"We move now to some footage shot more recently, in Angola," said Penna, matter-of-factly.

The next scenes passed almost without comprehension on Gerard's part. It was difficult to say if they were more horrible than the films he had already seen. Bodies burned hard, limbs scattered, hollow sockets where eyes had once been all rushed out at him.

Gerard began to rise. Bianchi, putting a hand on his shoulder, forced him to sit again. The horror show continued. More flames, efficiency ratings, and death. The screen went blank, and the lights snapped on. Gerard was ashen.

"I had no idea," he said weakly.

"Who'll believe that? Certainly not the pope. And he'll find out about it, I'll make sure of it. And what about the press? Think what they would do with it. The Sindona affair didn't cause too much of a stir—too complicated. This is a Church scandal everyone could understand. . . . Now, I ask you again, will you give me a loan?"

"I . . . must have time to think."

"If I give you time to think, you'll figure a way out of it."

"I cannot give you a decision now. I don't even know if I can move that much money without the pope finding out about it. Please, Alessandro, give me some time. Until tomorrow . . . please."

Bianchi relented. "You have until nine-thirty tomorrow

morning. I'll come here tomorrow. Remember, do not attempt to sell anything, and, of course, I can count on you not to tell anyone what we have discussed here. If you have not seen fit to arrange my loan, I shall make sure that the evening papers from London to Rome are carrying stories about the Church's rather gruesome investments. . . . How would that look? And quite apart from what it would do to your Church, think of the consequences for you personally. People, the pope, everyone would want to know more about the papal purse. They'd turn a searchlight on you—you would never escape. I know money, Gerard, and I know how you work. If you cannot work in secret you cannot work at all. Of course, that is the least of your worries. . . ."

Gerard's eyes flickered across Bianchi's face. "What other worries have I?" He spoke with scarcely a trace of emotion.

"Well, after tomorrow, Gerard, you wouldn't have a job, would you? You would be Gerard Cardinal Van Doorn, the man who made only one mistake. You'd be disgraced, ruined. Instead of being allowed to work for a few more years and then to retire with applause for a job well done, you'd be forced to leave and . . . tell me, do you people still go into monasteries and do . . . what is it called? Penance?" He asked the last question with an exaggeratedly polite air of curiosity. "Well, whatever would happen to you, it would be a shame to destroy all that you have worked for, wouldn't it?"

Gerard nodded absently.

"But," said Bianchi, "it's up to you. . . ."

Bianchi saw Van Doorn out, safe in his conviction that he had his loan. It didn't bother him in the least that he had, on the whole, enjoyed the session that had extracted it.

By midnight, as he waited for Amex's call, Gerard had regained his composure. He had been badly frightened, he admitted that to himself, but in the hours between Bianchi's performance and the present, he had managed to strip away

114

his fears and concentrate on his dilemma. It was now simply a set of problems to be solved. It was a feeling, he reflected, not unlike the panic one experiences at school when turning over an exam paper and finding that none of the questions resemble the subject studied in class. Only after a little thought did the calm and the familiarity return.

At first Gerard had almost acted on impulse—rushing to sell his Bianchi stock before the European markets closed and breaking the Senatron news to Anthony himself. But he had stopped himself. Curiously, the destruction of the Prefecture or his own downfall were not his only reasons for doing so. He didn't want to be forgiven by Anthony. Forgiveness—or even punishment—at Anthony's hand Gerard would have found eminently distasteful.

Indeed, Gerard had formulated a new plan. It involved making an ally, a strong one, of Bianchi. Finance makes, and had already made, strange bedfellows, but it was a small price to pay if it worked. Gerard would be free, once again, to conduct his business away from the prying eyes of an amateur.

13

IN THE DAYS before Anthony became pope, people paid little attention to Martin except to note his intelligence and suggest, occasionally, that Anthony get rid of him and hire a more conventional secretary, preferably an Italian. As private secretary to the pope, however, Martin found for the first time that he had become a figure of some importance. There were grumblings from some quarters that Martin was too young for such a delicate post, but Anthony had made his wishes clear on the subject, and there the matter rested. Martin was flattered a little by his new-found prominence, yet was still uncomfortable when a lordly cardinal would whisper obsequiously: "I know His Holiness is busy, Father Sykes, but if you could persuade him to see me, if only for a few minutes, I would be so grateful. . . ."

There was a dizzying amount of work to face, and Martin's days began early and ended late. By far the more onerous of his duties was handling Anthony's appointments. Politicians and movie stars were the most anxious to receive an audience. Politicians knew that photographs taken with the pope were good for votes, and movie stars felt that the occasion added luster to what might be a tarnished reputation. Before an audience was granted, backgrounds had to be checked out to avoid the embarrassment of the pope's associating with, and perhaps appearing to sanction, someone who might be tied to some pursuits less than saintly. Martin spent a good deal of his day trying to find out if the corruption charges brought against a big-city mayor were ever proven, or if a particular starlet had, as rumored, made a name for herself as an actress in pornographic films. It was an arduous and frequently embarrassing task, and one that Martin hated.

Although his desk was covered with paper, he impulsively called Rafaella and asked her to lunch with him. Even before he had hung up he felt guilty about shirking his work, but he ignored the guilt and slipped out to lunch early. Again he felt that sense of elation at seeing Rafaella. It was a chance to relax.

They met in the square in front of the portable post office in St. Peter's square that was Rome's busiest and most efficient. It was no secret that the Vatican moved mail faster than the Italian government did. As they walked toward the street, Rafaella stopped and looked around her. She stood rooted, staring at the colonnade, the Basilica, and the palace like a tourist or a pilgrim seeing it all for the first time.

"Once a year, until I was sixteen, I used to go to the town my mother was born in, in Sicily. Sette Bagni, it was called. I stayed with my grandparents." She continued to stare as she spoke. "My grandparents had a maid—she had been my mother's maid once, her name was Magdalena—a very devout woman but with a sort of medieval superstition about her. She used to talk about coming to Rome and seeing all this, the pope, St. Peter's, like it was the end of the world, millions of miles away. Of course I lived here, and as a rather blasé teenager, I couldn't understand what all the fuss was about. Besides, all sophisticated sixteen-year-olds are atheists, you know." She smiled at Martin but didn't move.

"And?"

"And what?"

"What happened?"

"I told Magdalena she should come to Rome. I told her my father would pay. But she refused. She didn't want him to pay for it because she knew that he didn't believe in God. Magdalena didn't like him; nobody in Sette Bagni did. I know that he made them uneasy. I never knew why, and I didn't want to know. Magdalena was always dropping dark hints about things that had happened before I was born, but when I asked her to tell me what she was hinting at, she refused. It's probably just another Bianchi story. And I've heard enough of those. Once before I left, she gave me some money and asked me to light a candle for her in St. Peter's."

"Did you?"

"No. What a little brat I was. I told her I did, though. Tell me, is there a statute of limitations on good intentions? Maybe I should still light the candle."

"Why not, if it'll make you feel better."

"Maybe I will."

"Tell me about your grandparents."

"They were civil," said Rafaella coldly. She began to walk again, quite quickly.

"That's all. Just civil?"

"They could hardly be much more, could they?"

"Why couldn't they?"

"They were the Marchese and Marchesa Della Porta. Italian aristocrats can be as stiff-necked as Prussians or the English. Added to that, they hated my father and they lived off him. They were penniless and they hated taking his charity. In return, they felt obliged to take me for the summer year after year."

"Come on," said Martin. "Italian grandparents, whether they are marcheses or not, smother their grandchildren with affection. . . ."

Rafaella cut him off abruptly. "They aren't very affectionate toward the offspring of a union of which they strongly disapproved. My mother was the center of my grandparents' life, and she married a guttersnipe with too much money and no manners. They thought he stole her away from them, and when she died they blamed him for it. You must understand, Martin, when you are Alessandro Bianchi's daughter the world looks a little different. It's him and me against the rest of the world, whether they happen to be related to me or not."

"What about the other side, the Bianchi grandparents?"

118

"I met them once. At my first communion. They were frightened to death of my father, I think. He probably supported them too."

Martin shook his head slowly.

"You don't understand, do you?" Rafaella's tone was cold and accusatory. "Grandparents, family—to you they all come from the pages of a fairy tale. Snowy-haired old ladies stuffing you full of apple pie, red-cheeked old men bouncing you on their knees. Not in the Bianchi family, Martin. I was always aware of it, even from the time I was a little girl. When I was in Sette Bagni, every day after lunch my grandfather would take me for a walk. I suppose he thought it was the least he could do. I knew he was ashamed to be seen with me because I was Bianchi's daughter. People used to stop on the street and kiss his hand because he was the *seigneur* of the village, the old baron, but I always noticed that these people looked at me in a funny way: curious but horrified, as if I were deformed or scarred. I knew it humiliated my grandfather, but he ignored it. What else could he do?"

Rafaella smiled ruefully. "One day the story of Alessandro Bianchi and Elena Della Porta will be a legend in Sette Bagni. Beauty and the beast."

"What happened to your grandparents?"

"They died, in time. Living on my father and hating him to the end, I'll bet," she said coldly. Then she added, "Let's eat."

They settled at a table in a small, plain restaurant on the Via Aurelia. It was full of workmen on their lunch break. Martin was more uncomfortable about the eyes on Rafaella than she was. As she slipped off her bulky sheepskin coat, her audience, as one, lost interest and returned to their food.

"They think I'm too thin," she said, and laughed.

She pulled a sheaf of papers from her handbag.

"Here," she said, "a present."

"What is it?"

"It's my article on the Church. Read it at your leisure."

Martin turned a few pages, reading a line here and there. "It appears to radiate authority," he said with a smile.

"How could it not?"

"You must have excellent sources."

"The best. But I'll need more."

"How come?"

"I want to do a follow-up story on Vatican finances."

Martin signaled for a waiter. "Lots of luck."

"Papa says that journalists have tried for years and failed to find out anything."

"Journalists and other priests."

Rafaella broke off a piece of the bread that had been thumped down in front of them. "You're keeping your eyes open?"

"Yes, but nothing for publication."

"Tell me about Cardinal Van Doorn."

"Off the record?"

"No."

"Tell me what you know about him first."

"He was born in Holland. He's been at the Vatican all his life. He does a good job, keeps his mouth shut, and people don't like him."

"You know as much as I do. As much as anyone knows."

"He was recently reappointed as the head of the Prefecture for Economic Affairs."

"How did you know that?"

"It was in *L'Osservatore Romano*."

Martin laughed. "You don't actually read that."

"It's a good way to get information."

"As I said; you know as much about him as I do."

"What do you think of him?"

"Off the record?"

"Sure, off the record."

"I don't trust him. Neither do a lot of other people."

"Does the pope?"

"More than he should."

"Why?"

"That's all I know."

Rafaella let the subject drop. Pushing too hard would get her nowhere.

They talked easily, ambling in no particular hurry or order from one subject to another. A couple of times their hands touched across the table by accident. Both of them noticed, but neither commented. The signora who ran the restaurant reapplied the rouge on her face and watched them. Priests these days, she thought huffily.

"Do you mind if I ask you a question?" asked Rafaella suddenly.

"No, go ahead."

"Have you ever been in love?"

"Yes," said Martin without hesitation, but he wasn't sure he wanted to go any further.

"Don't tell me any more," said Rafaella. "I just wanted to know if you had."

"Why, do you think that when you wear one of these it's impossible?" He fingered his collar.

"No, I just thought you might not admit it. To yourself or to others."

"It's nothing to be ashamed of. Besides, it happened before I was ordained."

"That makes it okay then?"

"It made getting ordained a little harder, that's what it did."

"But you were ordained anyway."

"Evidently," Martin said with a smile.

Rafaella squeezed his hand as it lay on the table. "You haven't asked about me."

"I'm too polite. . . . Okay, have you ever been in love?"

"Nothing that ever lasted . . . it's always been my fault."

"Your fault?"

"I'm looking for something that doesn't exist. It makes staying in love rather difficult."

"What are you looking for?"

"Perfection," she said sheepishly.

"Who isn't? But I think there comes a time when it doesn't matter much."

"You speak like someone who has found it."

"No, someone who has learned to live without it."

They parted at the restaurant. Martin hurried back to work, but Rafaella lingered over the last of the wine. The restaurant was empty and the staff stood around, bored, waiting to clear Rafaella's table. She sipped at her wine, making herself sad, wondering if, had things been different, she would have found what she was looking for in Martin.

She roused herself suddenly. Things *weren't* different, and she knew she would never know.

14

ALTHOUGH HE HAD a car at his disposal, Gerard, who had never learned to drive, took a taxi to the Bianchi offices. He was ushered into Bianchi's presence immediately. He liked the deference he received; it was so different from the offhand air with which he was treated outside of his own department at the Vatican.

"Well," said Bianchi, "I had no idea you would look so confident, Your Eminence. You didn't look well when I saw you last. It frightens me a little. I can only imagine that you have wormed your way out of my proposition."

"I have capitulated," Gerard said evenly. His voice came nowhere near suggesting surrender. "I have decided that it would be best for me to . . . to cooperate. But I must have the voting proxy returned, and I hope you realize that I shall be divesting myself of the Senatron stock."

"The proxy will be returned when our transaction is complete. As for the stocks, you would do well to hold on to them. Senatron is one of the few of my subsidiaries that is making a profit in fact as well as on paper. Don't worry, I have no intention of blackmailing you."

"Isn't that what you've done already?"

"Blackmailing you further, in that case. But it is an unfortunate choice of words . . . we simply have a business arrangement. It happens every day."

"How odd. I cannot recall ever having heard of anyone borrowing money—one hundred million dollars—at no interest before."

"Call it, then, a corporate act of mercy."

"I have made arrangements for an initial draft to be paid into an account with the Banco Santo Spirito here in Rome. The money is coming in a rather roundabout fashion, so it will not be available for several days."

"How much?"

"Ten million dollars, to start with . . ."

"Twenty," said Bianchi.

Gerard shrugged his shoulders to show that Bianchi was asking a lot, like a child who demands to be carried on a hot day. "Very well, twenty. . . .

"But there is one thing we have not discussed," Gerard said casually.

"What?"

"Collateral. I do think I should be getting something in place of many millions of dollars."

"But you are, Gerard. You are being allowed to live out your days in a position of absolute trust and security."

"I wish it were that simple. I want something from you that will help us both."

Bianchi's face darkened. Here it is, he thought. The catch. He should have realized that Gerard would not just roll over.

"From this moment forth, Alessandro, your destiny and mine and the destinies of our respective concerns are inextricably linked. If I fall, you fall. If Industria Bianchi collapses, I go with it. You think you have gotten a loan, but what you have, in fact, is a partner. We are yoked together, you and I, and we must make sure that nothing happens to either of us. One must take care of the other. . . . I have a problem—that means you have a problem. It is a problem that you can help me with, and in helping me, help yourself. There is no stronger motive than self-preservation, and if you help your partner in the meantime, so much the better."

"Problem? My last problem has been solved. I have what I need."

"No, you fail to understand. If one of your tankers runs aground and kills some sea birds and what have you, I could say, 'Well, it's Bianchi's tanker, it's his problem.' But if *all* your tankers run aground, and if *all* your workers go on strike, and if the world suddenly decides that it doesn't need Bianchi this or Bianchi that, then it becomes my problem. I am loaning you money, and it will be missed if it is not paid back. What threatens you with annihilation threatens me."

"And you, Gerard, are you threatened?"

"As I said, I have a problem."

"And what is this problem?"

"I am watched. Watched closely. There was much opposition to my reappointment. My enemies—and they are the power just at the moment—don't think I should be kept on in such an important post. But they cannot tell the Holy Father that—or rather, they cannot insist that I be removed. So they wait and watch and hope that I make a mistake. Well, I've made a mistake—two mistakes in fact. But you are the only person who knows about them . . . Senatron and this loan. You know how damaging that information could be in the wrong hands. Well, the wrong hands are anybody's outside of yours and mine. I keep rather a tight rein on things, but I cannot do everything. Therefore, I am afraid that this news might leak, that someone may find out something. You can see how disastrous that could be for both of us, don't you?"

Bianchi nodded. "It seems to me that this is something that only you can do anything about. But you said that only I can help."

"The person who poses the greatest threat in this regard— the person who would do anything to destroy me—is a young man known to you."

"An employee of mine?" said Bianchi. He wondered if Van Doorn was slipping slightly. There was the fevered fear of persecution in his voice.

"No. Nor one of mine. A young priest named Sykes, Martin Sykes."

"I've met him. He seems harmless enough."

"He is far from harmless. He's a viper. If he were to find out about our arrangement . . . well, he'd lose no time in telling the pope and the world. You see, he's the pope's private secretary. A rather delicately placed thorn, for us."

"For you." The last thing Bianchi wanted to do was get involved in some squabble between priests.

"No, for us."

"What have I got to do with this?"

"I believe he sees a great deal of your daughter."

Bianchi became very angry very quickly. "Who told you that?"

"The Vatican is a very small town. Word gets around when the secretary to the Holy Father is seen escorting a pretty woman about."

"And . . . ?"

"And I would like you to find out if anything, *anything* untoward, is going on between your daughter and Father Sykes."

"No," said Bianchi flatly. "I won't do it."

"Why not?"

"I will not drag my daughter into this."

"I think," said Gerard deliberately, "that it is somewhat unfair of you to make me take all the risks."

"You made the mistake."

"You ran your business into the ground."

The two men glared at one another for a moment.

"There is no sense," Gerard said, "in bickering. We must have something to safeguard ourselves against discovery. A trump card . . . it's not much of a trump, but it is something. Sykes is the person in the position, and with enough malice, to do the most damage. Some of the other cardinals would like to see me ousted, but they are limited in what they can do. Cardinal Lepore of the Secretariat for Non-Christians—you've never heard of him, and neither has the outside world. But he's powerful here, and a liberal. He'd dearly like to get rid of me, but how can one cardinal spy on another? It would be like sending the President of the United States to Russia to spy on the Politburo. If Cardinal Lepore started asking questions, people would say to themselves, 'Why is the Cardinal for Non-Christians interested in the goings-on in the Prefecture for Economic Affairs?' And they would have a point. But Sykes, on the other hand, as secretary to the Holy Father has no limits on what he can be 'interested' in. On top of that, he's young, determined, and would be very happy if I were to be caught in a compromising position. He can rifle through any file he chooses and I suspect he'll be heading my way soon. He is the person, short of the pope himself, we must watch most closely. Do you see? He's close to the Holy Father, a friend of his. The pope, for some unknown reason, puts great stock in what he says. Information on Sykes is protection against anything the pope might find out."

"I blackmail you, so you blackmail me, so I can blackmail my daughter, so you, in turn, can blackmail the pope." Bianchi shook his head slowly, ruefully.

"Alessandro, how unlike you. Next you'll say, 'What is the world coming to?' Besides, blackmail is an unfortunate choice of words."

"But true."

Gerard had had enough of semantics. "Do you see that this must be done?"

"Yes."

"And will you do it?"

"I suppose I must."

"Good, then the collateral is secure."

Bianchi found the notion of watching his daughter repugnant; on thinking about it, the thought of her with Sykes was even more so. He tried to banish the thought from his mind, but the harder he tried, the more fixed the image became. He saw her, for a split second, naked, her long hair falling down her back, smiling and pushing herself up against Sykes, dressed, paradoxically, in a cassock. It was a ludicrous image, he knew, but it didn't make his loathing any less potent.

"I'll let you know what I find out," he said, as Van Doorn rose.

"Thank you. You understand that it is important. . . ."

Bianchi nodded glumly.

"I'll notify you when the first drafts of money come through."

"Good," said Bianchi with finality. "Let me show you out."

An hour later, in his office, Gerard received a phone call from Salvatore, who told him loudly and agitatedly that Anthony, at the following day's general audience, would remove the prohibition against artificial birth control. Another bombshell. Salvatore sounded as if he were on the verge of a coronary and babbled about another sodality meeting. Gerard had stopped listening. He smiled. Anthony's announcement was a welcome diversion; people would not be too interested in the doings of the Prefecture. The announcement—about which Gerard cared little—could not have come at a better time.

15

A LAIN CARDINAL LE BREWSTER hated opera. He found it
too long, too loud, and embarrassingly overacted. Staying awake through a full performance was almost impossible;
if he managed to stay awake through most of one, he considered his duty done. Unfortunately, he was often in danger
of torture by opera. He was a popular man, and Rome's
elite, thinking mistakenly that a clever, cultivated man like
LeBrewster would enjoy opera, invited him frequently. He
declined as often as he could in good grace and accepted the
rest of the invitations with well-concealed anguish.

That night he was due to attend a performance of *Il
Trovatore* as a guest of the French ambassador. But for-
tunately, now he could not. The pope had phoned late in
the day and invited him to dinner. An informal dinner and
a chat, Anthony had said. It sounded delightful. It was also
a perfect excuse, one that would certainly satisfy the French
ambassador. Alaïn had wasted no time in communicating the
news to the embassy, implying, diplomatically, that dinner
with His Holiness was a cross that every music-loving cardinal had to bear. The French ambassador accepted defeat
gracefully, and honor was satisfied.

Anthony received LeBrewster warmly, as he always did.

"This is a great honor for me, Holy Father," said Le-
Brewster, smiling.

Anthony shook his head and laughed wearily. "Not you
too, Alain. I get so tired of the bows and curtsies, the 'by
your leaves, Your Holiness,' and the 'if it pleases Your

Holiness.' Alain, do me a favor and just say 'hello' as if I were an ordinary human being again."

"Hello, my Lord Pontiff," said Alain, laughing.

"Nice try. I give up . . . come sit down. I suppose you had to break some terribly important engagement tonight. A dinner party at which your attendance is required to avert a world war, something like that?"

Anthony ushered Alain into a small sitting room as he spoke. It was warm and well lit, more cheery than the state apartments, plainly a room to be lived in rather than admired. Anthony's single extravagance, his costly stereo, gleamed on a corner shelf. Ranged around it was his huge record collection.

"The opera. I had been invited again," said LeBrewster, as if he had been invited to attend a beheading. "It was no great loss, I can assure you. You have no idea quite how terrifying it is to realize that you shall spend the rest of your life being invited to the opera."

"You are very gracious, but I'm sorry to have upset your plans."

"Upset! You were a godsend! I loathe going, but sometimes I cannot avoid it."

"That's what you get for being a social lion," said Anthony, in mock reproach.

"In the face of *Il Trovatore*, I become an antisocial lamb. And who could blame me? Certainly no one with ears."

Anthony rose and went to the record player. "Let this soothe you," he said, extracting a record from its sleeve. He wiped the disc carefully with a cloth before putting it on the turntable.

"What are you playing?"

"The first act of *Tannhäuser*," said Anthony casually.

"What are you trying to do? Send me to an early grave?" said LeBrewster, alarmed. "Come on, what are you really putting on?"

"Bach, the Goldberg Variations."

"Perfect. You're a music lover so you'll appreciate a story about Bruckner."

"Bruckner! I feel the same way about Bruckner as you do about opera," said Anthony, vehemently but good-naturedly.

"How unfair! Bruckner was a good Catholic! He was a simple soul . . ."

". . . as all good Catholics are," put in Anthony.

"Of course, look at me. . . . Anyway, let me finish. So as Bruckner lay on his deathbed, he worried constantly about meeting with the Almighty. A friend consoled him by saying that he didn't have a thing to worry about, as Bruckner was sure to be the organist in heaven. Bruckner was a great organ virtuoso, you know."

"I gathered."

"Well, this piece of information appeared to calm Bruckner for a few minutes, until his friend noticed that the elderly composer had once again become agitated. He asked what was wrong. 'How can I be the organist in heaven?' Bruckner cried. 'Bach was a greater organist than I was.' 'Don't you worry about Bach,' said his friend, 'he was a Protestant.' "

"It's hard to believe," said Anthony, laughing, "that people once actually believed that Protestants were damned."

"People still believe it! I would be willing to wager that there are people who will sleep this very evening within the Vatican secure in the knowledge that Protestants go to hell as a matter of course."

"Don't mention any names; I don't want to hear you bearing false witness," said Anthony.

Marco entered with a tray of aperitifs. Alain and Anthony were silent until he left.

"You know," said Anthony quietly, "before I was elected, I had no idea the Vatican was such a quiet place. I feel completely cut off. . . ." He swirled his Campari in the glass for a moment, looking into the dark red liquid as if he expected to see something besides ice. "Once when I was quite young

—about seventeen or eighteen, I suppose—I went climbing, hiking really, in the Appenines. My family owned a lodge up there, high in the hills. While I was up there, there was a heavy unseasonal snowfall, and I was stuck in the lodge for a week—snowbound. I wasn't too worried, though. I had plenty to read and lots of food and firewood, and I knew that the *guardie forestale* would come for me eventually. The *guardie* are, what do you call them? Forest rangers. When they finally came I found that I wasn't that happy to see them. The guards couldn't understand it—they thought I would dance for joy. . . . I feel now much as I did then—snowbound, alone, cut off—but now there is one big difference. Up there in the hills, I was calm, at peace . . . at peace with myself, with God, the world. Now it's simply emptiness I feel, without bearings. It's a little frightening."

"The office imposes its own solitude," said LeBrewster. "People wonder why popes are not more outgoing, more 'human,' the way John was. What they can't know is that it is like being in the eye of a hurricane. It's calm, up here, in the Palace, in the Vatican; people rarely speak above a whisper. But just below you, just above you, surrounding you is turmoil, pain, sorrow—and you must bear it all and change it for the good if possible. It's hard, I know, to make one's mark on the world, particularly when one is using as unwieldy an instrument as the Church. It takes a forceful personality, a man of strength. I, for one—and I am not alone —am convinced that you are well equipped to try."

He smiled reassuringly. "Look at what you've done already," LeBrewster continued, waving a cigarette he had not paused to light. "And people respect you for it. . . . Do not be afraid of your power, Anthony, it is yours to use, that is why you are here now; to exercise your power." He lit the cigarette. Anthony was staring at him intently, as if LeBrewster were explaining the workings of some complicated piece of machinery.

"You know, I keep my ears open, and the word I get is that your actions to date are being well received. You have shown in a few months what the last three popes have been unable to do in three reigns. You have shown Catholics that the Church is finally responding to change, to the times. If your pontificate were to end tomorrow, you would already have done immeasurable good. But there is much more time and much more to do. . . ." He exhaled heavily, smoke eddying out of his nostrils.

"Tell me," said Anthony abruptly, as if he were trying to wake himself up, "were you surprised when Gerard was reappointed?"

"Surprised? I was astonished! I almost came to you to protest, but after I had thought about it, I realized that you had made a very good decision. The conservatives have taken it as a sign that you are responsive to their point of view."

"I reappointed him because he can continue to do a good job. It had nothing to do with politics."

"Anthony," said LeBrewster seriously, "don't put too much trust in Gerard. Let him work with you, by all means, but don't give him a free hand as Gregory did. He's too old a dog—and too cunning and headstrong—to learn new tricks. He has an absolute mania for security. The Sindona affair shocked him no end, and there's no telling what he could be doing."

"I have asked him for a complete list of the Church's holdings, but I must say he's dragging his feet a bit."

"You don't have a complete list already? *Insist* that you get one."

"Alain, do you suspect something?" Anthony looked troubled.

"I am from Marseilles, Anthony; I am naturally suspicious." He lit another cigarette and chuckled.

Dinner was announced, and they went into a lavishly decorated, jewel-box dining room. The furniture was ponderously Louis Quinze, all curves and curls and angels and cupids; an indiscriminate mixture of the sacred and profane danced on the ceiling above them. They surrounded a picture of the marriage feast at Cana; it was by no means the best fresco in the Vatican, but it fit in well with the dining room.

Talk at dinner was easy, rarely touching on matters of any importance. LeBrewster was a delightful dinner companion at all times, but that night, sensing that Anthony needed diversion, he outdid himself in witticisms and stories that were genuinely amusing. A servant or two hovered behind them.

"You know," said LeBrewster, "your election got me into a great deal of trouble."

"Really?" said Anthony quizzically. "How so?"

"My mother," said LeBrewster, laughing. "She's in her nineties, but I am still her little scoundrel Alain, red hat or no. She called me up from Marseilles and gave me a good tongue-lashing. 'Why aren't you pope?' she asked. 'You could have made your old mother happy, but no, not Alain. . . .'" He laughed. "She even read one of my old report cards from school. It must have been fifty years old, but she still had it. 'Alain could do so much better if he tried harder. He has brains but lacks ambition. . . .'"

He laughed some more. "I can still hear old Sister Martina berating me—she taught me when I was ten years old. Oh! She had a cruel tongue."

"I was just the opposite," said Anthony. "I was the pious little boy whom no one could stand. I did well in school. Always on time. Always neat. My school chums must have hated me. But I was atrocious in mathematics. I'll never forget that my math report card read once: 'In Anthony's case as far as mathematics is concerned, we can only hope that he adopts the school's motto as his own: *orare laborare*—to pray, to work.' Well I prayed and prayed and prayed and didn't do too much work. I never got the hang of it. But I became more pious and more solemn, a difficult little boy."

"*Now* I know why you're pope." LeBrewster laughed. "I should telephone Mama. 'He may not be pope, but your little Alain can add and subtract.'"

They finished eating and retired again to the sitting room for coffee and brandy.

LeBrewster settled himself in an armchair. With his coffee in one hand and a cigarette in another, he was content. "You know what I find amusing?" he said expansively. "Your assistant, Father Sykes. I see him now constantly besieged by men who prior to your election wanted him deported. He handles them very well . . . a very good young man. I wish we had more like that."

"He is keeping an eye on Gerard," said Anthony. "There is no love lost between those two. He's impetuous, Martin is, but very little escapes him. You know, before I brought him to the Vatican he worked in Peru. . . ."

"No, I didn't know that." LeBrewster sipped his brandy.

"He made himself very unpopular with the government there. They asked him to leave—in fact they demanded it."

"Really? Why?"

"He worked up in the mountains, in the midst of the most wretched poverty. There was a group of young priests working together to try and make things a little easier for the people. Martin wasn't content to stop there. He impressed upon them that they deserved better from their government, and in doing so managed to stir up some unrest. Some demonstrations—nothing violent. An army investigator decided that Martin was to blame, so out he went."

"He was lucky to get out when he did. The regime's attitude toward the clergy is not healthy."

"Tell me what's going on there? What do you know?"

LeBrewster sat back in his armchair and pulled hard on his cigarette. "We have something of a problem there."

"What exactly?" Anthony asked, his brow furrowed.

"Well, the most vocal anti-government figure there is a man called Carlos Ferreyra. Technically, Father Carlos Ferreyra. He's a young man who petitioned to be released from his vows."

"Was he?"

"Well, no. You know how long these things take. He's been living openly with a woman. There's no doubt that he's serious about leaving the Church."

"So he joins an ever-increasing statistic. I don't see the problem."

"Well, word got out somehow that the Peruvian government was importing at great expense some kind of weaponry —I don't know what. Father Ferreyra led a band of a thousand or so out to the port to stop the ship unloading. The army moved in, people got killed—one of them was Ferreyra's female companion. He ended up in jail."

Anthony shook his head. He was about to speak when LeBrewster stopped him.

"But there's more. Both the Archbishop of Lima and the papal nuncio are old-fashioned men. They were offended by Ferreyra's sexual behavior and were terrified by his political activities. Early on he was suspended as a lecturer at the Catholic University, but I guess that is reasonable. Once he landed in jail though, Sanz-Guerrero, the nuncio, visited him and told him that as far as the Church was concerned, he was no longer their—our—responsibility."

Anthony's features darkened. "By what authority?"

"His own, apparently . . . he thought he was doing the right thing. He didn't want the regime to have an excuse to victimize other members of the religious orders. Remember, to his way of thinking, Ferreyra is not much of a priest."

"But my God!" said Anthony. "He knows the Church is denied to no one in need."

"I would say," LeBrewster added soberly, "that Ferreyra is in great danger."

"Then we shall have to see that he gets out of danger. I want the secretariat of state to issue a statement condemning the action and calling for Father Ferreyra's release."

"We shall be accused of defending an excommunicant."

"Christ defended thieves and murderers."

LeBrewster shrugged his shoulders and smiled. "You just might have a point there. . . . Now I must leave you." He crossed the room to the window. "Please don't let it be snowing," he said plaintively. He looked out to see the rooftops below him dusted with a light fresh snowfall. Something caught his eye. He smiled. "Come here," he said to Anthony. "I want to show you something. You see that light? That is burning in Gerard's office. A loyal servant . . . he works till midnight every night."

"Highly commendable," said Anthony.

"It certainly disproves what Pope John said when asked how many people work at the Vatican. 'About half,' he said. He forgot about Gerard."

The two men laughed, though Alain felt that Anthony's laughter was a little forced.

"Good night, Holy Father," he said. "Thank you for saving me from the opera."

"I'm glad we had this evening together," said Anthony. "Thank you."

In the cold corridor outside the apartments, LeBrewster paused to put on his overcoat. A Swiss Guard stood in the doorway, unseeing. LeBrewster thought about the light in Gerard's window and Anthony's forced laughter. Alain shrugged his shoulders. "Perhaps he had heard the story about Pope John before," he said to himself.

"*Buona notte*," he said to the Swiss Guard, who saluted smartly in return. LeBrewster strode off, whistling softly.

Had someone been watching LeBrewster as he made his way through the long corridors, he would have thought that the cardinal was slightly tipsy and without a care in the world. It would have been far from the truth. LeBrewster was deeply concerned about what he had heard that night. While he remained convinced that Anthony alone of all the liberals could be pope, he suspected that Anthony would be needing his help more than he had thought at first. Anthony's naïveté about Van Doorn was particularly disturbing, but not nearly as disturbing as the thought of what Gerard could be up to. The Prefecture had been spinning on its own axis, remote from the workings of the Vatican, like a planet on a slightly eccentric orbit. It was no accident either. LeBrewster did not know Van Doorn well—no one did—but he knew him well enough to know that nothing with which Van Doorn was involved was an accident. Le-Brewster could feel himself slipping once again into the role he had played with Gregory, Anthony's predecessor: a combination of father, guide, and spy.

16

THE SWISS GUARDS at the sacristy gate had long ago become used to seeing Martin jog by their post every morning, rain or shine, at six A.M. They waved and smiled when he passed, and on those rare occasions when he happened to be late, they would point accusingly at the clock on the archway and pretend to be annoyed. They were always glad to see Martin, because his arrival meant that their long shift was coming to an end. By the time he jogged back through the gates an hour and a half later, the guard had changed, there were people around, and no one paid much attention to him; the new guards were always grouchy and businesslike, not having been awake for very long.

Martin rounded the colonnade and turned into the Via Conciliazione; the ornamental lanterns on the marble pillars that lined the street were still burning. At that time of the morning it was hard to believe that a few hours hence the cafés and the souvenir shops would be filled with tourists, the street itself stagnant with traffic. Sometimes Martin stopped dead in the center of the street to look back at St. Peter's. In the moments of pale half-light the Basilica looked, in contrast to the rest of the city sleeping around it, awake and watchful, the twin arms of the colonnade never more protective. It was a comforting sight.

Somewhere off to his left, in the clutter of buildings behind the roadway, Martin could hear a rooster crowing. Someone had been unable to resist bringing a piece of the country with them to the city.

Martin started to run again, conscious of the sound of his

feet and breathing. He passed the Hotel Columbus, once the palace of a Renaissance cardinal, then passed the tiny cinema that showed nothing but Westerns—were clerics particularly fond of that type of film? At the Piazza Pio XII that caps the street, Martin ran directly out into the intersection, an act that would probably cost him his life if attempted two hours later. But at that hour there was no traffic, the signals just going through the motions, green to amber to red, as if they were bored, like the guards at the gate.

After the Piazza, Martin crossed the road to run along the raised embankment beside the river. Invariably, as he passed the chocolate-brown bulk of the Castel Sant'Angelo, the *guardiano* shouted, *"Buon giorno, pazzo!"*—"Good morning, crazy." Martin laughed and waved, reflecting that he probably did look a little crazy running along at that hour in his ragged black gym shorts with "Georgetown" stenciled on one thigh and his Boston Red Sox T-shirt. Italians prefer to get their exercise together, running and kicking a soccer ball for hours on end, and usually at a more reasonable hour.

The best thing about Martin's morning run was that he thought of nothing in particular. As he moved, so his thoughts moved, drifting from the past through to the future. A sudden recollection of a home run he had seen hit at Fenway Park when he was eleven might give way to a snatch of a song he had heard on the radio, and that, in turn, would fade, to be replaced by a line from a book he had been reading the night before. Martin made no attempt to hold on to, or to pursue, these thoughts as they ambled through his mind. He just let them slide away to be replaced by something else.

After the Castel Sant'Angelo came the uninspired building that housed, according to the stern lettering over the door, the Foundation for the Protection of War Widows and Orphans. Here Martin always had the same thought: which war? First? Ethiopian? Second? All three? Then came the Palace of Justice, "more palace than justice," the

Romans said. The palace was a gargantuan nineteenth-century disaster that had begun to collapse as soon as it had been built. It was constantly bedecked with scaffolding and ladders; restoration was continuous.

At the Ponte Margherita he stopped, leaned on the parapet, and looked to see how the current was running. If it was fast, the water rose high on the pillars of the bridge, boiling as it broke. If slow, the water was sluggish, not even lapping at the granite piles. Today the river was running fast; there must have been rain in the hills. The stronger the better: it made rowing that much more strenuous. At the base of the embankment was a boathouse, an old rotting houseboat floating on barrels and garbage that housed the grandly named "Rome Society of Rowers." One day the boat would sink, and that would be the end of the society. For now, however, it housed a few old single sculls and a chair or two; the rest of it was filled with dust and junk. Martin had joined the club several years earlier, but because of his odd hours he never saw the other members—there weren't more than a dozen active ones anyway. Martin got all the club news he needed, actually a good deal more, from Vittorio, the ancient *guardiano*.

Vittorio, like the guards, was happy to see Martin. He had spent a long night among the rotting timbers and rats with only a bottle for company. During the war, some American soldiers had taught Vittorio a few words of English—most of them graphically obscene—and he had plagued every foreigner within earshot with them for forty years.

"Hey, Martino!" he shouted when he caught sight of Martin on the embankment. "You gotta match! My face and your ass!" It was one of the rare instances when the old joke made sense. Vittorio had never bothered to find out what the words meant, and no one had ever told him. He said them because he liked the sound of them, blissfully unaware that he insulted himself and members of his family almost every time he opened his mouth.

"Hey, Martino!" he added, "my old lady got V.D." He pronounced the initials "veedy." "You think the Cards win the Series?"

"Not this year, Vittorio, the Red Sox," said Martin, in English.

Delighted to be addressed in English, Vittorio replied in kind. "You gotta match! My face and your ass!" He laughed out loud, exposing a wide expanse of very red gums.

They always talked for a moment in Italian. Vittorio usually reported the lewd nocturnal doings on the riverbank, and how he, Vittorio, had turned down the invitations of a dozen or more comely *puttane*. "Free, for nothing," Vittorio would exclaim, blowing a lungful of wine-tinted breath at Martin. Vittorio was one of the rare Italian males who considered priests men like the rest of them.

Martin put a shell in the water and stepped in. He pulled strongly on the oars, shooting the boat out into the current. It gripped him immediately and pulled him downstream. Martin eased forward in the tiny rolling seat and pulled a good tight stroke. The ends of the oars dipped in the water and fought the current; the shell inched upstream. Another stroke and Martin hit his stride, slicing the shell into the current and feeling the satisfying stretch of the muscles across his back. He exhaled heavily and struck with the oars again.

Gerard. Martin continued to mistrust and, perhaps, fear him. Anthony's reappointment of Van Doorn made a good deal of sense, but it nagged at Martin. Anthony had a tendency to see only the good in people; Martin tended to be more guarded in his judgments. He had no proof that Van Doorn had done anything untoward, and he probably would never have the proof—Van Doorn was too clever to get caught. But Martin knew he had to try. If Gerard were working against Anthony, he had to be stopped; Martin must find out what Van Doorn was up to before he went too far.

The night before, Martin had played a hunch. During that dinner at Rafaella's home Bianchi had spoken so knowingly of Van Doorn—perhaps, he thought, there was a link between the two.

Martin had spent the night employing an old Vatican-watcher's trick. To find out in which companies the Church had placed its money, one had to examine the board of directors. If the Church had money invested, a prominent layman, someone close to the Church—a member of the aristocracy, perhaps—was sure to be a member of the board. In Industria Bianchi's case, Martin could find no name he recognized. Martin had had a lot of trouble getting hold of a Bianchi prospectus. He had been forced to wheedle one out of Giuseppe, Gerard's weasel-faced assistant, who had looked suspiciously on the request. Martin claimed that he had a pet charity and wanted to approach the wealthy Bianchi board members for donations. It was a common enough ploy in the Vatican, but Giuseppe had been unconvinced. It was a bad move on Martin's part. He had come up empty-handed, and his interest in Bianchi would be directly reported to Gerard, he was sure of that.

"Hey, Martino, you gotta match?"

Martin smiled over at Vittorio. He pulled harder on the oars and edged upstream, but not quite as far as he thought he would travel. The current was stronger that morning than he had felt it in months. Could there be an early thaw in the hills?

Rafaella. Her article had been a pleasant surprise. She handled her subject well—Martin had seen the most experienced journalists come to grief when confronted with the Vatican. While Rafaella's piece was by no means the last word on the subject—there would never be a last word, probably—he knew that a layman who read it would come away with a clearer view of the traditionally hazy inner workings of the Vatican. Martin recognized a number of his own thoughts and fears in her piece. It flattered him that she

143

had thought enough of his opinions to all but adopt them as her own.

He wondered idly what he would do when Rafaella left. Martin had not made many friends while at the Vatican, and though he hated to admit it, he was lonely. He enjoyed the time he spent with her. She made him feel as if he were a part of the world at large, a world not entirely governed by protocol and whispers. Was it more than that? He didn't really want to think about it. He had stopped rowing, his knees pulled up to his chest; the current had brought him well below the boathouse. He struck again with the oars, deeply this time, trying to move as much water as possible, trying to lose his line of thought in the process. His thoughts whirled like loose snow and settled again.

He had heard from an old friend, a priest with whom he had worked in Peru. The letter was an unsettling one, obviously written in a hurry; Martin could smell the fear rising from it like poisonous fumes.

If a friend of mine in the American embassy had not promised to send this in the diplomatic pouch, I would not be writing now.

Carlos Ferreyra is in jail, and rumor has it that the Church is disavowing any connection with him. His sins are minor compared with how he and many others are being sinned against. I for one cannot believe that the Church has abandoned him. How could it? It is unthinkable.

Martin pulled grimly on the oars. Peru, he thought, is where he should be, doing something useful, not in nice safe Rome spying on cardinals and running after the daughters of industrialists. . . . He must speak to Anthony about Ferreyra. He would want to do something.

Had Martin noticed the man on the bridge photographing him, he would have thought the man was a tourist given to rising early.

Although he had been in Bianchi's employ for years, Umberto Scarfone could not recall the last time his boss had spoken to him. Scarfone didn't expect to get much in the way of attention from Bianchi, who, after all, was an important man, and what was Umberto but a driver? But now Marietta had said that the *padrone* wanted to speak to him. Umberto wondered if he was in trouble.

As jobs go, Scarfone considered himself lucky. He looked after the four or five cars that Bianchi kept in the barn-cum-garage behind the house, drove to town on errands, and met people—usually Industria Bianchi executives—at the airport. Scarfone was not allowed to look after the Mercedes; that was kept separate, in another garage, like a thoroughbred kept away from the herd. The German driver took care of the Mercedes—washing it, servicing it, everything. Umberto supposed the *padrone* was afraid that an Italian would put a bomb in it. As if Umberto would do a thing like that, him a Sicilian like Bianchi. Umberto's station had declined over the years. Once, in the days when rich Italians didn't need bodyguards to keep them alive, Umberto had been Bianchi's personal driver, but now there were *tedeschi*—Germans—for that job. They were welcome to it. It was a nice twist, thought Scarfone, bringing Germans to Italy to work, instead of Italians going to Germany.

So, Umberto considered himself lucky. Bianchi had been poor once himself, so he paid well. There wasn't much work, and most of the time Umberto could be found in the kitchen talking with Marietta, the cook, and her half-deaf husband Pietro, the gardener. Pietro could do a very funny imitation of the Germans trying to speak Italian.

But recently all that had changed. Umberto had been given a real job. One of the Germans, Klaus, had given Umberto a gun and asked him if he knew how to use it. Sure, he knew. Hadn't he been the shooting club champ in Messina three years in a row? To prove it, he had gone with Klaus to the range the Germans had built on the grounds and shot a few targets. For Umberto, used to shooting at moving clay pigeons, the stationary cut-out targets had been easy. He had shown that German a thing or two. Umberto had been given a car and told to follow Signorina Rafaella, to protect her.

That had been a surprise. He didn't even know that Signorina Rafaella was back from the United States. He liked her—he had driven her to school when she was young —and he was glad to have the assignment. *Dio!* but she had grown pretty, though maybe a little thin, he had thought when he first saw her. He had followed her closely, and because she was so pretty, he had admired her every step of the way. There was no trouble from the Red Brigades—only from men who pretended to faint when she walked by, and who shouted things at her.

"Let them put a finger on her and they'll get a surprise," Scarfone had said to himself. She didn't know he was following her so she had gone about her business, whatever it was, unselfconsciously. After a few days on the job, Umberto was sure that he could kill for her, if it came to that.

Now Bianchi wanted to talk to him. Why? He had been doing a good job.

Bianchi received him in the study. It was a lovely room, with french windows looking out over the lawns to the lake in the distance. The carpets were very thick, and the shelves were lined with books. It was a quiet room; the ticking of the clock was the only noticeable sound. In so delicate a room, Bianchi's coarse features looked a little out of place; it was a room for a tall man, with an aristocratic bearing. He was sitting behind the heavy antique oak desk when Umberto came in. He looked happy to see Umberto, and Umberto knew why: I remind him of the south, of home, he thought.

"Sit down, sit down," said Bianchi. "Would you like a cigarette?" He offered Umberto an open box, full, and he took one. Not bad, American cigarettes. Marlboro.

"Grazie, commendatore." Umberto had the Italian habit of giving a title to anyone of importance: *brigadiere, dottore, professore* . . . *commendatore* seemed to fit Bianchi best.

Bianchi looked at Umberto and realized that he had the perfect face for a shadow. He was middle-aged and dark, not too short, not too tall, a touch of gray in his hair; his cheeks bore evidence of a childhood bout with smallpox. He wore a cheap dark suit and a tie. A face in the crowd.

"I'd like to congratulate you, Umberto. Klaus tells me that you have been doing an excellent job of looking after Signorina Rafaella." Bianchi had discarded the Roman dialect that he had acquired and spoke to Umberto like a Sicilian, so as to lessen the gap between them.

"Thank you, *commendatore*, but it is an easy job. . . ." He smiled with pride. You didn't get praise from the boss every day.

"Tell me," said Bianchi, sounding as if he were only casually interested, "does she go to the Vatican much?"

"Oh yes, *commendatore*. I have followed her there a lot. Once or twice I almost lost her in the crowds, but I managed to keep an eye on her."

Bianchi opened a large manila envelope and took out a photograph. It was a picture of Martin in pale black and white, taken with a telephoto lens. He was rowing. "Does she see this man often? He slipped the photo across the desk and Umberto examined it.

"Yes, quite a bit. Usually they eat together. Lunch, most of the time. Twice, no, three times they have had dinner. Sometimes they just walk." Umberto had instinctively liked Martin when he first saw him. He didn't know why. Maybe it was because he could see how much Rafaella liked him.

"But they have never . . ." Bianchi didn't finish the sentence, hoping Umberto knew what he meant. Scarfone had a fair idea, but was too respectful to put words into his employer's mouth. He waited for Bianchi to finish.

". . . they have never gone to a hotel together, gone someplace where they could . . ." he decided that it was best to say it straight out ". . . sleep together."

"Oh, no, *commendatore*. Nothing like that." In spite of himself, Umberto was surprised at the question. It must be a terrible thing for a father to suspect his own daughter, and an even more terrible thing to want to know if he were right in his suspicions. Besides, Rafaella was old enough to do as she pleased.

"Well," said Bianchi with resolve, "if they ever go someplace that isn't in public, I want you to phone this number"—he pushed a piece of paper across the table—"and tell whoever answers who you are and where you are. A man will come and meet you. Tell him where Rafaella and this man are"—he gestured toward the photograph—"and do whatever he tells you to do. Don't you tell anyone about this. Got it?"

"*Si, commendatore*." Umberto didn't like this at all.

"Good, thank you," said Bianchi, rising and offering his hand to Umberto. "Here, take some more cigarettes. . . ."

Both men thought the same thing as they parted. It was a low game, spying on your daughter.

17

W ELL," said rafaella, "I think I might make a pilgrimage to Sette Bagni."

Martin shifted the telephone from his right ear to his left. "Sort of sudden, isn't it?" he said. "I thought you were never very happy there."

"I've thought about it, though, since we spoke. It's something I've been ignoring for a long time, for years really, and it dawned on me that I should exorcise my private demons now, before it's too late. Besides, I have an idea for the magazine that ties in, too."

"What's the idea."

"Well, the south is Italy's perennial problem, and it has to be covered. Instead of writing the usual 'no jobs, no money, no future' piece, I thought I would look into the possibility of doing a profile of a small Sicilian town, and what better choice than Sette Bagni?"

"Indeed."

"But look," Rafaella continued, "I need some advice."

"At your service."

"I want to give something to the local parish church in Magdalena's name. I could make a donation, I suppose, but I'd rather give something she can be proud of, that she can point to. Any ideas?"

"Well," said Martin, "you could give a piece of plate for the altar. That's traditional. Something that could be displayed on the Feast of Saint Rafaella."

"Was there a Saint Rafaella?"

"Well, no, actually. There was a Saint Rafael. He 'troubles the waters' in the Gospel. According to John."

"Just what I always wanted to be, a water-troubler."

"Not bad work, if you can get it."

"Funny. Now what about a present?"

"How about a monstrance?"

"A what?"

"A monstrance. In Italian they call them *ostensori*. It's an ornate holder for the host. It usually has a piece of glass in the center of it, and gold rays emanate from it. It looks like a crucifix without Christ. It's used during benediction, to venerate the host. Do you know what I mean?"

"Yes," said Rafaella, remembering but not saying that she knew someone in New York who had found an old monstrance in an antique shop and made a lamp out of it. "That sounds perfect. Where does one *buy* a monstrance?"

"Well, there are some ecclesiastical furnishing shops around the Via Santa Chiara, near the Pantheon, but if you want something special—really first-rate work—I know an old goldsmith near the Palazzo Farnese. A dying breed, an artisan, that sort of man. Cantankerous though."

"Expensive?"

"Yes . . . but nothing a Bianchi can't handle."

"Unfair, Martin."

"Sorry. Borelli might charge two million lire for some of his better pieces—two thousand dollars. But for a friend of mine . . . who knows." Martin laughed.

"You've got a friend in the monstrance business who can get one for me wholesale, is that what you're telling me?" Rafaella laughed too.

"Look upon it as a discount to those of us in the trade."

"He sounds fine. Will you come with me?"

"Of course. I wouldn't let a young woman within one hundred yards of Borelli without chaperoning. But can you wait till this, evening?"

"Of course."

"Right-hand fountain, eight o'clock?"
"Fine."
"Bring your checkbook."

As Umberto followed the taillights of Rafaella's car into a turn on the Lungotevere Testaccio, he knew at once that she was headed for the Vatican. He felt uneasy. He hoped she was just going off to the movies or to a quiet late dinner. It was late, later than any time he had followed her before. He wondered if tonight would be the night. He hoped not.

He followed her through the tunnel under the Gianiculum and into the Via Santa Ufficio. He saw her pull up at a parking place—finding one that easily was a miracle. The sort of luck that only beautiful rich women have, he thought. He pulled his car unceremoniously onto the sidewalk. She got out of the car and almost ran into traffic in her haste to cross the street. She stuck out her hand and stopped two lanes of cars, Roman-style, and crossed. The drivers honked, called her a few names, and drove on. Umberto, still sitting behind the wheel of his car, watched her and smiled. Her father's daughter, no doubt about that. He got out of his car to see her better. She was dressed warmly and casually, bundled up in her sheepskin coat. In the gloom of the night he could see her meet a man. The man in the photograph? The priest? Yes. They touched, but did they kiss? Umberto couldn't tell.

As they walked back through the square toward him, Umberto's heart sank. The priest . . . but without his collar. They looked like any young couple going out on a walk. Tonight was the night. Umberto could feel it.

Umberto got back into his car and waited for Martin and Rafaella to get into theirs. Instead, they kept walking, rather quickly it seemed to Umberto, as he scrambled out of his car to keep them in sight. Did they know they were being followed? Were they walking quickly to lose him, or simply because it was cold? He couldn't lose them tonight of all nights. . . .

They crossed the bridge and walked down the Corso, mingling with the evening crowds, window-shopping, walking idly. Umberto could see that they were talking easily. Once in a while they laughed. Rafaella laughed more than Martin—he must be quite funny, thought Umberto, but too polite to laugh at his own jokes. At the Via Baullari they turned into the forest of streets of the Campo dei Fiori. As they stepped from the bright lights of the Corso into the dark of the side streets, Umberto saw Rafaella slip her arm through Martin's. Umberto nodded grimly, his suspicions proven.

Martin felt the tug of her arm through his and had to work, for a moment, not to look or act surprised. She looked up at him, a teasing smile playing about her lips.

"Is this allowed?" she asked.

"Are your intentions pure, my child?" he said, hoping he sounded as if he were joking.

"As driven snow."

"Then it is allowed," he said. He was immensely flattered.

They were silent for a moment. Rafaella couldn't help feeling that they fit well together. She drove off the thought. It could never be. She didn't even want to consider it.

"Who is this man we are going to see?"

"His name is Bruno Borelli. His family have been goldsmiths for hundreds of years. He made some pieces for Anthony. Anthony gave a chalice and suborium to an order of nuns from his home town on the three-hundredth anniversary of the founding of their order."

"And he's likely to have something ready-made, off the rack?" Rafaella sounded doubtful.

"You can never tell."

———

Umberto watched them enter a ramshackle old building. He waited a moment and then followed them in. Standing in the stairwell, he watched them stop in front of a door on the floor above him. He retreated into the street and wrestled with his conscience for a moment. His moral sense told him to leave them alone. His sense of self-preservation told him that Alessandro Bianchi would not make a good enemy. He tugged on his ear, a nervous habit, and then slowly walked away, to look for a public telephone.

Borelli was a huge gruff man wearing stained overalls and work shoes that clumped heavily on the wooden floor. His face was almost completely covered with a shaggy white beard, and he had an unlit cigarette in his mouth. When Martin introduced Rafaella to him, he gave her a rapid once-over. He approved. His workroom was large and cluttered, the walls sorely in need of whitewash. Scattered about on work tables were the tools of Borelli's trade: pliers, hammers, tinsnips. A large vise was screwed securely into a block of wood. On a scored and beaten old desk was a sheaf of papers, all of them scrawled over with sketches and designs for crucifixes, chalices, croziers, suboria, and a dozen other types of religious paraphernalia. In the corner an electric forge glowed.

Borelli picked up a box of matches from the table and held them, as if against the wind, in his large hands pitted by contact with hot metal. He lit his cigarette and began coughing at once.

"My doctor says I should stop," he said between hacks. "I think he's right." He wiped his eyes and added, "I hate my doctor." His voice rumbled, heavy with smoker's phlegm.

"Martino, how are you?" he said in Italian, shaking hands. "I see your boss has a new job. You must know about it. It was in all the papers." He winked at Rafaella, encouraging her to enjoy the joke.

"No," said Martin, playing along, "I didn't hear. What job?"

"I don't know," he said straightfaced. "Something in the government. Pope, I think."

"Well, he didn't tell me."

"Just like a cardinal. All secrets . . ." Borelli began to laugh, a laugh which degenerated rapidly into a cough. "I'm going to die soon, God willing. Now. What do you want?" he almost bellowed. "I'm about to close up. I want to go home, eat, and then play with my fat wife. If I can get her away from the television and Tenente Kojak, that is."

Rafaella was undaunted by Borelli's show of impatience. She knew how Italian men liked to play.

"I want to buy a monstrance," she said.

"A monstrance! What would a girl like you do with a monstrance?"

"I want to give it to the Church."

"They got one already. Right, Martino?"

"I think they should have a spare," said Rafaella, laughing.

"Martino, you've brought a little saint. When was the last time a young virgin wanted to give something to the Church. Not since Luther, I'll bet."

"Times change," said Martin.

"A monstrance," Borelli continued. "I'll make one for you. Like this." He shuffled through some papers and drew out a sketch. "Come back in two years. Ten million lire. Good night." He turned his back on them.

"Come on, Borelli, you old bull," said Martin, "we need a monstrance."

"What is this? Some kind of party you're going to? 'Guests are asked to provide their own monstrance.'" He stubbed out the cigarette on the tabletop. "You come in here, in the middle of the night, and ask me to hand over a monstrance. What do you think this is? A *supermercato?*"

"Do you have one or not?" Martin demanded.

"I got one."

"Can we see it?" said Rafaella.

"Sure," he said amiably, a huge grin spreading over his face. He retreated into a back room only to return a moment later with a linen sack. "This is a beauty," he said reverently.

He opened the sack and placed the monstrance gently on the table. It was beautiful. It was made of silver and gold, both metals finely worked, and it rested on a base of onyx. At the top of the column was a crystal. Gathered round it were golden shafts, emanating from it like sunbeams.

"You put the host in here," said Martin, pointing at the crystal.

"And then you dance around it like a bunch of Indians," said Borelli sourly.

"Signor Borelli is a Communist," said Martin matter-of-factly, to explain the remark.

"Damn right I am, and proud of it." He lit another cigarette, no coughs this time.

"And you make religious articles?" said Rafaella, surprised.

"What's wrong with that?" Borelli bellowed indignantly. "Didn't Manzù make the doors of St. Peter's itself for John the Twenty-third? Manzù was an atheist!"

Rafaella looked at Martin for confirmation of the fact.

"What can I say," he said, shrugging his shoulders, "it's true."

"Times change," said Rafaella.

Umberto hadn't expected to be met by a photographer. Now this is getting really low, he thought. Bianchi wants photographic evidence of his daughter fucking a priest. Umberto could tell that the man was a photographer by the bulky aluminum briefcase he carried. The man was short, overdressed, and wore too much after-shave. Umberto disliked him instinctively.

The man was businesslike. "Where are they?"

"Up there," said Umberto, gesturing toward the second floor of the building they faced.

"Which window?"

"That one," said Umberto, pointing.

"Dammit. All shuttered up. We can't photograph them with the telephoto. We'll have to get inside."

"How can you take a picture now anyway from outside. It's dark."

"Heat-sensitive film. They generate a lot of heat, these couples." He laughed unpleasantly. Umberto frowned in the darkness. He didn't like this little creep to talk about Rafaella that way.

"You've done this before?"

"Sure, lots of times . . . divorce mostly."

"There's no divorce in Italy."

"Smart boy," said the man, patting Umberto on the cheek. Umberto almost punched him. "But there's divorce in Switzerland, Austria, Germany, and France—all neighbors of *bella Italia*—and my photographs stand as evidence in every one. Besides, we'll be getting divorce soon, and then business will pick up."

"So what do we do now?"

"You kick the door in and I take the picture," the man said matter-of-factly.

"Are you crazy? This is supposed to be a secret. Why don't you just go upstairs and ask them to pose for you?"

"Look," said the photographer, annoyed, "my boss told me to get these pictures no matter what. . . ."

"But they're not supposed to know."

"Once the evidence is in the camera it doesn't matter. Who is it anyway, his wife?"

"His daughter," said Umberto miserably. How had he gotten mixed up in this?

The man whistled softly. "Don't get many young ones. Usually, it's some old broad fucking some gigolo or some old guy fucking some whore. This will be a pretty picture at least."

Umberto grabbed the photographer by the collar and

shoved him back against the wall roughly. "Shut up, you little bastard. Don't talk like that or I'll beat your head in." Umberto dearly wanted to. It would make him feel better. The photographer pulled himself free.

"Sorry, sorry," he whined. "I didn't realize you were a friend of the family. . . . You meet all kinds in this business," he muttered to himself.

"So now what?" said Umberto gruffly.

"We go upstairs," said the photographer deliberately, as if he were explaining to a child. "You kick the door in and I take the picture."

"What happens if the door doesn't give?"

"Chances are, we'll be fucked."

"What if he turns nasty?"

"You take care of him. You've got the muscle. But they never do, they're too surprised. I'll bet you one of them shouts, 'Oh my God.' One of them always says it."

He took out a camera, snapped on a flash gun, and made a few adjustments. "Let's go."

"I made this beauty for the Archbishop of Livorno," said Borelli proudly, "but I'll sell it to you."

"I wouldn't want to upset your plans," said Rafaella.

"I'd rather sell it to you," said Borelli adamantly.

"Why?"

"Because you're prettier than the archbishop, and besides, I trust your check more than his."

"I wouldn't," said Rafaella.

"Neither would I," said Martin.

"Shut up you, what do you know?" shouted Borelli.

"How much?"

"Eight million."

"Forget it."

"Good," said Borelli, wrapping up the monstrance, "I'll forget it. *Buona notte, signorina e monsignore.*" He saluted.

"Four million."

"Come on, *signorina*, for a Bianchi the price should be ten times that."

"I'm a poor Bianchi."

"And I'm Tenente Kojak. How do you do?"

"Six million."

"Six million five hundred and thirty thousand six hundred and seventy-four lire."

"That's a precise figure."

"I can also do cube roots in my head. Do you want it for six million five hundred and . . . whatever I said, or not?"

"Six million five hundred and twenty-seven thousand," Rafaella countered. She was enjoying herself.

". . . twenty-seven thousand three hundred and fifty-two."

Martin laughed. The extra sum was under fifty American cents.

"Sold."

"I'll wrap it up. That's a thousand lire extra."

"That's okay," said Rafaella casually. "I'll wear it."

At that moment the door crashed open and a flashbulb exploded. Umberto and the photographer stared at Martin, Rafaella, and Borelli. They stared back. It was hard to say who was more surprised.

The photographer reacted first.

"*Scusi,*" he said, and broke for the stairs. With a roar, Borelli leaped after him, bringing him down on the landing. As they fell, the suitcase split open, scattering bits of camera everywhere. Borelli raised his huge fist to punch the photographer, who cringed and blanched. Borelli stopped himself. He picked the man up roughly and shoved him back into the room. Martin, Rafaella, and Umberto hadn't moved.

"Now what the hell is going on?" Borelli shouted.

No one spoke. They stared like deer caught in the lights of a car.

"WHAT IS GOING ON?" Borelli's voice shook the building.

"Ask him," said the photographer meekly, pointing at Umberto. "He's the boss."

"Maybe to you he is," said Borelli. He turned to Umberto. "Okay, *padrone*, what is going on?"

Umberto didn't know whether to look horrified or contrite. The image of a very angry Alessandro Bianchi passed before his eyes. Suddenly Rafaella recognized him.

"Umberto," she said, her voice trembling. "You're Umberto, aren't you?"

Umberto nodded glumly.

"You work for my father."

Umberto nodded again.

"And you followed me here, at his orders?"

"Yes, Signorina Rafaella." Umberto felt deeply ashamed.

"Why?" A tear ran down her cheek.

"Your father wanted to find out if you and this man . . ." he pointed at Martin.

"To find out what? If we what?" Rafaella pushed away the tear with the heel of her hand and took hold of herself.

"To find out if you . . ." he decided to use Bianchi's words ". . . if you were sleeping together."

"What?" said Martin, aghast.

"And he sent a photographer too?" said Rafaella.

"He wanted evidence . . ."

"Why?" Rafaella's mouth had set itself in a determined line. Her nostrils flared. "Why?" she repeated. "Answer me."

"Why would he do a thing like that?" Martin asked, genuinely puzzled.

The photographer looked from one face to another and wished fervently that Borelli would let go of his shoulder.

"Because . . ." Rafaella began. She looked around the room, trying to comprehend what she had heard and seen. Suddenly she caved in, like a sandcastle reached by the tide. She leaned against Martin and began to cry, very quietly but deeply. Martin could feel her stomach clenching.

She buried her face in his chest and sobbed. He felt as if he were holding something very fragile; he was unsure of what to do with his hands. He stroked her hair tentatively. Then held her close. She was warm and soft against him and he could feel her tears soaking through his shirt to his chest. Her sobs broke, one on another, and her hands gripped at his shoulders.

Borelli turned to the two men, who stared.

"Get out of here, you bastards," he said quietly. The photographer fled as soon as Borelli spoke the words. Umberto turned at the door, as if to say something.

"Go!" roared Borelli. Umberto went.

He closed the door behind him. "I'll go make some coffee," he said. Neither Martin nor Rafaella heard him.

Rafaella turned her tear-streaked face up to his. "I'm so sorry," she whispered.

"Don't be . . ."

"But I am," she said, with difficulty. Her throat was tight and dry. "I can't help it. I've mixed you up in this terrible thing. This Bianchi madness." She laid her cheek against him and wept some more.

"Come and sit down," he said. He backed toward an old daybed standing in a corner, strewn with clothes and papers.

They were silent for a long time.

After a while, he eased her head up so that she looked into his eyes.

"Rafaella," he said gently, "I think I know why this happened."

"It's my father," she said, sniffing. "He's gone crazy."

"No," Martin said, "it's me. He was after me . . . through you."

Rafaella looked puzzled. "What do you mean?" She sniffed some more.

"I know this sounds egocentric, but I think this whole thing was set up to catch me."

"You?" Rafaella stared at him, wide-eyed.

"Yes. It's a long story. And it has to do, believe it or not, with the Church."

"The Church?"

"Gerard Van Doorn."

"The head of the Prefecture for . . . money or whatever it is?"

"That's right. Van Doorn and I are enemies. He wants me out and I want to get rid of him. We're working against one another, trying to come up with something damning about each other. I suspected that there was a link between your father and Van Doorn. If there is, and if I expose it to Anthony, Van Doorn goes. It was just a shot in the dark, but I obviously touched a nerve."

"If Van Doorn is doing business with my father he's doing it against the pope's orders?"

"Absolutely. An alliance between Bianchi and the Church is something the Church couldn't stand for."

"He's that bad?" said Rafaella. Her voice sounded hollow.

"You know the kind of reputation your father has. . . ."

"Only too well . . . but why would Van Doorn get involved with him?"

"I don't know. But he's become a ruler in his own right in the most important practical Vatican office. He could do a lot of damage to Anthony's plans if his power isn't checked. Anthony refuses to believe it, so he must be shown. Van Doorn must go. . . . So I've been snooping, trying to find out anything I could. They retaliated by trying to get some compromising information on me. If you and I had been found together, I would have been finished, and out of Gerard's way. Maybe out of the priesthood. Anthony couldn't afford the scandal in his position."

"Do you think they'll try anything else?"

"I don't know. It depends on how much is at stake."

"A lot, do you think?"

Martin nodded. "Must be."

Borelli came in with some coffee. "All hell breaks loose

just as I'm about to close a sale."

"The deal stands," said Rafaella.

"Thank God," said Borelli, "the Borellis eat this year."

"I think it's a good idea, you going to Sette Bagni," Martin said.

"Yes. I don't think I could face my father, just at the moment."

"It'll do you good, getting away for a few days."

"Yes," said Rafaella bleakly. "I suppose it will."

As they left, Borelli said to Martin: "Funny friends you have, Martino," and looped an arm affectionately around his neck. He turned to Rafaella.

"Come again, signorina, the next time you need a monstrance. . . ."

Gerard liked to use the time he spent waiting for Amex to call unwinding, reading usually, and having a cup of tea. He made it himself on a hot plate that stood in an alcove in the hallway outside his office. Because he was a meticulous man, he had a proper china teacup, milk jug, and sugar bowl kept in the cupboard for his exclusive use. He hated to drink out of paper cups; he didn't like the feel of the paper against his lips. He always made a pot of tea with two spoonfuls and rarely finished it all. It was wasteful, he knew, but he wouldn't use a teabag. He swore he could taste it.

He put a cloth on the tray, the cup and the sugar and milk on top of it, and carried it into his office. He put the tray down on the desk, and looked through the papers lying there for a photocopy of the article from the financial pages of the *Berliner Tagblatt* concerning a company in Germany Gerard had investments in. He found it, poured the tea through a strainer, and let it set to cool for a moment. He put on his glasses and tried to read.

A large part of Gerard's long-lived success lay in his ability to harness his extraordinary powers of concentration. He attacked whatever task he had at hand single-mindedly and worked at it, as one would loosen a knot, until he had finished with it. But that night he failed. As soon as his eyes touched the page, his mind slid off, unable to concentrate. He knew why he was having trouble; he was preoccupied, gnawed by doubts, as he turned over the events of the day in his mind. He dropped the article and closed his eyes.

Gerard had taken his first step on the tightrope that day; he had started on a course which, once begun, offered no retreat. Salvatore's words, in another context, came back to him: "We must be the net below the tightrope. . . ." If Gerard fell, Salvatore would not be able to catch him—and Salvatore probably wouldn't if he could. He would be as horrified as the rest.

That morning, without ceremony, Gerard had delivered a bulky morocco-bound folder to Martin Sykes with instructions that it should be given to Anthony without delay. It was a complete financial statement for the Church including everything, from the accounts in the banks in Switzerland and eight other countries, the gold, the bonds, the shares, right down to the annual collections taken for the Vatican in Catholic churches all over the world—Peter's Pence it was called. It even included the receipts from the Sistine Chapel tourists. If the Vatican owned some priceless treasures, surely, thought Gerard, this report ranks in value, if not esthetics, with the Pietà and the Last Judgment. Everything was there: information that speculators in every financial center on earth would have sold their souls to obtain. Everything except Senatron.

Sykes had smiled politely when he received the report and asked if Gerard would like to see the Holy Father. Gerard declined. He tried to make the handing over of the report appear to be an occasion of the merest routine.

"Disturb His Holiness? No, it's not necessary. I'm sure he has more important things to do. . . ."

Gerard had looked hard at Martin Sykes and thought: I've handed you the gun. You just have to be clever enough to find the trigger and pull it.

If Martin or Anthony compared the latest report with the ones rendered in the past, Senatron's absence would not be too noticeable. Portfolios changed; it was a natural enough occurrence in business. If, for some reason, they should start investigating what each of the invested companies in that report actually did, Gerard was sunk—probably. If they worked forward, starting, say, with the financial year before last, he was finished. There would be no appeal. If they began checking with the latest report—and why should they be concerned about any other?—there was no mention of Senatron, so he was in the clear.

Another, more pressing, thought, one that had not left his mind for a moment that day, pushed itself to the fore. Would they notice the shufflings of cash and bonds that Gerard had painstakingly worked out, the maneuvers which amounted to Bianchi's loan? Gerard had been careful to couch the report in terms that appeared understandable. He could have made it impenetrable to all but the most knowledgeable financial analysts, but that might indicate that he had something to hide. Rather he made it mildly confusing; it was safer in the long run.

And what about next year's report? By then there would be a decline in liquid assets by . . . how much? How much would Bianchi end up demanding? Where would the cash come from next year, when it was time to reckon with Bianchi and Anthony once again? His work, *his money*, was evaporating before his eyes. Gerard pulled off his glasses and rubbed his eyes. This was the first big lie. How many lies would follow? He didn't know. He just didn't know.

Gerard turned his chair and looked out the window. A faint light burned behind Anthony's window. Gerard could picture Anthony sitting in his white soutane, the report open on his lap, reading intently—perhaps referring now and then to old reports. Was he building a case? Or would that task be left to Martin Sykes?

Had he made a mistake? Had he let some little fact slip

through, something inconsequential that could blow the lid off the whole thing, something that would expose the lie?

Sykes must be kept at bay—that was imperative. Giuseppe reported that Martin had been sniffing around the Bianchi prospectus. Did the Bianchi prospectus include Senatron, which was, after all, a separate company? Or was it made up simply of information on the parent holding company? Gerard went to the bookcase that stood in the corner and took down his copy of the bulky Bianchi profile. Under the heading *Chemical Subsidiaries and Licensees* there was a terse entry: "Senatron Corp., 1243 Worcester Avenue, Framingham, Mass. 02163, U.S.A. Guido Penna, liaison, Industria Bianchi (Chemicals) Milan." Penna—that was the young man who had shown the films. He'll keep his mouth shut; Bianchi would make sure of that. Gerard replaced the book on the shelf, somewhat relieved. There was little there that Sykes could latch on to.

He turned to sip his tea. It had grown cold. He was considering making another pot when the phone rang. Gerard glanced at his watch. Amex was on time.

18

For her eighteenth birthday, when she was still Daddy's little girl, Alessandro Bianchi had bought Rafaella a midnight-blue Bristol sports car. He had eschewed Ferraris and Maseratis, too common in Italy to be really distinctive, in favor of the Bristol, because it was so rare and because it allowed him to show the world that his daughter could have anything she wanted. He knew that the Bristol works in England only turned out about twenty-four cars a year, and Rafaella's model had cost him forty thousand dollars. He considered it money well spent. She was a natural driver, with good reflexes and strong nerves. She drove the car as if it were an extension of herself.

After leaving Borelli and Martin, Rafaella drove the little Fiat she had been using back to her father's home, packed a bag, and went out to the garage to see if her Bristol was still there. It was, the garage lights glinting on its smooth paint-work. It was lovingly cared for by Umberto, who drove it once or twice a week, had it serviced regularly, and polished it himself, just to keep it trim. Rafaella wanted to get to Sette Bagni quickly, by the following afternoon, if possible, and the Bristol was just the car she needed.

She glanced at her watch: twelve-ten a.m. She estimated that she would be in time for the eight-thirty ferry to Sicily. But she would have to hurry.

She slid behind the wheel. Everything was right. The seat was firm without being hard, the controls placed just right. It was a familiar feel, like a comfortable pair of shoes. The interior of the car was filled with the businesslike smells of leather and walnut, mixed with a faint scent of gasoline. Instinctively, she groped in the glove compartment for her string-backed driving gloves. She found them, not really surprised that they were still there, pulled them on, and clenched her fists to loosen the gloves slightly. She turned the key.

The engine turned over at once. She could barely hear it; only the faintest vibration told her the motor was running. The needles of the panel instruments glided into place. She ran a practiced eye over them, checking each one, like a pilot before takeoff. Gas, fine. Oil pressure, fine. Battery, fine. She wondered idly if Umberto still took the car to Graham, the English mechanic who lived in an oil-caked warren in Tiburtina, and who was godfather to virtually every English sports car in Rome. He claimed to have once raced Bentleys against Nuvolari.

One of the German guards stuck his head warily into the garage. He lived in an apartment above the garage and had awakened as soon as the engine started, rising automatically to investigate. Rafaella noticed that the man's face relaxed almost imperceptibly when he recognized her behind the wheel.

Rafaella rolled down the window. "Tell Marietta to tell my father that I shall be gone for a few days."

He nodded gravely, as if memorizing the message.

"Will you open the garage doors?"

He nodded again and opened them wide. As Rafaella drove by him, she saw he carried a gun in his left hand, close by his side, as if he didn't want her to see it.

She eased the car slowly down the driveway, the engine emitting a satisfying growl. At the gate the guards peered curiously into the car, as if expecting to see someone else. Rafaella wondered if they had been sneaking the car out at night to impress the prostitutes on the Via Veneto.

As they opened the gates and let her through, Rafaella hit the accelerator and roared out, negotiating the turn onto the Appia Antica in a single motion. The guards stared after the rapidly disappearing taillights.

Rafaella found her way to the *autostrada*, empty at that time of night, and pointed the car south. She felt wide awake, refreshed, and a little excited. She loved to drive long distances at night. It made her feel remote from the sleeping scenery she passed, remote and at peace. At times she needed nothing but her car and the road that stretched only as far as the beam of her headlights.

She reached Naples a little ahead of schedule. It was the time of night when even the most innocent of women look like whores and all the men look guilty. She coasted through the quiet streets, eager to get the car back out on the road and up to speed again. Off to her right she could see the lights of the island of Ischia. Rafaella recalled for a moment the summer she had spent on the island. She had been sixteen, a guest of a schoolmate and her rich family. It was the summer she discovered boys, and she had fallen in love four or five times in six weeks. Rafaella flushed and smiled at old, buried embarrassments newly remembered. Life hadn't been that easy then either, she thought, smiling to herself.

The whores along the *autostrada* on the southern edge of the town had built fires in the breakdown lane to keep warm. Rafaella wondered why they bothered; it wasn't a cold night. Then the headlights of the Bristol picked up a long line of women holding their coats open, like flashers in a New York subway. They were naked under their imitation minks. Rafaella shrugged it off; Naples was that sort of town.

Her mind coasted back to the events of the evening. Borelli and Martin, the scared faces of Umberto and the photographer seemed very distant. She could recall the scene vividly, the words spoken, even the flash of the bulb, but it was far away—like a film she had seen before, years earlier. After she thought about it a little longer, though, the details seeped into her brain, and suddenly the whole incident reassumed its grotesqueness. She felt the hot prickling of tears behind her eyes. She gripped the wheel tightly and pressed harder on the accelerator.

To her surprise, she felt not the slightest shame at crying

in Martin's arms. Unlike other men she had known, there had been no need, no reason to prove anything to him. To be strong or weak in front of him added up to the same thing —his simple acceptance of her, without reservation. Martin, she realized, was becoming less of an enigma to her. Upon meeting him she had thought that he was somehow not quite human, a shell of a man with an empty space where his feelings should have been. Priests were generally thought to have answers to every question, even if they were the wrong ones, but Martin didn't, and he cheerfully admitted he didn't. It was refreshing. She acknowledged to herself frankly that she was attracted to him but wondered if her wanting what she could not have was merely a ruse to cure herself of wanting altogether. The question was too complicated to be dealt with, she decided, and she contented herself with the knowledge that Martin would always be there to help her if she needed him. That was a luxury she had rarely been offered.

The road was rising now into the mountains, and as she approached Cosenza, Rafaella realized that the car was low on gas and that she hadn't eaten since lunch the day before. She didn't want to stop, but Cosenza would probably be the last large town before Reggio Calabria.

Cosenza is a gloomy town ringed by mountains, heavy with the mistrusts and superstitions of the Calabrese. Late at night it was as inviting as a tomb.

A sleepy attendant serviced the car. Inside the station Rafaella could see a coffee bar, with the heavy ornate espresso machine dominating the counter.

"Can I get something to eat?"

The attendant pulled the nozzle of the gas hose from the tank, nodded sleepily, and gestured to her to follow him.

She had two cups of strong coffee and two rather stale sandwiches.

"How long will it take to get to the ferry at Reggio?"

The attendant leaned against the counter and thought for a moment, as if he were doing sums in his head.

"Two hours," he said, "if you move."

Rafaella smiled. "I'll move."

Two hours later Rafaella leaned stiffly against the fender of the car and watched the ferry lumbering heavily into position against the pier. It was a beautiful morning, the sun playing on the water and beginning to warm the towns of Reggio Calabria and Messina that faced one another across the narrow straits. She was tired and cold, and she gripped the paper coffee cup she held tightly, as if trying to absorb its warmth. She'd reach Sette Bagni by lunchtime, on schedule.

It always came back to Gerard, Anthony thought.

"He was spying on me. Hoping to get something on me, which he considers tantamount to getting something on you." Martin gripped the arms of the chair as he spoke. He felt a bit guilty about hitting Anthony with this first thing in the morning. Fatigue showed in Anthony's face. He had worked until early morning every night recently.

"Martin," said Anthony warily, "how can you be sure that Gerard had anything to do with it?"

"Who else? I cannot believe that Bianchi was seized with paternal jealousy. Rafaella is a grown woman. If he wanted to know about us, all he had to do was ask. She would have given him a straight answer. Instead he wants pictures, evidence. It's like something out of, I don't know, Mickey Spillane or someone like that."

"An Italian woman can live to be as old as Methuselah, and she's never more than a little girl to her father. You must know that. Bianchi would never permit his daughter to have an affair with a priest. The slightest suspicion on his part would probably drive him crazy with anger."

Martin flushed. "But we weren't—"

"I didn't say you were. I'm just saying what it must have looked like to Bianchi."

"But Gerard. What about him?"

"What *about* him? There's nothing in this that links Gerard to Bianchi," said Anthony sharply.

"I have a hunch."

"That isn't good enough."

"It isn't good enough if they are trying to get at you? This is a threat, Anthony, a threat against you and your ministry." Martin was acutely aware that he was talking louder than he should.

"I know you do not like or trust Cardinal Van Doorn. It's a dislike and a mistrust that you share with many people," Anthony said. "What reason would he have for trying to protect himself in this way? Have you done anything that would lead him to suspect you of trying to damage his position?"

"Nothing major . . . I . . ."

"Like what?"

"I asked a few questions, looked a few things up. . . ." Martin said sketchily.

Anthony was angry now. "By what authority?"

Martin said nothing. The two locked eyes for a moment. Martin looked away.

"You will return to your job, and in future you will not do us the profound disservice of investigating things that are none of your business. You must learn not to make wild accusations against prominent members of the Curia without proof. Your snooping can be read as a vote of no-confidence from me against a senior member of my ministry. This blackmailing attempt, or whatever it was, must be seen as a family matter between Rafaella and her father. As far as Rafaella goes, Martin, I cannot forbid you to see her, but I can suggest that you don't." Martin was aware that Anthony had spoken the last words with a note of compassion in his voice. Anthony was telling Martin not to fall in love.

Anthony turned toward his desk.

"Thank you, Martin, that will be all."

"Thank you, Holy Father."

After Martin had left, Anthony rested his head in his hands. There was, he was sure—though he would never admit it to Martin—a degree of truth in what the young priest had said. Gerard was becoming more and more evasive, and an agreement with Bianchi could make him dangerous. An agreement between the Church and Bianchi was not a pleasant prospect. But Anthony couldn't allow himself to be swayed by hearsay. He brushed the thought aside and turned to a sheaf of papers LeBrewster had given him. They dealt with the worsening situation in Peru.

"We must meet," said Bianchi.

"Why?" said Gerard warily. He wanted to keep his meetings with Bianchi to an absolute minimum. Having Bianchi on the phone was bad enough. A call had to go through the switchboard and across Giuseppe's desk before it reached Gerard. Bianchi's name would be mentioned at each point. People would talk.

"We must meet because we are in trouble."

Gerard knew from Bianchi's voice that the trouble was serious.

"What kind of trouble?" He fought to keep control of his voice.

"Serious trouble. Sykes and Rafaella know that we are watching them. The people I hired gave away the whole damn thing."

Gerard almost hung up. "Alessandro," he said feverishly, "do they know about . . ."

"They don't know anything—yet."

"Do they know I'm involved?"

Bianchi laughed. "What happened to our partnership, Your Eminence?"

"I have a lot to lose," said Gerard weakly.

"Who is to say which of us has more to lose?"

"We shouldn't talk about this now," he replied quickly. "I'll meet you."

"When?"

"Tomorrow."

"Where? Should I come there?" Bianchi knew what Gerard's answer would be, but he enjoyed baiting him.

"No, no, don't come here. Do you know the tomb of the Scipios? It's right on the road to your house—you must pass it every day. It's beyond the Baths of Caracalla."

"What are you going to do? Give me a history lesson?"

"We don't want to be recognized."

Bianchi laughed. "How readily you priests adapt to cloak-and-dagger work."

Gerard could not tolerate teasing. "Tomorrow at the tomb of the Scipios at five o'clock."

"That is convenient; how thoughtful of you, Your Eminence."

Gerard hung up. He began to think hard. He had his powers of concentration back.

19

RAFAELLA SAW AND HEARD nothing on the drive back from Sette Bagni to Rome. She drove mechanically, the gears almost changing themselves as she sped northward; she felt quiet, alone, and numb. The headlights from approaching cars burned into her eyes, but she did not see them.

She wondered if the trip had not been a huge mistake. By going, Rafaella had forced out things that were better left unknown. Magdalena had said: "I knew you would come one day. I was waiting for you. What I tell you, you must never forget. . . ."

Magdalena was blind and hunched over, misshapen. People aged hard and grotesquely in the south, Rafaella knew that, but the change in Magdalena over ten years was astonishing. Her face was dry and deeply lined, her hands feeble and hideously gnarled with arthritis.

"I have some disease," she said, "I don't know what it is. The doctor at the Communist clinic told me that I should be in a hospital, but I won't go. I'm going to die here, where I have lived. Don Silvio comes to visit me. He's a good man. . . ."

Rafaella had been impatient for the old woman to tell her the secret of which she had spoken so dramatically. But Magdalena would not be rushed. She rambled, talking of people and events from the past about which Rafaella knew nothing. Every so often she mentioned Elena, and her features softened. Elena was Rafaella's mother. But very little was clear to Rafaella, until Magdalena said: "And then Bianchi came . . .

174

"Bianchi is a bad man. I shouldn't say that in front of you, but he's evil. He sent me money to keep my mouth shut and I will, I will. There's no worry there . . . except to you, Rafaellina. You deserve to know."

"Deserve to know what?" Rafaella eased forward to the edge of her seat to catch every word of the old woman's faint voice.

"Your mother was beautiful, tall and fair, like the ancient Greeks were supposed to look—that's what Don Silvio says. But I don't know anything about that. To me she looked like an angel . . . sometimes it would make me cry to look at her, she was so lovely. I was her friend all her life, and later I was her maid too. I lived in a little room above hers, in the old house. She was so *good*, Rafaellina, so good, like a saint. When she was young she talked about being a nun, but I wouldn't let her. I didn't want to see all that beauty wasted. . . ." Magdalena lapsed into silence, her sightless eyes, pale and ringed, staring inward, in rapt admiration of the memory of Elena.

Magdalena roused herself. "Then Bianchi came. He was young and rich and thought he was so smart. He made a fortune in the war. Some say he pimped for the American soldiers in Messina. We didn't like him, with his big talk and his car and his friends from the city. He thought he was better than us. His family had lived in Sette Bagni for years— his father used to make bedsteads. Did he ever tell you that, huh? No, he's too big a man to remember something like that. . . .

"Bianchi used to wait outside the church on Sundays in his big car, and as we left, he'd go up to Don Silvio and give him ten thousand lire for the poor box." Magdalena grimaced. "Trying to impress us with his money! Bah! We were all horrible to him—except your mother. She was kind to everyone. Even Bianchi. And look how he paid her back. He should be dead, not her."

"What? What did he do to her?" Rafaella was not sure she wanted to hear the answer.

"He and his friends, they raped her. Like she was a heifer." Magdalena spat into the fireplace. "And then he killed her. Killed her in the end . . ."

Remembering it now in the car, Rafaella felt the dizziness, the faint waves of nausea all over again. Now she knew. Now she knew all she needed to know about Alessandro Bianchi.

She arrived in Rome around three A.M. She roused a night porter at a pensione on the Via Due Macelli and cried herself to sleep.

The next morning she made an appointment to see her father. He sat behind his big desk looking sullen, like a boy caught stealing.

She planted herself firmly in front of him. "I am here to say that from this moment onward you are dead for me. . . ."

"Rafaella, I think you're overreacting. A father likes to know who his daughter is seeing . . ." He was aware of how ludicrously feeble his words sounded.

Rafaella laughed at him. There was no mirth in her voice; it was a nasty, strangled laugh. He had never seen her so hard. There was hate in that laugh and hate in her eyes. She frightened him.

"I don't give a damn about your cheap hoodlum tricks. The photographer, the spies . . . you've done worse, much worse." She was almost whispering.

A chill came over Bianchi. "What?"

"I spent yesterday in Sette Bagni . . ."

"Oh God," said Bianchi.

". . . you died there."

"Don't believe what they say. They hate me there. I suppose you believed what that old hag had to say? She hates me most of all." He spoke calmly but was starting to panic.

"She hates you for good reason."

"What did they tell you?" Bianchi had begun to sweat.

"Magdalena told me about how kind my mother was to you and what you did to her in return. Who were the others who raped her? Some of your fellow thugs?"

176

There had scarcely been a day since then that Bianchi hadn't thought of it.

It had been hot. He had been courting Elena for months, bringing her presents, flowers. Giving money to that damn church. And her father, the old marchese, wouldn't even let him into the house. Alessandro would wait until Elena went out for a walk to see her. She would never take the presents he brought for her. Sometimes she would take the flowers, but never the jewelry. She always smiled when he approached her, but then she always made people feel welcome.

He remembered it so well. She was walking in the olive groves above Sette Bagni. Alessandro knew that she walked there in the afternoons. The groves caught the faint breezes off the sea, and they would rustle her dress and toss her hair just a little.

Alessandro had waited for her. She came as he knew she would and had smiled when she saw him. This time, though, instead of making small talk and trying to make her laugh— he could never make her laugh—he had asked her, straight out, if she would marry him. She looked horror-struck for a moment and then regained her composure. No, she said, she could never marry him. She made him feel like he was some kind of monster, something unclean.

He left her and went back to Messina to get drunk with his friends. He told them the story. They said that she had made a fool of him. With a word and a smile, Elena had sliced off Bianchi's balls. Then someone reminded him about the Sicilian law. The law said that a woman who had been raped by a man—and the man's friends, someone had sniggered—had two alternatives. She could send the man to jail or marry him. No one had ever heard of a man being sent to jail—who would marry a woman who had been raped? No one would want her or respect her. Bianchi had been so drunk. . . .

They found her in the olive grove still. She was sitting reading, tilting her book to catch the last rays of the afternoon sun. The six of them had stood there staring at her. She

was so lovely—her long hair glinting in the soft sunlight—
and she looked up at them and smiled. The sun was behind
them, so she couldn't see the looks on their faces. For a second Bianchi knew he couldn't go through with it. Then
Giacomo said, "Come on!" and they fell on her like wolves.

The whole affair was kept quiet, and Elena refused to
marry him—until she found out she was going to have a
baby. After they spoke their vows at the church in Sette
Bagni, she never said another word to him, never let him
touch her, never smiled.

A week or so after Rafaella was born, Elena killed herself
with some pills the doctor had been giving her for pain. She
had suffered the pain in order to save the pills until after the
baby was born. Bianchi knew now that when she spoke her
marriage vows, she had also made the vow to kill herself.
Bianchi was important enough to keep it quiet. Only Magdalena knew . . . she had found the body . . . and now
Rafaella, who had found the ghost.

His daughter was still standing in front of him.

"What do you intend to do?" he asked quietly.

"Nothing. Unless you cause any more trouble for Martin.
If you do, the entire world will know the sordid story of
Alessandro Bianchi. Every paper, every magazine in Europe
will carry a story about you and how everything you touch
turns to filth. Don't worry, they'll still buy your refriger-
ators and your stoves and sail on your ships and stay at your
hotels, but they won't respect you. In every corner *taverna*
they'll be laughing at you. They wouldn't say anymore:
'Alessandro Bianchi, the almighty industrialist' . . . or 'Alessandro Bianchi, we need two or three more like him to fix
this country up.' And you won't be able to live with that,
will you?"

Bianchi sat silent for a moment.

"I am your father," he said weakly. The color had drained
from his face. Looking at him, Rafaella could imagine him
getting old and dying. Alone, now.

She felt no pity. Her anger remained white-hot. "I have

six fathers," she said coldly, "and I don't know any of them." She strode out of the office. Bianchi put his head down on the desk and began to weep, quietly, so his secretary wouldn't hear.

Rafaella's hands shook so badly she could hardly hold the telephone.

"Martin?" she said, her voice laced with tears. "Please meet me someplace. Now . . ."

Part Three

M ONSIGNOR SANZ-GUERRERO was badly frightened. On his desk in front of him was a statement from the chief of police. It read:

Father Carlos Ferreyra, who was assisting police in their inquiries into the incident at the Calloa basin, leaped to his death from the fourth story of police headquarters at Avenida Hidalgo 36. Police are investigating.

20

M ARTIN FELT a sharp bolt of fear when he heard Rafaella's tortured voice on the phone. There was a note of bewildered terror lurking there, terror that aroused, without warning, a confused, tangled glut of emotions from him. For a moment his carefully packed feelings came loose, as a thousand dreadful fears raced through his mind: Rafaella hurt, in trouble, kidnapped. The truth had been so much worse.

Not knowing where else to go, they met at her hotel. Rafaella looked tired; her face was shadowy and gray, her clothes wrinkled and limp, as if she had slept in them. Martin was reminded of a woman he had seen once in Peru. She had been hit by a car, and she lay by the side of the road, quiet and wan, shielded by her pain from the crowd that gathered around her shouting for a doctor, a priest, the police. Something seemed to have cut Rafaella off from the rest of the world. She spoke with little emotion, reporting the harrowing facts of her journey—the rape, the suicide, her talk with her father—as if she had read them in an official document, a police report. She had forsaken her delicate cigars for cigarettes—the cheap kind, Nazionali—and she pulled on one after another, until the room was heavy with smoke.

She finished her tale abruptly, as if her voice had been cut off. They were silent. The sounds of the street below Rafaella's window traveled up to crease the silence of the room. Martin felt uneasy, excluded as he was from Rafaella's sorrow. He found himself listening distractedly to the furious buzz of a far-off Lambretta and the deep, humor-filled shouts of a workman calling for his lunch. Somewhere a woman yelled back at him.

Rafaella roused herself. She had been sprawled on the unmade bed, as if thrown there. Martin sat awkwardly in the room's single straight chair.

"I look like hell," she said, staring into a mirror and fiddling distractedly with her hair.

Martin could do nothing. With the woman by the side of the road, the simple act of telling her that he was a priest had been a reassurance, a gesture that told her she did not face her pain alone. He had held that woman and she had leaned against him, deriving strength from him. But with Rafaella he could not step away from himself and be her priest, her ordained link to comfort. Nor could he comfort her as a lover might; now it would be only a hollow gesture. He felt the helplessness of a stranger.

"What will you do now?" He was sure he already knew the answer to that question. She would be leaving.

"I told you, I have an article to do."

Martin shook his head. "Surely that doesn't matter now."

"Now more than ever."

"Why? I would think you'd want to get out of here."

"No. Not yet."

"What difference would an article on Vatican finances make at this point?"

Rafaella breathed deeply, straightening her back as she did so. "If you're right and my father is involved with Cardinal Van Doorn, I want to know how and why. . . ."

"Out of revenge?"

"Partly. But more than that. For twenty-seven years now I've loved—adored—a stranger. Alessandro Bianchi and my father are two different people. Now I want to know everything about him: his business, his secrets. I'm here to report on Italy—Alessandro Bianchi is Italy. His story should be told."

"Rafaella," said Martin slowly, "I think you'll end by hurting yourself more than you've been hurt already."

A sharp look of anger crossed Rafaella's face. "Martin," she said, "don't hand me some priestly line about revenge being no one's business but God's. Right now it's all I've got. I'm going to find out about Bianchi and Van Doorn. You can stay out of my way or you can help."

"Anthony told me to stay away from Van Doorn." He hoped he had not shown how much her abrupt tone hurt him.

"You're out then?" Rafaella spoke as if she had been speaking to a servant.

"No. I'm not out . . . I don't know."

"Well, you've got to do something."

Martin looked around the room, to the door and then back to Rafaella. "I'll keep my ears open. Remember, there's no hard evidence to link them."

"So that's what I'll look for first, and if I find anything you can give it to the pope. It would make a difference if I found out something, wouldn't it? He would want to know then, wouldn't he?" Before it's published, she implied.

Martin hesitated a moment. He had seen LeBrewster leave Anthony's office that morning carrying a copy of the financial report. It could mean nothing, but it might also mean that Anthony was having his most trusted friend take a long, close look at Gerard.

"Yes," he said finally. "I think Anthony would like to know if there was anything."

"So we'll have to find something."

Martin spoke firmly. "Rafaella, this isn't your affair. I don't think you should get involved."

"And I shouldn't have gone to Sette Bagni either, but I did. From now on, anything Alessandro Bianchi does is my affair."

Martin said nothing.

Rafaella sighed heavily. "I'm going out to the house to collect my things." She glanced at her watch. "He won't be home yet. I can get in and out without seeing him. Would you care to go for a ride?"

"No, I have to get back."

In the lobby Martin said, "You'll be staying here?"

Rafaella nodded. "It's not the Hassler, but I don't imagine my father could find me here. If he's looking, that is."

Martin started to walk back to the Vatican and suddenly felt weak and tired, as if it were late at night instead of mid-afternoon. He slipped into a taxi, and as it stopped and started through traffic, he searched his mind for the words he had failed to find to reassure Rafaella, to transmit to her some of the strength he had given to that woman on the road to Lima. But he had not loved that woman. And even now, he could not say, and would never admit, that he loved Rafaella. He stared at the meter as it clicked off and remembered his words to Rafaella the night they had met: only fools think they have all the answers.

There was always an empty sadness about the tomb of the Scipios—a warren of sepulchers set in rock on the outskirts of Rome, largely forgotten. Under a gray sky, ringed by cold pines, the tombs—resting places of the Scipios, a great family of ancient Rome—were places of pure melancholy, Gerard thought, looking around him.

He wondered why he had chosen this place. It was convenient to Bianchi's house, and that was all. He paced the gravel path around the mausoleum, restless and pensive, glancing every so often at the sky. He had forgotten his umbrella. On the brightest days this was a dark place; in the cold of an early evening, the gloom was palpable.

Bianchi was late, and his absence made Gerard uneasy.

He sat on one of the pieces of broken masonry that lay scattered about and rested his chin in his hands. Surrounding him were the graves of conquerors. A Scipio had defeated Hannibal, another conquered Spain and Asia Minor, and yet another had claimed North Africa for Rome. All that, Gerard thought, before Christ, before there was a Church, in a time when the Vatican Hill was a sunny place, famed for the poor quality of its wines. So long ago.

Gerard straightened suddenly. What did he care for history? He had made his own mark on the world. Where Scipios had once conquered, there could now be found the mark of Gerard Cardinal Van Doorn. In Algeria he had financed a winemaking corporation large enough to rival the French and the Italians; coal mines were worked in Catalonia because he had breathed life—money—into them. He, too, had achieved wonders. He must never forget that, he told himself.

He looked up quickly. Bianchi stood over him, bundled up in a heavy black overcoat. He noticed that Gerard had forsaken his cassock for a somber suit and tie, in which he looked distinctly uncomfortable.

"This is a hell of a place you've chosen," growled Bianchi.

"It seemed suitable," said Gerard stiffly. He was beginning to realize how much he loathed Bianchi.

"It's certainly suitable for what I have to say." Bianchi did not sit down. Sitting below him, Van Doorn felt threatened.

"And what do you have to say?"

"It's finished. I'm not going to have any more to do with you or your schemes. We made a bargain. You supply me with money and I won't tell your damn pope about Senatron. That's as far as I go. We forget about Rafaella and the priest. You only have to keep the money coming to stay out of trouble with me."

Gerard was not going to allow himself to be pushed around by this man. "No. You won't get a cent."

"That would be a huge mistake on your part, Gerard. Play this game by my rules, or you'll end up in serious trouble."

"And you'll be bankrupt." What was Bianchi, after all? He was more hoodlum than businessman.

Bianchi's face darkened. "You'd destroy yourself to destroy me, wouldn't you?"

Gerard didn't hesitate. "Yes."

"Why?" Bianchi's voice was flat, lifeless.

"Because," said Van Doorn airily, "I have a feeling I'm doomed anyway. Because if I fall, I won't be alone. I've worked too hard. . . ."

"You will be doomed as long as you continue to be a stubborn fool!" Bianchi spoke loud enough to have his voice carom in a dull echo off the surrounding stones. "You have only one thing to worry about: whether or not the pope finds out about the money you have put into Senatron. Stop payment to me, and rest assured that he will find out. Beyond that you are free."

"I don't think it is quite that simple. Because of your bungling you have managed to alert your daughter to the fact that we are interested in her doings with Sykes. If Rafaella knows, then Sykes knows, and if Sykes knows, the pope knows, and if the pope knows, he's going to start looking into my affairs. I don't have to tell you that my affairs lead directly to you. If you hadn't mismanaged the whole affair we would be in the clear. Instead we could end up fighting for our lives. Don't come to me with your clumsy threats of blackmail; you have already shown yourself to be an inept conspirator. Remember, I am not some second-rate competitor that you are trying to put out of business. I have more money behind me than Bianchi Industries could accumulate in a century. I have survived in this game, not through brute force, but by skill. I took huge losses and turned them into something. When you are faced with losses, you resort to crime." The cardinal was amazed at the flood of words he had unleashed. He ran his fingers through his hair. It was unlike him to boast.

Bianchi flopped down next to Van Doorn. He stared at the gravel. Muted traffic noises rose from the city around them. Beyond the wall and the trees there was the street. There was the faint squeal of brakes, but neither of them paid any attention.

"Now," said Gerard calmly, "let's review the situation.

Does Rafaella know that in watching her we were actually watching Sykes?"

Bianchi nodded. Van Doorn's spirits sank.

"How do you know?"

"Because she came and told me. She said that if we caused any more trouble for Sykes she would . . ."

"She would what?"

"Nothing. We just can't use her, that's all. Forget it."

"You mean Rafaella is threatening you with something. Good God, Alessandro, you have been careless."

Bianchi turned to face Gerard angrily, but said nothing.

"So Sykes is safe. He is free to dig and snoop until he uncovers something. Then he will go straight to the pope, and you and I are finished." Gerard spoke matter-of-factly.

"Perhaps he won't find anything. Perhaps he won't bother to look."

Van Doorn looked at Bianchi as if he were crazy. "Is that a risk you are willing to take?"

"Perhaps," said Bianchi slowly, "if Martin were out of the way . . ."

"Of course," said Van Doorn sarcastically, "a little accident for Sykes could be arranged. What about Rafaella? She would be on to the pope so quickly we wouldn't have time to call a lawyer, and the next thing you know we would be facing murder charges. Are you mad?"

Bianchi cleared his throat. "I notice your objections are not raised on moral grounds."

"I . . ." Gerard was amazed. Bianchi was right. He hadn't given a moment's thought to whether it was right or wrong. Just dangerous.

"So," said Bianchi, on the offensive, "you would not be adverse to removing your enemies, if you thought you could get away with it." Bianchi shuffled his feet in the gravel. "It seems to me that Sykes can find out anything he wants, but if there is no pope to report it to, any information he can get hold of would be worthless. He would be, you might say, the voice of one crying in the wilderness."

Gerard jumped up as if he had been stung. "You must be joking. You are joking, aren't you?"

"It was just an idea," said Bianchi.

"Well, forget it. This instant."

"Do you reject it on practical or moral grounds, Your Eminence?"

"Both! A plan like that would never succeed. Who would assassinate the pope? Furthermore, I would never be party to a thing like that. It would be insanity."

"It would be insane, but not immoral, is that it? As for a plan not succeeding, it could be made to work. And from what I've heard from you and from what I've read, you might be doing your Church a favor."

"I cannot believe I am hearing this."

To be truthful, Bianchi couldn't believe that he had said it. He had brought it up to bait Gerard, but as he thought about it, he wondered if there wasn't something to it. A single stroke and all his problems would be solved.

Gerard's brain whirled. "Alessandro, think. How could a plan like that be accomplished? Anthony is constantly surrounded by hordes of people. An assassin would be caught immediately. There are more than Swiss Guards surrounding a pope, you know. The crowds are filled with Italian security men." What am I saying, he thought.

"Oh God!" said Bianchi, "His Holiness is surrounded by the crack forces of the Italian security police. That's a different story." Bianchi laughed. "His Holiness is as good as dead."

"Shut up," Gerard snapped.

"Forgive me, Father, for I have sinned," said Bianchi nastily. He rose and brushed himself off. "If Sykes finds out nothing, we are in the clear. If you renege on our bargain, you're sunk. If the pope finds out about you, I'm sunk." Bianchi kicked at some gravel. "Be careful that no one finds out, Gerard, because I don't intend to sink. You can bet on that. As for my idea, let's just bear it in mind. Just in case of an emergency. Good night." He turned and walked away.

"Alessandro," Van Doorn called after him.

Bianchi stopped. Gerard walked to where Bianchi stood. "They do not know yet," Van Doorn almost whispered. "They do not know about you and me. As long as we are not linked we are safe." Gerard sounded badly scared.

"That's right, Gerard. Let's keep it that way." He walked toward the gate. The cardinal waited a few minutes then followed him.

Gerard had not driven to the tomb, and as he was unlikely to get a taxi in that quiet neighborhood, he decided to take the bus. He hated public transport, and he hated buses most of all. They were usually so crowded. A light, cold rain was beginning to fall, and it clung to his clothes. He turned up his collar and stood waiting miserably in the deserted street.

He was not aware of the dark blue sports car coming along the street until it pulled to a stop next to him. Van Doorn knew little about cars, but this one was not Italian and it was obviously expensive. A young woman with long red hair was behind the wheel. She rolled down the window.

"May I give you a lift?" she asked.

After leaving Martin, Rafaella drove through the Piazza Venezia, around the marble extravagance of the Vittorio Emmanuele Monument, and turned into the dense stream of traffic on the Via dei Fori Imperiali. At the monstrous F.A.O. headquarters, she turned again, passing the Baths of Caracalla and into the Via Porta San Sebastiano. Here she increased her speed, accelerating easily through the empty streets.

She thought about doing an article on Cardinal Van Doorn and wondered if the editors in New York would go for it. She couldn't see any reason why they shouldn't; they had liked the piece on the Church so far, even though the instant reporting of events by the major newsmagazines had stolen some of her thunder.

She was so engrossed in her thoughts that the sight of her father's car parked on the road ahead didn't register until she was well past it.

Without thinking, she hit the brake. The car squealed to a halt. She sat in the middle of the road, engine idling, looking at the stately prow of the Mercedes in her rear-view mirror. There was no chauffeur, no follow car with the guards—at least she couldn't see any. She checked the license number. The car was her father's, she was sure of that. Rafaella sat with her head cocked, like a retriever listening for the rustling of a bird. What was her father doing parked in front of the . . . what was that place? Rafaella dimly remembered a school trip there years earlier. Why was Bianchi visiting historic sites on a gloomy winter afternoon? Perhaps he wasn't with the car at all. Maybe it was one of the guards. But she knew that special care was taken of the car, and it was unlikely that one of the guards would risk leaving it exposed while he took in some ancient history.

Rafaella's curiosity was aroused. She backed up and turned into a wooded driveway nearby. She was going to find out what was going on.

She had to wait a long time, longer than she expected. She was beginning to get impatient when Bianchi emerged and walked quickly to his car. He drove away without a glance in her direction. Following Bianchi by a few minutes came a short man of about Bianchi's age, dressed in dark clothes. He wore wire-frame glasses. Rafaella doubted that he was Italian. Looking at him, she was suddenly—firmly—convinced that it was Cardinal Van Doorn.

The man paused in the gateway a moment, looked up and down the road, crossed the street, and stood under the little metal flag of the bus stop. It had begun to rain.

Rafaella turned on the engine and swung out into the street, but instead of turning right, toward home, she turned left, back toward the city. When she drew up next to Gerard, he did not appear to notice her. When she asked him pleasantly if he wanted a ride, he hesitated, and then, as if to avoid being rude, got in.

"Where are you going?" asked Rafaella, shooting a glance at her passenger.

Van Doorn hesitated for a moment. "Please do not go out of your way . . . any place would be convenient."

"I'm in no hurry. Where are you going?"

"Rather far, I'm afraid, across the river."

"Well," said Rafaella, "how do you like that? So am I. Where to?"

Gerard became more uneasy. He told himself that he needn't. Her questions were reasonable enough. She was just a young woman giving an elderly man a lift on a rainy evening.

"Viale Mazzini," he said finally. He would be able to get a taxi from there.

"That's above the Vatican, isn't it?" Rafaella asked evenly.

"Yes, yes it is." It seemed to Van Doorn that she was driving terribly slowly, missing green lights on purpose. For a split second he wondered if he was being kidnapped.

"You're not Italian, are you?"

"No, no. I'm not."

"I could tell," said Rafaella, laughing, "by your accent. You speak Italian very well. Where are you from?"

"Holland."

"Really? Where in Holland?"

"Leiden." Van Doorn had begun to sweat. He told himself he was being ridiculous. The events with which he had had to contend recently had made him jumpy, overly suspicious.

"And what are you doing in Italy? You can't be a tourist, not with Italian like that."

"I'm . . . I am a translator. Dutch to Italian."

"I don't imagine there is much call for that," said Rafaella.

"But what do I know about it?" She laughed a little more. "That's a beautiful ring you're wearing."

Van Doorn screamed inwardly. He had taken off his cassock, but he had forgotten his ring. How stupid! He wondered how many people knew what a cardinal's ring looked like. If the girl knew, she gave no indication of it. He moved his hand to hide it.

Rafaella saw the movement and remarked with a laugh, "Don't worry, I'm not going to steal it."

Van Doorn managed a weak smile. "No, of course not."

Rafaella crossed the river, drove along the Lungotevere and through the tunnel under the Gianiculum. They were very near the Vatican, but well off course for the Viale Mazzini. Rafaella could see that her passenger was getting edgy. Once again Gerard wondered about kidnapping.

"Where are you going?"

"Shortcut," she said.

She pulled up in front of the Vatican at the sacristy gate. Two Swiss Guards in their rain capes looked on as she stopped. Gerard's heart sank. Rafaella half turned in the seat.

"Nice to have met you, Cardinal Van Doorn. I am Rafaella Bianchi. Tell my father I shall be thinking of him."

Standing in the rain a moment later, Van Doorn could only stare after her as she drove away.

21

MARTIN WAS SURPRISED to hear from Rafaella so soon.
"Martin," she said, her voice filled with excitement,
"I've got something."

"Got what?" He cradled the phone deep under his chin,
as if to prevent someone from hearing her voice.

"Van Doorn and my father. I saw them together."

Martin started. "Where?"

"They met around five-thirty at the tomb of the Scipios,
near the gate of San Sebastian."

"*Did* they?" That was it, the definite link between Bianchi
and Gerard. Martin felt a shimmer of excitement run through
him.

"Yes. Afterward I gave the cardinal a lift."

"You what?"

"I wanted to make sure it was him. Besides, he looked so
pathetic in the rain."

"Did he recognize you?"

"How could he? He didn't know what I looked like. But
I introduced myself to him when I let him off."

Martin smiled. Rafaella had a flair for the dramatic.

"What did he say?"

"Nothing. He just looked sick."

"That's pretty emotional, for him."

"What will you do now?"

Martin thought for a moment. "I have no idea."

"Why can't you just go and tell the pope what I saw?"

Martin's brow furrowed. "No, not yet. Right now it's
your word against his."

Rafaella sounded a little annoyed. "Isn't that good enough? He's not before a jury, after all."

"Anthony will want more. It would be better to find out what they are up to, exactly."

"Will you try to find out?"

Martin hesitated a moment. "Yes," he said at last, "yes, I will."

"How?"

"I think I'll probably . . . just a moment." His voice trailed off. LeBrewster had come into the room. Martin swung the mouthpiece of the phone away from Alain, burying it in the shoulder of his jacket.

"Sorry to disturb you, Father Sykes, but would you join the Holy Father and me in the Holy Father's apartments as soon as you can?"

"Of course, Your Eminence, I'll come immediately."

"No great rush," said LeBrewster. "Finish up here first."

Martin's eyes dropped to Anthony's appointment book. There were no more meetings that evening. He had a feeling the conference with Anthony and LeBrewster would be a long one. He returned to Rafaella.

"Martin? What's going on?"

"I'm not really sure. Anthony and Cardinal LeBrewster want me to see them right away."

"Do you think it's about Van Doorn?"

"I have no idea, but it seems likely."

"This could be your auto-da-fé."

"I hope not."

"Good luck. Let me know what happens."

Martin hung up and sat there for a moment. If this was about Gerard, he faced it with a clear conscience. He had heeded Anthony's warning and had not gone near Gerard's affairs. At least, not yet.

Anthony looked grave and pale when Martin entered. He felt a little like a boy summoned to the headmaster's office.

LeBrewster was half sprawled on the couch in the room, his heavy frame sinking into the soft cushions which puffed up around him. Martin smiled to himself. LeBrewster was the only person in the world who could look at ease in the presence of the pope. It was a trick Martin had not mastered, despite his long friendship with Anthony.

Anthony smiled at him. "Please sit down," he said, gesturing toward a chair. "Martin, Alain and I have decided to include you in our discussion because if there is an expert on this matter in this room, it is you."

Martin relaxed a little. If this was about Gerard, Anthony had had a change of heart. Martin realized that he could probably thank LeBrewster for that.

"Yes," said LeBrewster, "you are the only one of us who has actually been to Peru. I had always planned to go there, but somehow I never managed to make the trip."

It was plain that the Van Doorn affair was the furthest thing from LeBrewster's and Anthony's minds.

"Alain has had some rather disturbing information," said Anthony quietly. Martin looked at the cardinal enquiringly.

"Monsignor Sanz-Guerrero informed us this morning that Carlos Ferreyra died in police custody sometime yesterday. They say suicide, but we've heard that story before. . . ."

Martin lowered his head into his hands. He felt leaden; this was striking too close to the nerve. It could have been him—maybe it should have been. Van Doorn, Bianchi, even Rafaella seemed very far off now. They had lost their importance.

"The government plainly thinks that we weren't interested in the welfare of a 'bad priest,'" Martin said after a long silence.

"They'll have to be shown that they were wrong," said Anthony.

"Anthony, a word of caution," said Alain, "a word of caution. This is a delicate matter. Be careful how you act. . . ."

Anthony looked disappointed. "Those are not very brave words."

Alain shrugged. "Sometimes brave words are not the right ones."

Anthony snapped upright in his chair. "We must make a stand. I want the secretariat of state to issue another statement."

"A statement?" asked Alain. "What kind of statement?"

"A statement showing our displeasure. Something that will let the junta know that they are being watched."

"It's your decision," said Alain ruefully.

"You don't agree with it?"

"It will ruffle a lot of conservative feathers."

"I can't help that." Martin could see that Anthony was angry, though with Alain or the generals or with himself it was impossible to say.

Alain stood up. "Anthony, you are probably doing the right thing," he said in a conciliatory tone. "It's just that my scheming politician's heart sees that it will make waves."

Anthony eyed him shrewdly. "I have your support then?"

LeBrewster opened his arms wide. "Have I ever denied you that?" He laughed his rich, deep laugh. "Of course you have my support."

"I am relieved. I'd hate to have you as an enemy."

"Impossible. Now, Father Sykes, we must leave the Holy Father. We all have work to do. . . ."

In the hallway outside Anthony's office, LeBrewster and Martin spoke for a moment.

"Anthony tells me of the problems you have been having with Cardinal Van Doorn and Alessandro Bianchi," he said in a conversational tone.

"The Holy Father didn't seem to be at all sure that there was a problem at all," said Martin a touch warily.

"He's a clever man, Van Doorn. I went over his report and couldn't find a thing amiss. But you know and I know and Anthony suspects that there is something wrong. That is the subject you're the expert in, isn't it?"

If Alain was trying to pump Martin for information, Martin wasn't giving any. "I don't consider myself an expert on anything."

"What a modest young man. . . ." LeBrewster laughed. "As for Cardinal Van Doorn, perhaps we are being unfair to him. Maybe he has nothing to hide. But . . . I doubt it." He sighed heavily. "I suggest you keep an eye on him." He gripped Martin's arm tightly. "For Anthony's sake . . . for everybody's sake. . . ."

Martin said nothing.

"And Martin," LeBrewster added with a smile, "if you need any help from me, just ask. . . ."

The next morning the secretariat of state issued the following statement:

His Holiness Pope Anthony I and the government of the Vatican State wish to make plain the displeasure felt over the current state of affairs in the ostensibly Catholic Republic of Peru. Therein has taken place an abrogation of human rights and dignity incompatible with the teachings of Jesus Christ, Our Lord, and the basic moral tenets of the civilized world.

Furthermore, the death of our brother in Christ, Father Carlos Ferreyra, following detention by the Peruvian security police, is an open act of murder. The Holy See and the Holy Father condemn this atrocity and hold Generalissimo José Sarmiento personally responsible for this heinous act.

Anthony I, Pont. Max.

Telegrams poured in supporting Anthony, but the Vatican was stunned. Anthony was breaking a time-honored tradition in Church policy: no direct involvement in the affairs of another state.

Within an hour after the statement had been made public, Gerard and Alban had received notes from Salvatore summoning them to a meeting that night. Gerard stared at the note for a minute, looking at but not really seeing Salvatore's spidery, irregular handwriting. He dropped the note and picked up the phone, dialed Bianchi's private number, and prayed, as he listened to the ringing, that Bianchi was alone. Here was a new, still rather vague threat. Anthony's blundering in politics just might close some profitable doors. People would start watching Vatican money very closely.

A voice broke onto the line. "Signor Bianchi is not in his office. I will transfer the call to him." The voice was female and professional.

Gerard wanted to make sure Bianchi was alone. "Where is Signor Bianchi?"

"He is in transit, in his car. I am the mobile services operator. One moment please."

There was a burst of static and then Bianchi's voice. "Yes?"

"This is Gerard." He could hear the airy roar of static and traffic on the line.

"What is it, Gerard?"

"Are you alone?"

"Of course I'm alone. I'm in my car, stuck in traffic."

"The chauffeur?"

"For Christ's sake, he's behind glass. He can't hear a thing I say. Besides, his Italian is lousy. What's going on?"

"It's your plan. The one we discussed yesterday."

Bianchi's voice was tight. "What about it?"

"I . . . I think we should go through with it."

"Why the change of heart?"

"I can't discuss it now." Gerard's hands were trembling. "We must meet again. Today." One stroke and it will be finished, all the problems solved. He must do it. Living with it would be another matter, something he could deal with later.

"This time I'll choose the spot. Via Firenze, number

twenty-two. There's an apartment there in the name of Riccio. Meet me there in an hour."

"Whose apartment is it?"

"Mine. I take women there." The phone clattered onto its cradle and the line went dead.

Gerard hung up slowly. He sank back in his chair and closed his eyes. One stroke, he told himself.

Monsignor Jorge Sanz-Guerrero had been the papal representative, the nuncio, to Peru for fourteen years. In those fourteen years the Vatican had paid little attention to him, and rather than being flattered by their sudden interest in his charge, he resented it. He was not an active diplomat; he minded his own business and kept his mouth shut. He knew there had been criticism of his work among the lower clergy in Peru, but Sanz-Guerrero had ignored it, convincing himself that it was the product of envy rather than conscience.

He had made a profession of ignoring temporal politics. When the text of Anthony's statement had been made public, he was indignant at first, and then very angry. Here he sat on a hornet's nest, and that ingenue pope in Rome was just stirring things up. No good would come of it, Sanz-Guerrero was sure of that.

Now he had to go and see the American ambassador. Nine o'clock at night, and the American ambassador wanted to see him. He had a nerve. . . . Sanz-Guerrero had half a mind to make an official protest to Rome about that communiqué. It got everyone upset. As if the Ferreyra affair hadn't been bad enough. Thank God it was out of his hands. The foreign affairs minister had spent all afternoon yelling at him. And what had he done? Nothing. Just his job, and look how they treated him.

Sanz-Guerrero was overweight, so he took his time going down the stairs to the entrance hall of his residence. There were too many stairs in the old house, he told himself. He wanted to move, but there wasn't enough money in the treasury for that.

Francisco, the driver, stood in the hall waiting to take Sanz-Guerrero to the ambassadorial residence. Sanz-Guerrero noted that Francisco needed a new uniform. Probably couldn't afford that either.

"Is the car out front, Francisco?"

"Yes, Monsignor."

Sanz-Guerrero waddled outside and, breathing heavily, lowered himself into the back seat of the black, ten-year-old Cadillac. Every time he got into the car he was reminded that Goyena, the nuncio in Mexico, had a brand-new Cadillac. It annoyed him no end.

Sanz-Guerrero sat pouting in a heap in the back seat. He was normally a bad-tempered man, and he was even more so when he hadn't eaten. He had just been sitting down to eat when the call had come from the ambassador. Sanz-Guerrero made himself more unhappy by telling himself that His Excellency the American Ambassador had probably eaten already. Americans took all their meals too early.

The tree-lined streets of the suburbs of Charcarilla were empty and the car sped along. Staring out the window, Sanz-Guerrero repeated the words "American ambassador" over and over again, like an incantation. He folded his hands over his stomach. Francisco glanced in the rear-view mirror and noted that the old bastard looked as if he had just been bitten on the ass.

It dawned on Sanz-Guerrero, as he looked out the window, that something was missing. The police patrols, jeeps bristling with aerials and guns, were not parked at the intersections the way they usually were. That was odd. There must be trouble someplace, and the police needed reinforcements. More trouble, he thought gloomily.

Without warning, a white car shot through a red light into the path of the Cadillac. Francisco swerved and hit the brakes. The front wheels of the big car lumbered up on the curb to the pavement, stopping crazily, at an angle.

"Francisco, damn you!"

Neither had time to see another car pull alongside. Sanz-Guerrero heard the shots but never saw the guns. The bullets ripped through the glass and bodywork, tearing at his cassock and pulling up pieces of the upholstery around him. The force of a bullet tore the pectoral cross from his chest and flung it through the shattered rear window onto the trunk. Francisco lunged for the door but died before he could put any weight on the handle. There was silence for a moment; then the guns raked the car again for a few seconds, just in case. The men in the car pulled their guns in and drove away sedately.

22

THE APARTMENT on the Via Firenze was well furnished, but lacked any of the touches that showed someone actually lived there. It was an immaculately clean and impersonal one-bedroom apartment in an anonymous building on a quiet side street. The few paintings and prints on the walls had obviously been chosen by a decorator; they were coordinated perfectly with the light pastels in which the flat was decorated. Gerard thought with distaste of the women Bianchi brought there.

There was no sign of Bianchi's guards. They probably knew enough to be out of sight—across the street, probably—when the boss was in the apartment.

"You took your time getting here," Bianchi said.

"I just wanted to make sure I wasn't followed."

"Just like in the movies," said Bianchi sarcastically.

They sat in the living room.

"So," Bianchi said, "it looks as if my plan is the one that will save us."

Gerard took hold of himself. "I can see no other way."

"Hardheaded Gerard Cardinal Van Doorn. It's an honor to work with you," said Bianchi unpleasantly.

The cardinal took a deep breath. "Simply killing Anthony is not enough. A new pope could be elected in a matter of days. A new pope who would merely continue Anthony's programs, a liberal pope with the same priorities and supporters, would do no good whatsoever—he could, whoever he might be, listen to Sykes if Sykes could reach him. When you first mentioned your, ah, plan, this problem looked insurmountable. But now I think I have solved it."

Bianchi leaned forward in his chair. "Go on."

"If Anthony were removed, and if a suitable successor was elected in his place, we would be in the clear. I have the successor."

"Who?"

"His name is Salvatore Di Nobili. He's the leader of the conservatives."

"Would he condone murder?"

"He doesn't need to know about that. We only need to make sure that he's convinced that only he can save the Church from ruin, and only through accepting the papacy."

"And how do you mean to arrange all this?"

"I know what will convince him," Gerard snapped.

"What?"

"A lie. Don't bother to ask me what; I won't tell you."

"Gerard, you don't trust me," said Bianchi sarcastically.

"Di Nobili wouldn't lift a finger to save me—or you—but he would, I am convinced, allow himself to become part of a plan that he thought would save the Church, save it from the ravages of liberalism. The Church, as Di Nobili sees it, is all but gone. He is convinced that he alone is capable of reviving it. He has come close to election twice—very close. He has considerable support in the college and has always had; only clever maneuvering on the part of the liberals has prevented him from being elected. He is getting old now, and he knows he'll never have another chance at the throne. If we can give him that chance, he'll join us. Anthony's actions have shaken up a lot of the moderates and the conservatives. If he had instituted his reforms over a period of years rather than months they wouldn't be worried. Popes aren't supposed to act as quickly as Anthony has. It upsets people, it upsets the Curia. We can utilize the disquiet that many people are feeling, and that vote would swing the election in favor of Di Nobili, I know it would. And once he was elected, we'd have no trouble convincing him to post Sykes as far away from Rome as possible."

"What's to stop him interfering with us after he is elected?"

"He will have been part of a plot against the pope, for one thing, and he'd take care to see that that fact didn't come out. Besides, Di Nobili is a member of the old school. He thinks that the Church is supported by people putting money in collection plates, and that the money is put in a nice safe bank. Also, he trusts me; he thinks I am his most devoted admirer."

"And are you?"

"No. I find him tedious," said Gerard primly.

"Are you sure he trusts you?" Bianchi knew that Van Doorn had a way of making his dislike for someone well known.

"Absolutely. Furthermore, at this moment, Cardinal Di Nobili is very worried, deathly afraid that the pope is sailing the Church into treacherous waters. Until today he would not have joined a plot like this, but His Eminence changed all that this morning. I think that Di Nobili is half convinced already that Anthony is the Antichrist. This morning Anthony released a statement condemning the Republic of Peru."

"Peru?" said Bianchi puzzled. "Who the hell cares about Peru?"

"The pope does. He denounced the leader of the government by name this morning. This may be difficult for you to understand, Alessandro, but in the Vatican an action like that is comparable to a country declaring war. It has never been done before, it is unheard of, and it is exactly what the conservatives fear most. Getting involved in politics, particularly the politics of the Third World—it is an explosive issue."

"Peru," said Bianchi shaking his head. He laughed quickly. "It may interest you to know that the Peruvian government has been placing some very handsome orders with Senatron."

Van Doorn paled. All the more reason.

"Incidentally, I notice you have been selling your Senatron stock."

Gerard was surprised and worried. Someone had been talking. "How do you know?"

Bianchi looked bemused. "Don't worry, no one in your office has talked. I found out on the other end. You've been selling it off in small batches, not enough to be noticed, except by me. I know what's traded in New York. You should hold on to it, you know, you'll earn a tidy sum of money."

Gerard shook his head. "It is not important now."

"No, I suppose not. So. The rest of your plan."

"How does one kill a man?" Gerard asked quietly.

"There are people who would do it. I could contact one now, here in Rome."

"No, no, no," Gerard said quickly, "we can't have some thug going into the Vatican waving a gun around. It must be done quietly, and there must be absolutely no possibility of a link to us."

"That means one of us must do it. That means you."

"Me? I could never."

"Poison him," said Bianchi. "That's the usual manner of killing popes, isn't it?"

Gerard's head reeled. "Poison?"

"Something in his food." Bianchi put both his hands around his neck and pretended to gag quietly. "You know what I mean."

"For God's sake, Alessandro! How can we get to his food? You cannot just walk into the papal kitchens and put something in his soup. Don't be a fool."

Bianchi laughed quietly. "The papal kitchen . . . how did I get mixed up in this?" He sighed. "You did not think this plan through, Gerard. Killing is not easy."

Gerard looked up, curious. "Have you ever killed a man?"

Bianchi's features set hard. "I have killed five men, Gerard. And don't think that this is something you could use against me. It was a long time ago, and I've taken care that there would be no way of proving it." Five men. His five "friends." After Elena died he hunted them down. No one missed them. Five fewer petty thieves in the Messina underworld was no one's loss.

Bianchi wasn't amused any more. He had taken risks before, plenty of them, now he had to take the biggest risk of all. "How much do you want Anthony dead?" His voice was deep and menacing.

Gerard composed himself. "I can see no other way."

"Then listen carefully. In Sicily people from all walks of life live with murder. People say that isn't true, but don't believe it, it's just crap they hand out to the tourists. Everybody knows that no one is spared the threat of death. Policemen, politicians, the wife of another man's mortal enemy —they die if they must. Children have been killed—even priests. And what is Anthony, after all, but a priest? Policemen are shot, politicians stabbed usually, women and children strangled. Each profession has its own way of dying in vengeance. Who kills? The *amici*, the friends, and do you know what the 'friends' are? They have been called many things: the black hand, the *cosa nostra*. . . . In the United States they used to be called the Mafia; now they prefer 'organized crime.' We Sicilians prefer 'the friends,' and one thing we know, they always kill for a good reason. Someone talks, someone gets in their way, someone slights them. Priests have talked, gotten in their way, slighted them, and they have died, like anyone else by their way, the way friends have reserved for them. Poison. In the communion host. It's a time-honored tradition."

"You cannot be serious," Gerard gasped.

"I ask you again. How important is it that the pope die?" Gerard closed his eyes. "Very important," he whispered.

"Then do it this way."

"I cannot."

"Conscience? How unlike you."

"I've . . . never been involved in anything like this," he said weakly.

"This is your last chance." He lit a cigar and relaxed. "It seems like a perfect plan. The host must pass through a dozen hands before reaching the almighty papal lips. You only have to make sure that it passes through your hands. And then, it is *out* of your hands. . . ."

"Salvatore would not go along with this if he knew."

"Then you must take care that he doesn't find out."

"But the poison itself. Anthony is a healthy man, if he suddenly drops dead, people will ask questions."

"There are poisons which induce a simple but fatal coronary. I will make inquiries. . . ."

"But . . ."

"And no one does post mortems on a pope; even I know that. Even the healthiest man under strain is liable to have a heart attack. My doctor warns me of them constantly. Anthony is bound to be under pressure. His death will stun the world, but no one will supect anything."

Gerard whispered, "This is preposterous."

"You're damn right it is. But because it is preposterous it will succeed. And please, Gerard, do not try to fool yourself that you are in a state of moral shock. It'll take a little getting used to, your new role, but I have faith that you'll adapt to it. Remember, you'll be doing everyone a favor."

Gerard sat immobile.

"Now," said Bianchi, rising, "I'm glad we got that settled. You will handle Di Nobili and I'll look into a suitable substance. Gerard," he said, laying a hand on his shoulder, "I have a feeling that this will be a fruitful partnership after all."

Bianchi led the way to the door. He walked like a man who has had a great weight lifted from his shoulders. Gerard, on the other hand, looked as if his burden had become even heavier.

An hour after Sanz-Guerrero's death in the streets of Lima, Anthony knew about it. A telegram had been routed at top priority through the U.S. State Department's high-speed lines, relayed through Washington to the embassy in Rome. A United States marine had delivered the telegram to the secretariat of state. From there it was passed to Martin, and from Martin to the pope. Anthony stared at the light brown paper for a minute and then let it fall lightly from his hand.

"Martin," he said quietly, "cancel my appointments for the rest of the day. Please ask Cardinal LeBrewster to come and see me, and tell the secretariat of state to stand by to release another statement." He followed Martin to the doors and closed them.

Before Martin could begin searching, LeBrewster entered hurriedly. He looked at Martin. "He wants to see you," Martin said. "Go straight in." Martin frowned. Word was out about the murder already; bad news traveled fast at the Vatican.

As the word spread, Martin began receiving calls. From the Vatican press office, the Italian foreign ministry, even an enterprising journalist in New York who had managed to get hold of Martin's number. Martin told them nothing. He knew nothing to tell. He glanced at the doors of Anthony's office every few minutes, and occasionally he could hear the edge of a raised voice.

After two hours had passed Anthony summoned Martin, using the quiet electric bell that ran from his desk to Martin's.

LeBrewster sat smoking the way he always did. Anthony looked pale and drawn. He's blaming himself, Martin thought.

"Martin," Anthony said, "please type this and give it to the secretariat of state for immediate release." He handed Martin a piece of paper. "Ask Cardinal Beauchamp to schedule a solemn High Mass for noon on Sunday."

"Yes, Holy Father," said Martin, withdrawing.

"Wait a moment, Martin . . ." Martin paused at the door. "Yes, Holy Father?"

"I would be honored if you would concelebrate the requiem with me on Sunday."

"Me?"

"Yes. You have a feeling for the country and the people we shall be mourning. Will you assist?"

"Of course, Holy Father."

Anthony smiled faintly, reassuringly. "Good. Thank you, Martin."

In the hallway outside, Martin looked at the paper he had been given. It was a piece of pale blue notepaper, the coat of arms designed for Anthony by the papal herald surmounting it. As a rule, Anthony's tiny writing was not easy to read, but now it was clear and firm.

The brutal murder of Monsignor Jorge Sanz-Guerrero in Lima, Peru, brings great sorrow to the Church and to our person. It does not, however, shake our belief in the morality of our position, nor does it weaken our will to resist the forces of tyranny ruling the unhappy Republic of Peru. We raise our voice to exhort the people of that state to throw off the shackles of dictatorship.

Monsignor Jorge Sanz-Guerrero and Father Carlos Ferreyra are martyrs for their faith and the rights of free men. We express the most profound hope that their deaths shall not have been in vain.

23

SALVATORE COUGHED, deep wracking coughs that seemed to pull at his throat. His shoulders shook and his eyes teared. Alban and Gerard stared at him worriedly; he was pale, his skin washed out and thin, like onion-skin paper.

"Salvatore," said Alban, concern showing on his face, "should I get you a glass of water?"

Through his coughing Salvatore waved away assistance. "No," he gasped. "I'll be all right . . ." He wheezed heavily. "Forgive me for interrupting. I'm fine."

"You should really be in bed," said Gerard. "You'll only make yourself more ill."

"It's only a cold," the old man replied weakly. "I'll be fine in a day or so. Unfortunately I was caught in the rain yesterday."

They had been sitting for two hours, three scared men. Anthony had been condemned loudly by Salvatore and timidly by Alban. Gerard had said almost nothing. He was waiting for the right moment.

"He is leading us toward ruin," cried Salvatore passionately. "One need only read a copy of this statement"—he waved a copy of Anthony's communiqué—"to realize that he would lead us to war if he had an army. He has exhorted the people of Peru to rise against their government. The man is insane!" He nervously rolled the statement into a tube. "He is mad! What will he do next?"

They sat quietly around the table when Salvatore had finished. Alban stared at a painting, a very bad picture from the eighteenth century, depicting the martyrdom of St.

Stephen. He felt nervous and sad, concerned for the Church. Salvatore was right. Anthony appeared to have taken leave of his senses—and there was no way to stop this madness.

"Fathers," said Gerard quietly. The two men looked at him, worry showing deep-lined in their faces.

"Fathers," Gerard repeated, "I see the deep concern you feel for the Church. You are good men, decent godly men; you feel the pain afflicted on the corpus of our beloved Church as you would feel tortures applied to your own selves. It causes me great pain to see you so distressed. Furthermore, I am sorry to say that I must add to your pain. It is my duty to inform you of a portion of the plan that Anthony has not made public, a scheme that only a few men know about and that Anthony thinks the world will never hear."

"What?" asked Salvatore. "What are you talking about?" Fear gripped him like a vise. There couldn't be more.

Gerard took a deep breath. He had always been a skilled liar, and he was confident that he could make them believe him. "I was summoned last night to Anthony's apartments. There, he instructed me to carry out a plan so outrageous, so immoral, that I could hardly believe my ears." Gerard could see that his words were inspiring terror in his listeners. They would not question him, that much was obvious.

"What? What did he tell you to do?" Salvatore stammered, almost choking on his words.

"In Peru at present there is a band of guerrillas, Communist-trained. They are savage men, as savage as the government of that country, if not worse. These guerrillas have been wreaking havoc on all parts of the population, women and children, civilians alike. I'm sure I don't have to spell out to you what kind of men they are. Even the most ragtag army needs money. Last night Anthony ordered me to make five million dollars in gold available to this band of thugs through intermediaries in Mexico. So you see, Salvatore, the Vatican does have an army presently operating in the field, a Communist army supported with Christian funds."

215

"No!" cried Salvatore.

"It is true," said Gerard quietly. "I protested, of course. I tried to make him see that such a step was not only dangerous but sinful. He refused to listen."

"And the money," said Alban. "Will you send it?"

"I will not," said Gerard strongly, "but Anthony pointed out that it could be done easily without me."

"What are we to do?" asked Salvatore.

Gerard spoke again. "I asked myself that question. How can this be stopped? I feel that this move more than absolves us from any oath of fealty we may have made to Anthony."

"Absolutely!" said Salvatore.

"To stop this monstrous plan, I believe, it would be necessary to stop Anthony. . . ."

Alban and Salvatore stared at him, puzzled.

"What do you mean?" asked Alban.

Gerard's voice dropped almost to a whisper, and he spoke quickly. "What I am about to propose must never leave this room—on this I must have your word."

Alban and Salvatore nodded gravely.

"Using the information I have received from Anthony, I propose to force him from the throne. I will threaten to reveal his plan to the world. . . ."

His words hung in the still of the room for a moment. Salvatore began to cough again, sharp cutting hacks, his eyes streaming. He bent over the table, forcing a handkerchief against his mouth. This time, though, Alban paid no attention to his distress. He stared at Gerard.

"You're going to *blackmail* the pope?" he asked incredulously.

"I realize that this is an extreme measure, and that it is one that runs counter to all the teachings we have always held sacred." Gerard paused for a moment, as if to consider the effect of his words. "Father, as long as Anthony remains as sovereign ruler, the Church is doomed and with it the souls of seven hundred million Catholics. That is the responsibility we bear, we three. Can we sit here and worry about how foreign this plan seems to our natures when the very fiber, the heart of the Church is at stake? Only drastic action can stop him and we alone have the means to effect it." Gerard stopped speaking, folded his hands, and looked around the room.

No one spoke for a full five minutes. Finally, Salvatore broke the silence.

" 'Be ye not equally yoked together with unbelievers: for what fellowship hath righteousness with unrighteousness? And what communion hath light with darkness?' Father"— Salvatore said slowly—"we must put aside considerations that would turn us away from notions of this kind. We must be guided by our conscience alone. We must break the yoke that binds the largest single body of people in the world to the mad ideas of a tyrant. Gerard, I feel my conscience is clear."

"It cannot be," said Alban, aghast. "We cannot do such a thing."

"Why not, Alban?" Salvatore stared at him.

"Because he is the pope, the Vicar of Christ," Alban replied passionately.

"He is *not* the pope, he is *not!* He was elected, true, but he was elected to lead the Church, to stand in that line that stretches unbroken back to Peter. He is supposed to be our protector; instead he leaves us open to attack. He has perverted the doctrines of the Church, Our Lord, Our God," Salvatore stormed.

He gripped the sides of the table, his eyes wide with anger. "The papacy, the Church, is supposed to be an island of calm in the roaring torrent of the world. 'The World passeth away, but the word of God abideth forever!' He has plunged us into the maelstrom of petty feuds and turmoils of nations. How can a man owe him allegiance when Anthony has so plainly poisoned the lifeblood of the Church? How can we stand by and permit ourselves the luxury of ignoring these crimes, when the life of our Church, a two-thousand-

217

year span, can end because of the stupidity of one man? No. Gerard is right, there is no other way."

Salvatore's ringing voice had filled the room. Alban had sat very still while he spoke, his mind pestered by this question. Alban had felt himself wavering, but Salvatore had spoken with such conviction, and he was so rarely wrong. Alban mopped his brow with a handkerchief and wished he had retired last year.

"It would be a crime," he said softly.

"It would be a crime against the laws of man, but would it be a crime against God?" asked Gerard. "And would it not be a graver crime to betray the trust into which God has delivered His Church? If it indeed is a crime, then I suggest that we make the sacrifice, take this crime upon our souls and trust in the boundless mercy of the Almighty."

Gerard's words gave them even more to think about.

"Do you not have eyes, Alban?" Salvatore asked quietly. "Can't you see what this man has done? If he had not committed terrible crimes would I, a loyal, devoted servant of the Church, entertain this plan for a moment? No, of course I wouldn't. Cardinal Van Doorn has shown us that this man is evil. With one voice he tells us—tells the world—of the value of peace and the sanctity of human life, and yet, behind the scenes, skulking in the darkness, he takes the money of the Church and uses it to underwrite death and suffering. How many times have we been told, how many times have we taught others, that the temporal life is of no consequence? That the life we lead on earth is only a prelude to our life in heaven? This is a basic fundamental teaching, and yet, our pope, the leader of our Church, has undercut this tenet, has invalidated the very foundation of faith. He must not be allowed to continue."

Gradually, Alban began to cave in before Salvatore's ardor. But he was still greatly troubled.

"How do you know he'll step down? He could refuse."

"He can't refuse. If his proposed actions were revealed to the world, the furor that would arise would be enough to drive him from office. He has the choice of resigning now, quietly, with some dignity, or in the face of the fury of the entire world."

"Can you confront him? And what if something were to go wrong? We could be ruined, disgraced." Alban shuddered.

"I can do it," said Gerard confidently. He could see that his taking charge greatly relieved his companions. "It will be done quietly, don't worry." The corners of his lips twitched in a smile. The night before he had read himself to sleep, not with the usual financial report but with a martyrology. He did not know why he had taken the rather dull book down from the shelf. Perhaps he thought of himself as a martyr, maybe Anthony was—he didn't know. As he turned the pages of the book, unopened since his student days, his eye had been caught by the entry on St. Expeditus, an obscure, perhaps mythical saint, revered in Germany and Sicily, whose name was invoked in times of great danger. Reading the sketchy details of Expeditus's life, he had been struck by the similarity of his death and the one he had planned for Anthony. More extraordinary had been the fact that Expeditus in Latin meant two things: "expedient" and "sent off." It was pure, inescapable irony.

Salvatore looked around him, worried. "No one must speak of this."

"Then let us give it a code name," said Gerard. "Expeditus. The expeditus plan."

"Expeditus?" said Salvatore, whose conversational Latin was rather rusty. "Why that?"

"It means to expedite," said Alban.

Gerard smiled to himself. Not even Alban knew of the shadowy Expeditus and his sacrilegious end. Gerard was beginning to feel a little lightheaded, as if the crime in which he was indulging was a strong draft of spirits, melting his usually practical mind and showing him, instead, the fresh face of freedom of action. But he had not finished with the explication of his plan.

"Of course, the election following the execution of our plan will be very important. To have Anthony replaced by a man of the same stamp would not benefit the Church. We must have a man upon whom we can count to flush out the poisons. I cannot think of anyone who would be better for the task than Salvatore."

Salvatore looked down and his eyes filled with tears. He had been offered another chance; surely the hand of God lay behind all this. From the blackest depths he felt his spirits rising. There was hope now, where before there had been only despair.

Gerard looked at Alban. "I think we can agree on that, can we not? Salvatore has shown himself to be a leader in the true spirit of our Church." Alban nodded. He had always trusted Salvatore.

"I am deeply, deeply honored, my friends," said Salvatore emotionally. He stretched out his hands to Alban and Gerard. "Together, when all this is behind us," he said in a voice filled with hope, "we shall rebuild our Church."

"It will be an honor," said Alban weakly, "to serve you, Salvatore." Something bothered him—apart from the magnitude of the act to which he was an accessory—something about "Expeditus."

"When will this take place?" asked Alban. "When will you . . . expeditus, you know . . ."

"Soon," said Gerard. "Before Anthony does any more damage. I think Salvatore should leave Rome. It is imperative that he is not connected in any way with this."

"I shall go south," he said, changing the subject, "to Santo Isodoro; it is my hometown, and I have a little house there."

"The warmth will do you good," said Gerard blandly.

"Do we need to know more?" asked Salvatore.

"No. You must trust my judgment."

"We must swear," said Gerard, "not to speak a word of this to anyone. We must not meet again until after everything is done. That is extremely important. We must part now and act normally. We hold the life of the Church in our hands—never forget that."

The three men nodded gravely. "Salvatore," said Gerard, "would you lead us in prayer?" Salvatore nodded, made the sign of the cross, and clasped his hands together fervently.

"Oh God, look with favor upon our endeavor . . ."

As Salvatore prayed, Gerard looked at his cohorts. They were old and stooped, hacked at by life. Gerard noted grimly that as Bianchi had transferred his burden to him, so he had passed on his to these tired, broken old men.

Gerard left Salvatore's apartment and walked to a public phone to call Bianchi's private number. The phone was answered immediately.

"Di Nobili has joined us," he said.

"Good. I have managed to locate a suitable substance to use. It's called Digoxin, a heart medicine, a stimulant, basically. A large enough dose will induce a coronary."

"Where did you get it?"

"I manufacture it—a subsidiary of mine, Schlieffen A.G. in Switzerland, a pharmaceutical concern. If you administer a dose of three and a half milligrams or higher, the attack will come about two hours later. Will the mass be over by then?"

"Yes, it will have been over for about an hour. He'll be back in the apostolic palace by then."

"So, I'll have the stuff delivered to you tomorrow. Today is Thursday . . . all our problems will be solved Sunday . . . about sixty hours from now."

"Don't deliver it. I'll fetch it myself. At the apartment on the Via Firenze. Meet me there tomorrow at ten A.M."

"As you wish. It makes no difference to me."

"It's safer this way."

24

ALBAN HAD LIVED in the same apartment for almost thirty years, and in that time he had accumulated a staggering number of books. They lay in piles on the floor, under the bed, stretched along the mantelpiece. The bookshelves that lined each wall of his study had long been overrun, the gaps between the tops of the books and the upper shelf stuffed with volumes lying on their sides. Alban moved through the clutter with easy familiarity, able to put his finger on almost any book at a given moment. Unfortunately, as he got older he noticed that he forgot the titles of books, something that made their location a little harder.

He sat at the oval mahogany table he used for a desk. The top was strewn with papers and books, files and folders, and rising from the middle of the chaos was an old-fashioned brass gooseneck lamp. The skullcap shade cast a pool of light onto the old book he was reading; he read slowly, a bony finger moving from word to word. Occasionally he would pause and close his eyes as he worked to translate an unfamiliar phrase. The book, a diptych, was written in Tzakonian, an obscure Greek dialect that had remained unsullied by Slavic incursions into Greece.

Every so often Gerasimus, Alban's cat, would settle himself on the book and demand to be stroked. Alban toyed with him absently and thought about what he had read. Alban loved cats, he always had one, and he named them all Gerasimus; if he changed names with every cat, he'd get mixed up. The Gerasimus he had now was Gerasimus the fourth. He named his cats for Saint Gerasimus, a desert father who had once tamed a lion. The lion had followed Gerasimus everywhere, and when Gerasimus died, the lion, brokenhearted, lay down and died with him. Alban doubted that Gerasimus IV would do the same for him.

Abruptly Alban got up, leaving the book open, put on his scarf and overcoat, and left. His rooms did not have a phone, and it was important that he speak to Gerard immediately. There was a public phone two blocks away. It could not wait until morning, so he hurried through the dark, cold streets.

Gerard was not in his rooms. Alban hung up, thought for a moment, and decided to call Gerard's office. The call was answered on the second ring.

"Gerard," he said breathlessly, "I'm sorry to be phoning you at this hour. . . ."

Gerard recognized Alban's voice immediately. "Not at all, Alban. What is it?"

"Well, I don't quite know how to put it. You see, your use of the word 'Expeditus' started me thinking, there was something very odd about that term, but I couldn't for the life of me remember what it was. Well, I looked it up this evening in a Tzakonian incunabulum of which I have a facsimile, and I discovered that there was a Saint Expeditus, a martyr who died in a most peculiar way. A horrible death— for sacrilegious reasons more than aesthetic ones, actually. His martyrdom was not as horrible as some, but it was rather horrible ecclesiastically—do you see what I mean? . . . Hello?"

Van Doorn felt an icy fear run through him. "No, I'm afraid I don't know what you mean."

"Well," Alban explained, "Saint Expeditus died with a poisoned communion host . . . and well, your mentioning his name out of the blue struck me as a little odd. . . ."

Gerard summoned up every ounce of will he possessed to keep his voice steady. "Alban, what are you suggesting?"

"Well, nothing really . . . Gerard, how is it that you are so sure Anthony will step down?"

Gerard's voice caught in his throat. He was aware of the ever-lengthening silence on the line. Somewhere, faintly, another conversation could be heard. "I have explained this already. . . ."

"Forgive me, Gerard," said Alban, "but I must ask you. . . . Do you plan to harm . . . the Holy Father?" Gerard heard, and feared, a note of strength in Alban's voice, a note he had never detected before.

"Alban," he said, fighting the quaver that threatened to force itself into his words, "I am amazed that you should think such a thing."

Relieved, Alban sounded like his old self. "No, it was silly of me, really. . . . I apologize, forgive me. . . ."

Alban hung up, much relieved but a little embarrassed. Gerard was a cardinal, a prince of the Church. How could he have thought such a thing? He began walking slowly back to his flat. At the corner he stopped, uneasy. He thought: among certain churchmen, betrayal had always been a potent weapon. . . . Did he trust Van Doorn? He walked a few steps more and stopped again. Had not St. Peter himself denied Christ? Alban stood in the middle of the road. A Fiat roared by him, missing him by inches. The driver shouted at him: "Old fool."

But Alban did not hear. He turned sharply on his heel, and walking quickly, started back toward the phone booth. He wanted to speak to Salvatore.

The phone rang many times, loud and lonely in the cavernous marble hall of Salvatore's apartments. Alban could imagine the sharp sound and cringed at the thought of awakening Salvatore's household. After several minutes, the phone was answered.

"Yes?" It was Bruno, Salvatore's manservant, his voice heavy with sleep.

"Bruno," said Alban breathlessly, "it's me, Father Beauchamp. I must speak to Father Di Nobili. Please . . ."

Bruno considered the request for a moment, trying to wake himself up. Finally, he spoke slowly: "He is not well. His Eminence is not well."

For a moment Alban considered dropping the whole matter—it was too fantastic a notion to disturb Di Nobili with at that time of night. "Oh . . . of course . . ." Alban reconsidered. "Bruno, I must insist," he said. "It is extremely urgent. . . ."

A long half-silence followed. Alban could hear Bruno shuffling away and, deep in the apartments, coughing. Finally, Salvatore's voice came on the line.

"Alban, what is this?" Salvatore sounded exhausted.

"Forgive me, Salvatore, but I must speak to you. . . . I have serious doubts about—"

"About?"

"About our discussions with Father Van Doorn, very serious doubts. . . ."

"Doubts?"

"Yes . . . something he said. Expeditus . . . it made me wonder if he weren't planning to harm the Holy Father. . . ."

Alban's words poured out in a torrent. "I am deathly afraid, Father. . . ." He explained, hardly pausing for breath, about the double meaning of "Expeditus," of Gerard's reassurance, of his own nagging fears. He finished, as he finished most sentences, abruptly. There was silence from Salvatore. The beeps indicating that Alban's time was up started. He felt through his pockets and jammed a token into the phone.

"Salvatore? Are you there?"

"Yes," he said. "These are serious allegations . . . ones I am sure are not true. . . . Have you any proof?"

"No, no, of course I haven't." Alban almost allowed himself a moment's anger. "No proof, just fears."

"Then I advise you to ignore them," Salvatore said loftily.

"Gerard is a prince of the Church, an ordained priest. . . . He wouldn't consider such a thing."

"No," said Alban, "of course not. . . ."

"Now," said Salvatore, "I think you should go home and sleep."

"Forgive me for disturbing you, Father."

"Of course, Alban, of course."

Salvatore hung up the phone and surrendered himself to Bruno, who hovered concernedly in the background. As he lay down to sleep again, he felt the fatigue trying to take command of him, like a drug. But he lay awake, his eyes open in the dark.

Gerard hung up, badly shaken. That had been too close. He waited a moment and called Bianchi.

"Alessandro, do you remember that you said that you had a man here in Rome . . . a man who would be willing to kill?"

"Yes," said Bianchi, "I remember. I thought we didn't need him."

"We need him now. For someone else."

"Who?"

"His name is Alban Beauchamp. He's a cardinal. He knows about the plot."

"He what! How did he find out about it?"

"Calm down. I told him a bit too much, I'm afraid. I am a member of a secret society—there are three members, me, Salvatore Di Nobili, and Alban Beauchamp—all cardinals and all conservatives. Beauchamp knows something about the plot because his support is essential in the election that follows. He had to be in on it. But he is suspicious. He's beginning to figure things out. I told him I was going to force Anthony to step down. But he suspects."

"Shit."

226

"I've managed to convince him that I am not going to kill Anthony, but if he should so much as breathe his suspicions to Cardinal Di Nobili, he'll withdraw. It's not a chance we can afford to take."

"Goddamn you, Gerard!" Bianchi shouted. "If this plan comes unstuck, so help me. . . . You've been a fool, and we are in trouble because of it."

"Shut up, Alessandro," Gerard snapped. "Can you arrange it?"

"Yes," Bianchi growled.

"Nothing obvious."

"No, no, damn you. He'll have a convenient little accident." Bianchi's voice was deep and surly.

"When?"

"Tomorrow sometime. What's his address?"

Gerard told him Alban's address, and Bianchi slammed down the phone.

25

L UIGI FELTRINELLI had been in the business of killing too long to make a mistake. For the most part, he enjoyed his work; it made him feel important, holding the lives of men he did not know in his hands. Feeling important, pretending he was better and smarter than he actually was, meant a lot to him. He was incapable of understanding the abstract fact of taking of lives: that every time he wielded a knife or pulled a trigger, he was ending the life of a man. But he knew well enough that his actions paid the bills. That was important. His mind was like a hand without a thumb; it could snatch at the theoretical, but never grasp it. He was in his middle thirties, always dressed neatly—never flamboyantly—and he liked women a great deal. They liked him.

He gazed idly at the apartment building, planning his way in. He took the trouble to go through careful preparations before each job, and he hadn't made a mistake yet. He hadn't even had a close call. He had no police record to speak of—a few minor incidents when he was younger, but nothing that distinguished him from a thousand other men who had been a little wild in their youth and who later settled down to lead anonymous, taxpaying lives.

This job would be easy. An old man—nothing violent, nothing dangerous. He only had to wait until it was late enough to get inside and make things look like an accident. He had done that sort of job before: people who wanted to inherit Granddad's money before Granddad had decided to kick. For this sort of job he was paid ten million lira, about ten thousand dollars. A piece of cake.

Alban awoke from a hazy sleep and lay very still. He could swear he could hear the water running in the bathtub.

"Gerasimus?" he called. But he knew that no cat could, or would, run the bath taps. In the darkness he could see nothing. He sat upright and listened for a moment and then lay back.

"Italian plumbing," he said to himself. The water wasn't running into the bath, it was just running through centuries-old pipes buried in the walls. He thought he knew every noise in the repertoire of his building's plumbing, but somehow this was one he had missed. It probably happened every night at this time. It had woken him tonight because he was on edge. He composed himself for sleep.

Silently, the door to his room swung open.

Alban lay for a moment and then opened his eyes again. He could sense that there was someone there. He stared until his eyes began to hurt. Standing above him in the darkness was a looming outline, darker than the night. A man.

Alban opened his mouth to cry out. A strong hand came out of the dark and struck him sharply in the throat. Alban made a high, scared, pain-filled sound, like that of a mouse caught in a trap. The blow was not enough to bruise him, just enough to close his windpipe temporarily and prevent him from crying out. He thrashed against the hands weakly. A fleshy thumb found its way to a point just below Alban's right ear. Pressure was applied there, and he blacked out.

Luigi was proud of that trick; just a tap behind the ear and they went out like a light. He checked to see if Alban was still breathing. He was. Luigi was relieved. There had to be water in the lungs or it wouldn't look like drowning.

He hauled the old man from the bed—he was very light—and carried him into the bathroom. He dumped him rudely on the floor. With some difficulty, Luigi stripped him of the long white nightshirt, the man's gangly limbs refusing to cooperate. Luigi swore under his breath as he worked. He didn't like the old man's smell, a mixture of sweat and food and cat. Eventually the unconscious man lay naked on the cold tiles, his pale white body showing every bone. "Christ," thought Feltrinelli, "they get to be such a mess when they get older." He vowed that he would never look like that.

Gently, he picked the body up in his arms and lowered it into the bath water. He rolled up his sleeves and pushed the gray head under the water. The man's limbs moved weakly for a moment or two then stopped. Luigi held the head underwater for about ten minutes and then pulled it up. He was dead. Then he snapped the dead man's head back smartly against the rim of the tub, once, twice, three times. He broke through the skin and a little blood oozed out through the wet hair. Although dead, the wound would generate enough blood by the time the man was found to make the accident look perfect. An old man slips in the bath, bumps his head, knocks himself out and drowns. Happens every day.

A big gray tomcat wandered into the bathroom. He sniffed at Luigi for a minute, raised his nose in the air toward the bathtub, and meowed. He raised himself on his hind legs for a second to look into the bathtub. He couldn't quite reach, meowed again, and looked at Luigi.

"It's a good thing you can't talk or you'd get a bath, too," he said to the cat.

He folded the man's nightshirt and returned to the bedroom. He remade the bed and laid the shirt out on the pillow. He turned on the bedside lamp. A perfect scene. As a final touch he picked up an open book from the desk, the one under the lamp, and laid the book on the pillow. He glanced at the book; it was old writing, some kind of foreign language.

He left the apartment quietly, using the front door, and walked down the steps. Elevators made too much noise.

On the street he walked briskly for ten blocks and then

slowed down. He turned into a corner bar and ordered a brandy. He took an exploratory sip, like a bather testing the temperature of the water, and then poured the drink down his throat. An easy night's work, he thought.

Salvatore Cardinal Di Nobili stared out into the black as the train cut through the night; the glass threw his reflection back at him. He was tired from the events of the last two days.

He felt feverish. His mind whirled and his head ached; he began coughing a deep chesty cough. He examined his handkerchief: green sputum covered it, and here and there were flecks of blood. He was so tired, yet he could not sleep. It was so far to Santo Isodoro. Tomorrow was Saturday, market day in the little town, a market that had not changed a bit since Salvatore's childhood. The piazza would be packed with people and livestock, bargaining, buying, selling, calling to one another, joking. It would be a happy day. When he had been a boy he had considered it the best day of the week. If he had remained there, a country priest, he could have spent every Saturday of his life in the market, laughing and talking with his flock. But things had turned out differently.

Salvatore's manservant Bruno clattered into the compartment. He had been standing outside in the corridor talking to someone he had met.

"Are you warm enough, Eminence?"

"Yes, thank you, Bruno."

"Can I get you anything, Eminence?" Bruno was a big man and looked after Salvatore like a nursemaid.

"No, thank you, Bruno." Salvatore smiled weakly.

"We will be there soon, Eminence."

Salvatore smiled and nodded, closing his eyes as he did so.

"I'll be in the corridor, right outside, if you need me, Eminence."

"Thank you, Bruno."

For the hundredth time that day he thought of Alban's startling confession of the night before and shuddered. He turned to face his reflection once more. If only I had stayed in the country, he thought. I would have died happy.

26

R ETURNING FROM his Saturday morning row, Martin
jogged past Alban's apartment building. An ambulance
was parked outside, and a few people stood gawking as a
policeman questioned a woman who sobbed piteously into
her apron. Martin recognized her. She was Beatrice, Alban's
housekeeper. He remembered how Alban had once mentioned that he would like to have a television set, but couldn't
afford to buy two. "Two?" Martin asked. "Why do you
need two?" "Because," Alban had answered, "I know that
Beatrice's family doesn't have one, and how would it look if
a single old man had one to himself and her entire family had
none at all?" Alban had eventually bought two TV sets. A
color model for Beatrice and family and a tiny black-and-
white set for himself, at which he would squint myopically.

Martin crossed the street.

"Beatrice, what's wrong?"

Beatrice glanced at him and then flung her arms around
his neck.

"*Oh padre Martino!*" she wailed. "*Il cardinale*, he's dead!"

Martin winced and groaned. Beatrice wept into his shoulder. Looking over her gray streaked head, Martin asked the
policeman what happened.

"She found him in the bathtub this morning. He slipped
and fell last night—hit his head and drowned. He was an old
man."

If Alban had died last night it was too late for extreme
unction.

"Was he in any pain?"

"I've got no idea. You a friend of his?"

"Yes," said Martin huskily.

"Too bad," said the cop, without much conviction. "Look, you want to do me a favor? Take the signora upstairs and settle her down. A doctor is coming, he's going to drive her home and give her a shot. Do you know if he had any relations?"

"In England maybe. He was English," he added dully.

"Yeah? Who'll take care of the funeral arrangements? Any ideas?"

"The Church will, he was a cardinal."

"Really?" said the cop, genuinely concerned. "Well, he's in heaven at least. My wife will light a candle for him. Can I take your name and address? Just in case, you know."

Martin gave him the information and then helped Beatrice, still sobbing, into the lobby of the building. The two of them crammed into the tiny elevator which moved slowly, like an aging butler.

The door of Alban's apartment was open. Martin led Beatrice into the tiny, sparsely furnished sitting room and made her lie down on the couch. As he went to the kitchen to make some tea, he passed Alban's bedroom. He went in and stared at the clutter of books and papers and smiled to himself, wanly. Poor Alban . . . A fat gray cat got up from the bed and stretched luxuriously. Martin scratched behind its ears, and it began to purr contentedly.

The reading lamp still burned next to the bed, and as he reached across to turn it off, the open book caught his eye. He picked it up and stared at the script. Tzakonian. That took him back to Father Mansfield's Greek class at Georgetown. Martin read a few words with difficulty.

"And Expeditus, a holy man of great age and learning was martyred through the use of a blasphemed eucharist. He died in great pain from the poisons, thus compounding the sins of the heathen slave."

Well, thought Martin, that was certainly a new twist. He wondered why Alban was reading about St. Expeditus.

Martin had never heard of him. Doubtless some convent someplace had sent a box of musty bones to Alban for verification that they were indeed the relics of the holy St. Expeditus.

The doorbell rang. Martin dropped the book and went to answer it. The doctor looked surprised to see a young man in shorts and T-shirt open the door.

"You're not the patient," he said.

"No," said Martin. "She's in there. She's had quite a shock."

"So I was told. You don't have to stay. I'm going to drive her home."

"Nothing I can do?"

"No, it would be better if she was left alone."

Martin left the building and walked slowly back to his room. He sat on the bed and removed his sneakers. Poor old Alban. He was one of those men who seemed to have lived forever. Now he was gone. It was hard to believe. He jumped when the telephone rang. It was Father Gioia.

"Father Sykes, I think there is something you ought to know. Cardinal Breakespeare-Beauchamp—"

"I already know, Father. Thank you.' He hung up, annoyed.

Salvatore almost had to be carried from the train to the car that stood waiting at the station. He had no strength left, and his face had taken on a yellow pallor. Bruno looked at his employer worriedly as he held him in his strong arms.

"Eminence, I must take you to the hospital."

"No," Salvatore wheezed, "I absolutely forbid you to. Take me home immediately."

It was a two-hour drive from the station at Potenza to Santo Isodoro. Salvatore slept feverishly, waking every few minutes to stare unseeing at the rough landscape bathed in bright morning sun. His mind spun, dredging up images both from the day before and half a century earlier.

After a drive that seemed to Bruno to last an eternity, they pulled up in front of Salvatore's sturdy little house, set on a hill above the town. Bruno helped Salvatore from the car and half carried him inside. Of course, the bed had to be made up—it was stripped down to the mattress when Salvatore was away—and Salvatore spent a terrible few minutes propped up in an armchair while Bruno worked quickly to prepare the bed.

Without warning, Alban's frantic voice from the night before came to him clearly, like a tape recording. He wished he could speak to Alban. What if his old friend was right? Gerard was not to be trusted. . . . "Bruno," said Salvatore quietly, "I must return to Rome."

"Quiet, Eminence," said Bruno. "Rest, rest . . ."

Gerard stared at the brown-tinted bottle with the cotton wad stuck in its mouth. He opened it and dropped two tablets onto the marble counter in his bathroom. Using the bottom of a cup, he mashed the tablets into a powder and swept it into an envelope.

The ciborium with the large host would stand unattended in the sacristy before being taken out to the altar. All he needed to do was sprinkle the powder on it and withdraw. It would be simple, he told himself. Simple. He took a quiet, perverse delight in the fact that he would be there to see the host administered, and that Martin Sykes, the person who had caused all the trouble in the first place would be the concelebrant. Martin would give the host to Anthony; Martin would be the one who dealt the blow.

Salvatore could hear a voice he didn't recognize.

"Pneumonia," said the voice. "It's gone too far to stop. At his age it could put a strain on his heart. Keep him warm and don't let him get agitated. He must remain still."

A tear coursed down Bruno's lined face. "Nothing can be done?"

The doctor scratched his head. "I don't think so. . . ."

"Can he see a priest?"

"Of course."

I am a priest, thought Salvatore. Are they talking about me?

Father Giovanni Battista Nicolosi thought of himself as a failure. Few of the people of Santo Isodoro respected him, and when children and pretty girls teased him in the streets, he flushed a deep crimson all over his face and neck. It was so embarrassing. They needed an older man here, not a young man like himself, just out of the seminary. Of course, he knew the real problem. It was not his maddening, lingering acne, although his nickname *foruncololo*, "pimply-poo," didn't help. It was because he was a northerner, too well educated for these people; they didn't understand his ideas. Neither did the local bishop, Monsignore Licato. Giovanni Battista was sure that his bishop hated him. But maybe one day he would be transferred, perhaps to Rome, maybe even into the Curia, or if he were really lucky into the diplomatic corps . . . London, Paris, New York. He closed his eyes and imagined it, thrilling himself.

The strident ring of the bell at the gate pulled him from his reverie. He hurried to answer it. The local children were in the habit of ringing his bell and then running away. One day he would catch them and sparks would fly.

Standing behind the gate was a big, burly man. Giovanni Battista had never seen him before. "Yes? What is it?"

"I'm sorry to disturb you, Father," said Bruno agitatedly. Working for Salvatore had taught him how to talk to priests to his best advantage . . . always apologize first. "I am Bruno Corelli. I work for Cardinal Di Nobili."

"Yes?" Cardinal Di Nobili was another thorn in Giovanni Battista's much pierced side. The villagers looked up to that man so much. To them he was already a saint. Once, when Giovanni Battista had placed a communion host in the hands of an old crone at Mass instead of putting it directly in her mouth, the old-fashioned way, she had berated him in front of the whole congregation. She had waved an arthritic old finger at him and croaked, "Wait till Cardinal Salvatore gets here. He'll stop this nonsense." Giovanni Battista had never met Di Nobili. He didn't want to.

"The cardinal is very ill, Father," said Bruno. "The doctor says he is dying. You must come at once and hear his confession."

The news stunned Giovanni. He had expected that Di Nobili would summon him from on high; now Giovanni had to minister to him as if he were an ordinary mortal.

"Yes, of course, wait a moment." He dashed into the house and grabbed a chalice, a host, some wine, and chrism. On the way out he jumped on his bicycle and rode to the gate. Bruno still stood there.

"I have a car, Father," he said. "We can drive."

Giovanni Battista hopped off the bicycle and let it fall to the ground with a crash.

Salvatore awoke as Giovanni Battista touched his forehead with the oil.

"Who are you?"

"I am the parish priest, Your Eminence. Father Nicolosi."

"What happened to Father Biagone?" asked Salvatore.

Giovanni Battista passed Father Biagone's grave every morning on his way to Mass. He had died in 1954.

"He's away," he said uncertainly, wondering about the consequences of lying to a cardinal, one on his deathbed at that. "He's on vacation."

"No, he's dead. I had forgotten. He was a lucky man . . . he spent his whole life in this lovely town. I hope you are that lucky, Father."

"Yes, Eminence."

"I never should have left. Never." Salvatore began thrashing feebly in the bed. Something was in the back of his brain, struggling to get out. His eyes opened wide and he gasped for breath. His pale lips were caked with saliva. "Father," Salvatore panted, "I have something to tell you, something you must not forget."

"Yes, Eminence, would you like to confess it?"

"No, no, no, no confession . . . listen." He raised his hand to grasp Giovanni Battista's sleeve weakly. "I do not want you to be bound by your oath. You must go to Rome. Now, right away. You must go and see Anthony."

"Anthony?"

"The pope . . . go see the pope."

"Oh," said Giovanni, feeling foolish, "the pope."

"If you cannot reach him, you must see Martin Sykes. Martin Sykes. Father Sykes. Repeat his name."

"Martin Sykes," said Giovanni dully.

"Tell him I am afraid for His Holiness. I am afraid that . . . before I came here . . . Alban was afraid that Gerard was planning to hurt the pope, to harm him. . . . I think he was right. Gerard has fallen away. I can see that now, he has fallen away. His vows, they mean nothing to him. The world has corrupted him. We meant to save the Church, not kill the pope. Tell Sykes to ask Alban about Expeditus, Expeditus." Salvatore half rose from the bed, and the movement brought on another terrible fit of coughing.

Giovanni Battista hated to see this old man fall apart before his eyes. He was raving, saying the most extraordinary things. They could not possibly be true. It was pitiful to hear him talk of the things that preyed on his mind when his defenses were stripped away.

The effort of all his talk had exhausted Salvatore, and he slipped into a troubled sleep. Bruno appeared at the door.

"Father," he said quietly, "I would appreciate it if you would stay. . . ."

Giovanni Battista smiled reassuringly. "Of course," he said.

In the late afternoon, Salvatore's eyes snapped open. He saw Giovanni Battista and smiled.

"You're still here," he said. His voice was tough and dry, and he smiled softly. "Could I have some water?"

Giovanni poured it out, and Salvatore took a few small sips.

"Father—I'm sorry, I have forgotten your name . . ."

"Giovanni Battista Nicolosi, Eminence."

Salvatore was calm now. "Father, did I speak in my sleep?"

"Oh, you said some things. Nothing very important or coherent."

"Did I mention Expeditus?"

"Yes, Eminence, but you were disturbed, that's all."

"Father, do you believe that I am lucid now?"

"Oh yes, Eminence."

"Then listen to me. What I said is true. I will not burden you with the details, there isn't time. Suffice to say that some men who should have known better have been foolish beyond reason. You must do as I say and see Martin Sykes, Anthony's secretary; there would be no hope of getting to Anthony. Go to the Vatican and find him. Tell him to ask Alban about Expeditus. Ask Alban first, he will explain. Then tell him to find Gerard Van Doorn. Are you listening?"

"Yes," said Giovanni Battista, gapmouthed.

"Good. Sykes will know who these people are. I don't know what Gerard plans to do, but it must be stopped. He kept referring to Expeditus, Expeditus. That's what he called the plan. Tell him that I didn't know what he could have been thinking of." Tears collected in the corners of the old man's eyes. "Tell him, tell Anthony, that I am deeply, deeply ashamed and that I beg his forgiveness. . . ." Sobs crept from Salvatore, his body rocking slightly on the bed. "I am so ashamed. . . ." He sniffed deeply. "Will you hear my confession, Father? You would be within your rights to consider me an excommunicant."

240

"I will hear your confession, Father," he said softly.

Salvatore's confession was short. He received the host, and lay back on his pillows. He stretched his hand out to the young man. "I thank God," he said, "that there are still priests like you. Unafraid, good, kind . . . while there are men like you there is hope, hope. . . . Never desert the people my son. Here is where the most important work is done. 'The good shepherd giveth his life for his sheep.' Now go . . . go to Rome. But return, for the sake of the people."

"Eminence," said Giovanni Battista quietly, "your blessing please."

"It is I who should ask your blessing."

"Please, Eminence . . ."

Salvatore raised his right hand feebly.

"When I return from Rome, may I call on you?"

"When you return, I shall be dead. God is merciful. Now go," he said in a whisper.

At the door Giovanni Battista looked back at Salvatore. He had turned his face to the wall, but he could hear him whispering, quietly, in prayer. . . .

27

For several hours pilgrims, tourists, ordinary Romans, the devout, and the curious, had been filling St. Peter's. The ushers of the church, the San Pietrini, young men in well-cut tailcoats, shepherded families, groups of nuns, and teams of Japanese tourists into this aisle or that. Despite the solemnity of the occasion, the ushers showed great good humor, laughing and winking at one another like attendants at a wedding of two large families.

Those who had friends at the Vatican did not enter through the main doors of St. Peter's. They came through one of the dozen side doors, flashing their huge red tickets which secured them good seats, up close, near the cardinals and other dignitaries. That night those tickets would be carefully smoothed and put away with the marriage licenses and the birth certificates.

In the sacristy Martin had the jitters, like an actor on opening night. He paced, staring about him at the comings and goings of the servers and deacons and the phalanx of Swiss Guards; he was impatient, yet scared of beginning. He had never celebrated Mass at the papal altar and was enough of a traditionalist to appreciate the honor. He wished his parents and sister could be there, but there had been no time. A few members of the procession stood around chatting idly. Martin smiled to himself. If only people knew how casual it all was.

Suddenly, as if switched on, the choir began to sing. Any moment now, he thought.

A burly Swiss Guard captain elbowed his way to where Martin was standing.

"Father Sykes?" he asked in a heavy German accent.

"Yes?"

"I am Captain Schroeder. There's a man at the arch of bells who insists on talking to you. He's a priest. Father Nicoloni, something like that. He says he must speak to you immediately."

"Not now," said Martin impatiently. "Mass is about to begin. He probably just wants a good seat."

"He said he has a message from Cardinal Di Nobili. Something about Cardinal Van Doorn. . . . I don't know, I'll tell him to wait."

"Van Doorn? What about Van Doorn."

"He wouldn't say. But he's awfully agitated."

Martin glanced at his watch. "Bring him in. . . ." He followed Schroeder to the door. The guard returned a moment later with Nicolosi.

"Father Sykes, thank God I have gotten to you. I am Father Giovanni Battista Nicolosi from Santo Isodoro. Cardinal Di Nobili is there, he is dying—he may be dead by now. He said that I am to tell you that he fears for His Holiness's life."

Martin recoiled. "What?"

The bells began to chime for twelve o'clock.

"He said you must speak to Alban," cried Giovanni Battista.

"Alban," said Martin. "Alban is dead."

All night on the train Giovanni Battista had repeated the names, Alban and Gerard; over and over again they had coursed through his mind. The shock of Martin's news was as strong as if he had known Alban himself.

"But . . ." said Giovanni Battista.

An usher approached. "Father Sykes, we are ready. . . ."

"I must go," said Martin.

Giovanni Battista snatched at his sleeve. "You were supposed to ask him about—" Blank. The word he had carried with him like a relic in a reliquary was gone. He breathed deeply and pounded his brain. Sykes looked at him as if he had lost his reason. "You must ask him about—Expeditus." He blurted out the word, like the shattering of glass.

A flash of light exploded in Martin's brain, and his features hardened. "Wait here until Mass is over. . . ."

"Father Sykes," a deacon whispered, "please . . ."

Martin ran to his place in the procession. Anthony had arrived in the sacristy; he stood alone, in the center of the two ranks of celebrants. Before him a young man carried a cross, another a candle. Anthony's head was bowed. Martin started toward him.

"Father Sykes," someone hissed, "stay in place."

"But . . ."

"*Stay in place.*"

They moved down the aisle into the nave of St. Peter's. The church was packed, and the faces that pressed against the railing blurred in front of Martin's eyes. A barrage of flashbulbs exploded, blinding him.

Usually when the pope enters St. Peter's, people sing and chant, clap and yell. Anthony loved it, laughing with the crowd and shaking hands; people would hand their babies to him and he'd bounce them for a second or two, bless them, and hand them back to their beaming parents. Today there was no joviality; if everyone in the crowd did not know the significance of the service, they knew after a glance at Anthony's troubled face that the day would be a solemn one. The crowd was silent.

In the silence, Martin felt alone. A chance meeting with a gibbering young country priest had caught him in a terrifyingly simple quandary: someone must be lying. But who?

At the altar, the procession stopped. Martin and Anthony ascended the steep steps. Anthony faced the crowd.

"*In nomine Patris, et Filii, et Spiritus Sancti.*"

The crowd rustled like a wheat field as they crossed themselves. In a low, throaty roar came the response: "*Amen.*"

Martin faced them:

"*Dominus vobiscum.*"

The choir responded:

"*Et cum spirito tuo.*"

Martin searched the assembled cardinals for Gerard. He could not find him. He struggled to fit the pieces of the puzzle together: Alban had died . . . he had slipped in his bath. Open on the pillow had been the book: *Expeditus, a Holy man of great learning . . .*

Anthony's voice filled the church:

"*Kyrie eleison.*"

"*Christe eleison.*"

Martin stared, horrified, at the ciborium containing the host. Was it possible that one was, in the words of the anonymous diptychtist, blasphemed? There was silence. Martin looked at Anthony. Anthony looked back, a little concerned, and nodded. Martin took hold of himself and turned to the microphone.

"*Gloria in excelsis Deo* . . ." He said the words mechanically; a few members of the crowd spoke with him. He finished, and Anthony, fearing another long silence, said quickly: "*Oremus.*"

The choir responded: "*Amen.*"

Salvatore had said that he feared for Anthony's life. He was to ask Alban about Expeditus. Gerard would do it. Do what? Salvatore did not know. But perhaps Alban had found out . . . and had died for it. The thought numbed him. The Mass, the greatest honor of Martin's life, had become a nightmare.

Martin stood stock still, staring into the crowd. LeBrewster, watching from a few rows away, wondered if he was ill. He hoped he recovered before the Gospel.

The Gospel was read in five languages: Italian, French, English, German, and Spanish. In honor of the priests who died, the Spanish was to be read first, followed by the Italian and English. Martin was slated to read the English.

The elderly Spanish priest read well, deep-voiced, in elegant Castilian. The lisping on the "s's" rushed through the sound system like a sharp wind. Martin did not hear. His mind worked feverishly. Gerard was in the congregation somewhere. Martin knew he had to see him, to know if Giovanni Battista was right. A glance would tell. Martin shook himself, opened his ears and heard French: *"C'est la parole de dieu . . ."*

Martin rose:

"The reading is taken from the Epistle of Paul the Apostle to the Romans. Chapter eight, verses twenty-eight to thirty-nine." His voice filled the vast space of the Basilica, booming out up to the dome and down again. *"And we know all things work together for good for them that love God, to them that are called according to his purpose. . . ."* He tried to read and keep his eye on the crowd. He lost his place twice.

Gerard's heart beat quickly and loudly as he watched from a corner behind the seats put aside for the diplomatic corps. An usher recognized him and tried to get him into a better seat. Gerard waved him away.

Sykes seemed very nervous and made a mess of the reading. Plainly, he had his hands full.

And so to the consecration. The ciboria filled with the hosts for the congregation were brought before Martin who blessed them. The two large hosts for the concelebrants were placed in his hands. Martin stared at the one stamped with the papal seal—Anthony's—and rubbed his thumb across its dry surface. A few specks of fine white powder stuck to his thumb. Martin trembled slightly and almost dropped the host. Expeditus. "He died in great pain from poisons . . . a blasphemed eucharist. . . ." In his hands he held a murder weapon. He could not consecrate it. He placed the host in the

246

ciborium, bowed, and whispered, not the words of consecration but a quiet, private prayer, asking forgiveness.

The servers came forward to receive the hosts for the
congregation. Martin extracted two and placed them in his
own chalice. Anthony knelt before him to receive the host.
He was shielded by the altar.

"*Corpus Christi,*" he said, holding one of the small conse-
crated hosts.

"Martin," said Anthony quietly, "that is the wrong one.
You must break the large one in two."

Martin pretended not to have heard. "*Corpus Christi,*" he
repeated, urging, beseeching Anthony to take it. Anthony
looked at him for a moment. "*Amen,*" he said, and took the
host in his mouth.

Martin turned and faced the congregation.

Suddenly, there was Gerard, kneeling with the cardinals.
A deacon worked his way down the line, administering
communion to them. Taking his chalice, Martin walked to
where Gerard knelt. His eyes glittered with hate and fear.

Martin put his hand into the chalice and removed half of
the large host.

"*Corpus Christi,*" he said.

Gerard knew he had lost. Martin was offering him the
easy way out.

"*Amen,*" he whispered and took the host into his mouth.
Martin stood over him, oblivious to the nervous glances of
those around him.

"*Amen,*" Gerard repeated.

Gerard left the Basilica before the end of Mass and hurried
toward his office. It was deserted on a Sunday. He sat down
at his desk and worked quickly. Speedily he produced memos
countermanding the maneuvers that gave Bianchi his loan,
and he dashed off a note to his secretary instructing the bank
to freeze all money already in account number 056-80003-

988-4 of the Banco Santo Spirito. Bianchi would never get a penny.

He walked briskly to his room. In the square he could see people streaming from Mass. Gerard sat and watched them for a while, until he felt himself going numb. He tried to mumble an act of contrition. His left shoulder and arm tingled painfully. He tried to pray. As he raised his arm to cross himself, a sharp pain shot through his chest. He staggered and fell heavily to the floor.

28

R AFAELLA AND MARTIN were having lunch at the restaurant on the Via Aurelia.

Martin arrived first and gazed at the bustling crowds of patrons settling down to their lunch. The workmen who had been there the time before were there again. They remembered Martin and exchanged among themselves glances and smirks and the odd gesture. They figured that the young priest was probably waiting for the same girl he had been with last time. They nodded to one another, smiling knowingly. They knew what these two were up to.

Martin didn't notice them. His thoughts were miles away. He knew he had changed, he could feel it. The events in Peru, the death of Carlos, and Van Doorn's terrible plan, all had altered him, shifted his focus. He had for the first time in years a sense of where he belonged and what he needed to do. He knew he still did not have all the answers, but he knew now that they weren't to be found at the Holy See. He knew which path he had to follow. Anthony would approve his decision to leave—no one knew better than Anthony the necessity of having to do what one felt to be one's duty.

Rafaella slid into a chair facing Martin. He smiled at her warmly; he would miss her, but it couldn't be helped.

"I thought I'd never get here, the traffic . . . the buses. . . ."

"This is our last lunch," he said lamely, and quite suddenly, he felt sad.

Rafaella's face dropped. "What do you mean?"

"I'm leaving the Vatican. I'm going back to Latin America."

"To Peru?" she asked, alarmed.

"I'd like to, but I'm not sure they'd let me in."

"But what about . . . what about Gerard and Bianchi? And, surely the Vatican is the place to be if you want to . . ." she groped for words. "If you want to consider your career."

Martin smiled. "I'm going back to Latin America for my 'career.' As for Gerard, I'm sorry to say he was found dead this morning. A heart attack."

Rafaella was dumbfounded. "I don't believe it!"

"It's true."

"My God . . ."

"He worked hard," said Martin evenly. "It was bound to happen."

But Rafaella wasn't listening. "You're sure you want to leave?"

"I'd be giving up more if I were to stay here."

Rafaella looked rather sad as she spoke. "You do what you think best."

"I shall . . . I'm sure this is the right thing to do."

"So this is the end."

"End?"

"The end of what never could have been, I suppose."

There was a long silence.

"What will you do?" Martin asked.

"I'll stay in Rome long enough to finish my articles and then . . . I'm going to go back to New York."

"Well, I suppose it's your home now," said Martin blandly.

"Yes," she said.

"Would you allow me to be a priest for a moment?"

"Are you going to suggest that I become a nun?"

"No, I'm going to suggest that you make a greater sacrifice than that. I think you should make peace with your father."

Rafaella's eyes widened and then narrowed.

"No," she said coldly.

"It's just a suggestion, but I think you may find that you need one another someday. It would be a terrible thing to find, on that day, that it is too late, that you've cut yourself off from the person you may still love most of all."

"I cannot. Not after what he did."

Martin ran his hand through his hair. "It's understandable; no one can blame you for feeling that way."

Neither of them felt much like eating, so their meal ended sooner than expected. Martin felt at a loss, unable to say anything. But he also felt closer to Rafaella then than ever before. They stood in the street, each not wanting to be the first to leave.

"Good-bye," she said abruptly, and turned on her heel. He grabbed her shoulder to stop her.

"Rafaella," he said, "promise me you'll think about what I said. About your father, I mean."

Rafaella nodded and started again. He pulled her back and held her close and tight. She could feel her body rigid and stern against his. It might have been the wrong thing to do, but he was doing it, not for her but for himself.

"Good-bye," he said softly.

Rafaella nodded and walked away quickly. Martin watched her go and wondered.

Umberto was surprised to see the dark blue Bristol with Rafaella at the wheel pull up the drive. Marietta had told him that Rafaella had packed her bags and left the day after that terrible night with the photographer and the priest. Umberto had thought that he would probably never see her again. He had also expected to be fired, but Bianchi had listened in silence to Umberto's account of what happened that night and never mentioned it again. Bianchi's not so bad, Umberto had thought, no matter what people might say.

Rafaella parked the car in front of the house and disappeared down the path that led to Bianchi's distillery.

The winemaking season had long passed, but Bianchi sat on an upturned barrel next to the press, in the semi-darkness of the rainy early evening. It was the only place he could be alone.

His daughter was gone; he didn't care about the business. He didn't care about the pope or Gerard or anyone else, just Rafaella.

Rafaella paused before the rough wooden door. She stood in the drizzle as it dripped off the trees around her and thought fleetingly of Martin, and of a woman smiling into the warm afternoon sunlight in an olive grove in Sicily, so many years earlier. Then she pushed the door open. It swung easily on its hinges.

"Papa?" she called into the darkness.

Frank Ritt had had a bitch of a Monday. Wall Street was always crazy after a weekend, and it seemed as if on that particular day all the craziness had been directed at him. All he wanted to do now was get the hell on the train, go home, have a few beers, lie on the couch with his wife, watch some TV, and go to bed.

But no. He had to sit here, after everybody had gone home, and make these hokey James Bond calls to Rome. Christ, he had been with Balter, MacReddie, Inc., for six years now and still old man Pershing treated him like he was some kind of goddamn office boy. He was going to talk to Pershing about it. It wasn't fair. He got home about two hours later than anyone else. Sarah complained about it, non-stop.

The second hand of the wall clock swept around toward twelve. Six o'clock. "Time to dial-a-spook," he said aloud. He picked up the phone and dialed the international access code, 011, then the country code, 39, then the Rome code, 6, and the telephone number.

Ritt had never been more surprised when the phone just rang and rang and rang.